TSALIX SILVERTHORN AND THE SCEPTER OF DESTINY

RICHARD M. SIDDOWAY

TSALIX SILVERTHORN AND THE SCEPTER OF DESTINY

For permission requests, write to the publisher at the address below:

Cayélle Publishing/Dagger Imprint
44349 Lowtree Ave Ste 114
Lancaster, CA 93534
www.CayellePublishing.com

Orders by U.S. trade bookstores and wholesalers. Please contact Freadom Distribution
Tel: (833) 229-3553 ext. 813 or email: Freadom@Cayelle.com

Cover Art by Robin Ludwig Design, Inc.
Interior Design & Typesetting by Gessert Books
Edited by Ashley Conner Editing
ISBN: 978-1-952404-18-4 [paperback]
ISBN: 978-1-952404-19-1 [ebook]
Library of Congress Control Number 2020941308

TSALIX SILVERTHORN AND THE SCEPTER OF DESTINY

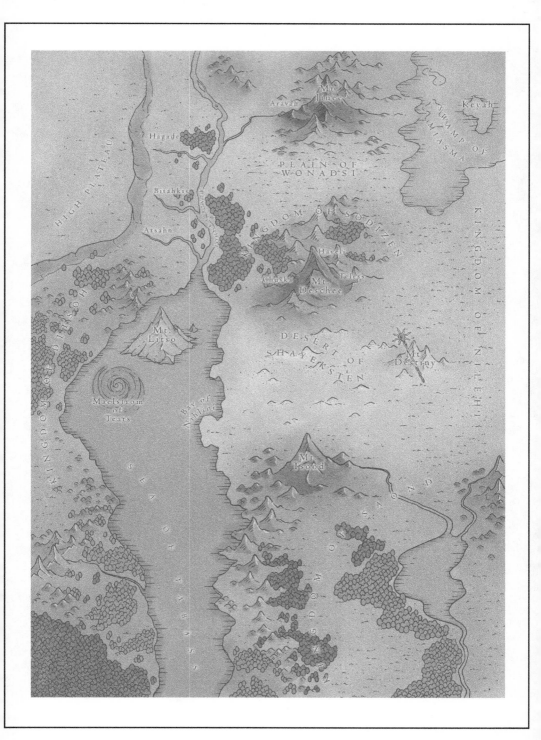

CHAPTER 1

T SALIX WEDGED HIMSELF INTO THE CLEFT IN THE ROCK, placed his ear against the smooth obsidian wall and listened. Above him on the steep hillside, huge polished slabs of stone perched precariously. Through the rock he could hear the footfalls of the approaching riders on their enormous wolacs. Tsalix listened intently, trying to read the signature of the heavy, armored six-legged beasts. Each one had a slightly different gait, and someone with an experienced ear could identify each wolac by its tread.

Tsalix grimaced as he thought he recognized the footfalls of Nash Doitsoh's wolac. The hoof beats were drawing nearer, and the young warrior forced himself even further into the crack in the rock wall at the base of Mount Jinee. He shed his breastplate to lose another couple inches, but still he felt as if his ribs were cracking from the pressure of the obsidian against his back and chest, until the crevasse widened and he popped into a small cave. He plummeted to the floor and took deep breaths, ignoring the pain in his bruised ribs, then reached back through the crack and retrieved his breastplate, sword, and knapsack. He could see his footprints outside the opening, but knew he had no time to obscure them.

Tsalix turned around and viewed his surroundings. In the dim light that filtered through the opening, he could see the cave's roof was just slightly higher than he was tall, and the room was about six feet in diameter. He pressed himself against a side wall when he heard the wolacs stop outside the narrow channel that led into the cave. They were breathing hard and whistling through their gaping mouths that were bracketed with two sets of enormous pincers.

Tsalix had met many men on the field of battle, but had never had the pleasure or the misfortune to have crossed swords with Captain Doitsoh, Prince Abadon's lion-headed henchman, although he had witnessed his ruthlessness often. Tsalix's mind raced as he tried to think what Nash Doitsoh's move might be. But before he could think further, a double-edged battle ax, a tsenil, was thrust through the cleft until it touched the back wall of the cave. Slowly the blood-red steel head turned and twisted as Doitsoh probed the cavern.

Tsalix slid silently until he forced himself against the front wall of the tiny cave next to the opening. Above the entrance in the dim light, he could see a narrow shelf of rock. Carefully he raised his body from the floor, and with his muscles straining, pulled himself onto the shelf. The head of the tsenil twisted and moved back and forth as much as the narrow opening allowed. It looked almost alive and as if it were trying to sniff out Tsalix's scent.

Nash Doitsoh's voice roared into the cave. "You are trapped, Silverthorn. Your footprints condemn you. There is no way you can escape. I know you are in there. Come surrender to me, and I will let you live."

The wolacs keened their approval.

Tsalix forced himself to lie silently on the rock shelf. His heart was beating so loudly he was afraid Nash Doitsoh would hear it.

One minute passed. Then two.

"I will count to three, Tsalix Silverthorn, and then my offer is withdrawn—and you will die!"

Tsalix tried to calm his heart and mind as he lay motionless on his stone bed. He knew if he surrendered he was a dead man anyway, despite Doitsoh's proffered amnesty.

"One."

The commotion outside the cave subsided as the other warriors silenced their steeds, watched, and waited.

"Two."

One of the wolacs stamped a foot and screeched a plaintive cry that echoed in the cave.

"Three."

The head of the tsenil was withdrawn from the cave.

"So be it. You have made your choice and sealed your fate," growled Doitsoh.

The sound of steel on stone rang loud and clear as war hammers pounded on the hillside, and a shower of rocks began to rain down into the opening of the cavern. With a shout from the men outside the cave, a slab of rock broke loose and thundered into place blocking Tsalix's exit and sealing his tomb.

"Sleep well," Nash Doitsoh roared, although Tsalix heard it only faintly through the pile of rock.

Through the stone, Tsalix's ears picked up the muted raucous laughter of Abadon's men as they turned their wolacs and rode away. One of them pounded the butt of his tsenil against the stone slab as a final goodbye. It sounded like a bass drum as it reverberated through the cave.

Tsalix waited a few minutes, hoping his eyes would adjust to the darkness of the cave, but it was black and he could see nothing. He slipped off the shelf, to the floor. Rocks the size of cobblestones had bounced through the opening, and he had to tiptoe to keep from stumbling over one or stepping on them and turning an ankle. He put his hands in front of him as he moved around the small room. There was no opening he could find except the fissure, which was now covered. He thrust his sword through the narrow gap against the rock slab, but there was no give. All the cave's walls felt like polished glass.

Despair filled his heart. He sank to the floor and rested his head in his hands. *How did this happen?*

The walls seemed to press in against him as he struggled to swallow the panic that threatened to fill his throat. It was all he could do to keep from screaming.

Air. I need air! Tsalix sprang to his feet and pressed against the polished wall.

After what seemed an eternity, he gave up and sank back to the floor. From some unknown spot, a feeble breeze alerted him that even though he might starve to death, at least he would not suffocate. The thought of food made his stomach rumble. He searched in the darkness until he found his knapsack. Opened it and retrieved a crust of bread and some hard cheese, and nibbled on them.

It was difficult to keep track of time, but at last he slipped into a fitful slumber. When he awoke, he could not tell whether an hour or a day had passed. He rose to his feet and shuffled across the floor with his hands stretched in front of him. Tsalix pushed several small stones out of his way with the sides of his boots until his hands felt the crevasse through which he'd entered the cave. By turning sideways and extending his arm, he could feel the slab of rock that blocked his exit. Again he tried pushing against it, but it was as solid as welded steel. Panic welled up within him, and he choked down the scream that filled his throat.

At length he cleared a space among the cobbles and sank down to the floor again. Although early on the battle field he accepted that death was inevitable, Tsalix had never thought it would come while he was so young, nor had he thought it would come without the feel of steel against his skin.

As he sat in the uncomfortable silence, his mind wandered to more pleasant days of the past. He was home in Aravah, eating dinner with his father and mother in the kitchen of their cottage. His mother had baked his favorite bread, and Tsalix dripped honey and melted butter onto its savory, soft center. In the darkness of the cave, Tsalix reached for the phantom feast before he sank into total despair.

What had brought him here? He had been summoned by the king to meet with him at his palace on top of Mount Deschee, near the center of the kingdom. Although the distance was normally only a three- or four-day journey, the way was treacherous because of the battle that raged between the two princes—Abadon and Johona—across the land. Nevertheless, upon receiving the summons from King Elosha's messenger, Tsalix had begun preparations for the journey. Everyone in his tiny hamlet of Aravah was aware of the dangers that faced travelers who left the safety of their homes, but Tsalix was determined to respond to the call of his king, no matter how dangerous his odyssey might be. His father had taught him well the need to obey.

He had returned to his home from the battlefront only two weeks before. The two years he had served in Johona's forces had toughened his body, but left him weary in mind and spirit. As much as he would have liked to have spent more time with his family, upon receiving the request from Elosha, he polished his armor, oiled the leather straps that held his breastplate in place, and sharpened his sword. He stood just over six-feet tall and was muscled from his time in the field. Twice during his time of service, he had to lengthen the straps to accommodate his growing body, and now his breastplate was almost too small. Nevertheless, he adjusted the straps once again.

His mother had watched quietly in the kitchen, with tears running down her cheeks as she watched his preparations, while his father sighed deeply and stroked his chin. Knowing the distress they felt, Tsalix decided to avoid a tearful farewell. Once his preparations were complete, he walked outside the humble cottage and took a long look at their farm. In the glowing moonlight, he could see that plants were beginning to emerge although it was still early in the spring. The two cows their family owned were muzzling the hay he had forked into the manger. He entered the barn and stroked the flank of the cow nearest the door. She shuffled her feet, turned her head toward him, and mooed, her breath perfumed with grass. A wistful smile crossed his lips as he patted her again before leaving the barn. He glanced at the house and saw his mother watching him through the open door. With a lump in his throat, he smiled at her and walked back into the cottage.

"Be careful, my son."

"I will, Mother. I'm always careful."

She wiped a tear from her cheek before she hugged Tsalix. Her head barely reached his chest. He put a protective arm around her and returned the hug. His father pushed himself to his feet from the bench on which he'd been sitting, and took halting steps toward the two of them.

"You've always been a great help to me." As he tried to control his emotions, he looked at their humble cottage. "I wish I could have given you more."

Tsalix released his hold on his mother and took his father in his arms. "You've given me more than enough. I vow that I will never do anything to bring shame to you."

They sat at the table and ate their simple dinner. Then with a final hug, retired to their beds. Tsalix lay awake, staring at the ceiling. Moonlight filtered through the window and danced on the wall. A spider web in one corner of the room reflected silvery strands to his weary eyes. At last he drifted off to sleep.

Before the sun rose the following morning, he slipped out of his house before his parents were awake, and crept along the path that girdled the foothills of Mount Jinee. Its black flanks extended through the low-lying clouds which always seemed to hide the top of the peak. Flashes of lightning forked from the clouds onto the side of the mountain, followed by kettle drum claps of thunder. Through the filtering layers of clouds, the sun rose and sent feeble light down on the lone figure lurking along the trail.

By noontime Tsalix had covered a considerable distance and slipped into a copse of pine to rest and eat his meager lunch of bread and cheese. As he peered through the trees to the plains below, a flash of light in the far distance caught his eye. The first flash was followed by a dozen more, and he realized the sun was reflecting from drawn blades as a battle raged. He shrank back into the cover of the trees, although he was that aware the battle was a dozen miles away and it was not likely he could be spotted. He was so weary of fighting that he could not stomach the thoughts of being pulled into another skirmish.

After an hour the flashes stopped and Tsalix wondered who had won and who had lost the encounter. The obsidian war had raged for decades, and it still was not clear who would emerge victorious.

He drank deeply from a small spring that coursed down the flank of the mountain, and prepared to continue his journey. He had but a few miles more on the foothill trail before he'd have to leave the cover of the pines and start across the valley floor, on the trail across the Plain of Wonadsi which led to King Elosha's palace on the summit of Mount Deschee. It was there between the two mountains that he felt peril was greatest, since there was so little cover and he would be exposed to prying eyes.

Slowly he raised to his feet, adjusted his breastplate, and shouldered his pack. His sword hung from its sheath on his left hip. As silent as a whisper, he slipped out of the pines and continued his journey. The sun slipped behind banks of clouds, sending ghostly silhouettes across the plain below. Tsalix had not taken a dozen steps on the trail before he heard the distant squealing cry of a wolac behind him. He broke into a trot and sought cover. Although Abadon had tolerated the village of Aravah on the flank of Mount Jinee, on whose side he'd built his palace, he was quick to mete out punishment to those who left the confines of the town.

A cleft in the rock appeared ahead, and Tsalix forced himself into the cave and found himself imprisoned in inky blackness. A blackness so thick he could feel it seeping into every pore. In despair, he again pushed his sword through the gap and felt the steel blade flex as it met the resistance of the slab of rock that entombed him. Frustrated, he sat and tried to think of any way he could escape from his prison, but no plan emerged. Although he had never been one to give up in the face of insurmountable odds, he felt powerless to find a solution to his predicament.

I wish I had awakened my parents before I left. They will never know how much I loved them, nor will they know what happened to me.

The thought sent a chill down his spine. He could think of nothing worse than never knowing what had happened to a loved one. He had never been good at farewells, and thought he had done his parents a favor by not waking them. Not only had he not said farewell to his parents, he had ignored his friends, Asur Longtooth and Kwercus Strongheart, who had been like brothers to him. They had invited him to sup with them the night before he left—*was that last night*—but he had chosen not to join them, wanting to spend time with his family. *How long have I been locked in here?*

"All because I followed the king," he whispered into the darkness.

Tsalix stood, faced the wall, placed his hands against it, and began to sob as emotions flooded over him. A slight tremor ran through his hands, followed by a stronger one. He wrinkled his brow in puzzlement, and then a stronger shock passed through the cavern. He lifted his shield over his head to ward off any falling stones when, with a mighty quake, the slab of obsidian that sealed the passage was thrown away from the cleft and a rush of fresh air filled the tomb. Cobbles fell from the ceiling and bounced from his shield.

Tsalix scurried across the floor and tried to wedge himself through the opening with a deep-throated groan, when the mountain heaved again and Tsalix was thrown out of the cave. More fist-sized stones cascaded down the mountain and bounced off his shield for several minutes, until the avalanche stopped. He pushed himself to his feet as another temblor shuddered across the trail, and another cascade of rocks bounded down the mountainside. He tried to jog down the trail as the earth heaved and buckled beneath his feet, and more than once he tumbled onto his knees and struggled to regain his footing.

Then, as quickly as it had begun, the quake ended and the earth became peaceful again. Tsalix looked through the trees at a quarter-moon that hung high above him.

How long was I trapped?

CHAPTER 2

ABADON PACED BACK AND FORTH ACROSS HIS THRONE ROOM. The earthquake had wakened him from a troubled sleep. Nash Doitsoh had reported to him the previous day, and he felt certain that Tsalix Silverthorn had been disposed of. But without proof he was unsure. So many of those foolish souls who had been summoned to meet with Elosha had been summarily eliminated by Captain Nash Doitsoh and his troops, but Abadon feared there were still others who would honor the call of the king. Honor and power, were they not what this was all about?

He had called for Doitsoh to return to the throne room. Now he knelt before the throne.

Abadon spun on his heel. "Go. Bring me his body. I must be sure."

The lion-headed captain bowed his head at his master and licked his leathery lips.

"He is encased in a tomb, Sire. It will take considerable effort to move the stone. I am certain he will trouble you no more."

"Do you dare question me?" Abadon barked at his captain, and rose to his full height.

His black eyes seemed to spit sparks.

Nash Doitsoh rose to his feet and shook his mane. "No, of course I do not question, Sire. I just wanted you to know how difficult it might be."

Abadon snarled, "Bring me Silverthorn's body. Do you understand?" He grimaced as he stared at Nash.

Without another word Doitsoh bowed again, gathered his cloak around him, and backed out of the chamber. Behind him, Abadon seethed. A huge map of the kingdom hung on one wall of the room. Each cardinal point was anchored by a mountain—Mount Jinee, where his palace stood, on the north. Mount Litso on the west, surrounded by the Sea of Tabass. Mount Tsood on the south, across the Desert of Shayeksten. And Mount Destiny, the Glittering Peak, on the east. In the middle of the map rose Mount Deschee—home of Elosha, his father, king of the realm.

On one side of the map was a parchment scroll with names of those whom Elosha had summoned to his throne. It had taken considerable effort, torture, and a fortune to extract those names. Abadon had drawn a line through the first six of the twelve men's names. The heads of these men were impaled on pikes that lined the path to the great portcullis, which guarded the entrance to his castle fortress. The crows had picked the flesh from them, leaving sun-bleached skulls.

Next on the list was Tsalix Silverthorn. Abadon dipped the quill in the fountain of ink and debated whether to draw the line that would show him eliminated. He placed the tip of the pen against the scroll, but before he drew the line he replaced the quill on the desktop. He pursed his lips and rubbed his forehead with his gnarled hand. His black locks fell forward as he began to pace again, scanning the floor before him. Back and forth he strode across the polished black floor of the throne room.

Abadon returned to the map and scanned its surface. The four mountains that secured the boundaries of the kingdom rose like silent sentinels. His fortress lay on the northeast side of Mount Jinee and was protected by a sheer cliff which dropped over a thousand feet in front of the castle walls. Access to the great fortress was restricted to a narrow path that wound up the side of Mount Jinee. Elosha's palace lay to the south, on the summit of Mount Deschee. Between the two mountains lay the deeply scored Plains of Wonadsi, nearly two hundred miles of low-growing scrub and cheat grass which made it impossible to hide.

"If he is truly dead, only five remaining men need to be sniffed out and destroyed," Abadon snarled. "Only five chosen ones that stand between me and victory."

He crossed the room to the window that overlooked the stairway that had been cut into the side of the mountain. Ten thousand men had cut the steps by hand—over half of them perished in the process.

Nash Doitsoh and ten of his soldiers were descending the path to the base of the mountain, where their wolacs were stabled. Lightning flashed and thunder shook the mountains.

"Victory is so near. So very near."

With determination on his face, Abadon returned to the list. The next name beneath Tsalix Silverthorn was Asur Longtooth.

"Why Longtooth? He has not been trained in battle. He is a farm boy. Perhaps it is time to visit Aravah again." He swirled his black cloak around him and marched out of the room.

CHAPTER 3

ASUR PUSHED ON THE HANDLES AND FORCED THE BLADE OF the steel plow into the earth. He called encouragement to Kelechog, his mule, who pulled on the traces. Row after row of rich soil yielded to the blade until the field was ready to be sown. Ten generations of Longtooths had farmed the field on the fringe of Aravah, and with his father's leg broken it had fallen upon Asur to prepare the fields.

He wiped the sweat from his brow with his sleeve, and drank deeply from the water skin that hung around his neck and shoulder. He cupped one hand, filled it with water, and allowed the mule to lap it dry. He smiled as the tongue tickled his palm.

In the southwest the sun was dropping behind the sawtooth ridge of the high plateau which defined the edge of the kingdom. He released the plow, led Kelechog to the barn, removed the collar and harness and hung them on heavy wooden pegs driven into the side of the stall. He poured feed into the mule's trough, made sure the water barrel was full, and sponged down the sweat-flecked animal. When he was sure Kelechog was taken care of, he stepped into the cottage. His father lay on his bed, with his leg elevated. On each side of his leg was a stave of oak circled with cloth bands. Asur's mother was finishing dinner in the kitchen. The aroma of mutton stew greeted Asur as he sloughed off his coat and hung it on the peg by the door.

"How went the plowing?" his father said.

"Well enough. I'll be able to sow the seed in the morn." Asur stepped to the sink and splashed water on his grimy face and hands.

His mother handed him a scrap of linen to dry himself.

"The winter rains have been good to us," he said. "The soil is rich and ready."

His mother, Mona, scooped a bowlful of stew and took it to his father, then returned and filled a bowl for Asur. As usual she said little as she and her son sat at the table with their stew in front of them. A loaf of thick-crusted bread was covered with a cloth. Asur broke a piece of the loaf for each of them. They ate in silence. When the meal was finished, Mona stacked the bowls in the sink and poured boiling water from a pot that had been simmering on the wood-burning stove.

"The stew was wonderful." Asur nodded. "You take good care of us, Mother."

Mona smiled and bowed her head. "Thank you." She reached into her apron pocket and removed a small scroll that had been sealed with the red seal of the crown. "This was delivered today. I did not wish to disturb you until you had finished your supper."

Asur took the scroll and broke the seal with his thumbnail. "Who brought it?"

"A man on horseback. He appeared to have ridden a long way. There were a dozen with him offering protection."

Asur unrolled the scroll. It was about six inches long and four inches wide. Written in script was a request that he travel to meet with King Elosha at his castle on Mount Deschee. There was no date, only a request that he come as soon as it was convenient.

"Why me?" he said, after reading the invitation to his parents. "I can understand why he'd want Tsalix to come. But why, in the midst of this terrible war, would he want me? I'm no warrior. I'm a simple farmer."

His father struggled to raise himself from his bed. "I do not know why, but I do know you cannot ignore a request from the king."

"You must go, as much as I fear you leaving," his mother whispered.

"It says when it is convenient." Asur tossed a lock of his dark red hair out of his eyes. "I'll sow the seed tomorrow and leave the next morn."

The water in the sink had cooled enough that he could rinse the bowls.

"I'll be turning in," he said. "I'll need to get an early start to finish the fields in one day."

He bade goodnight to his parents and climbed the stairway to his bedroom in the loft.

His mother watched until he closed the door at the top of the stairs. Then she turned to his father.

"I feel foreboding," she said. "There is a chill that has settled in my bones."

"Aye, but he must go. I fear the ancient prophecy may be realized in our son. We'll have to give him a happy face when he leaves."

"If I can. If I can."

CHAPTER 4

"YOU, BOY," THE HORSEMAN CALLED TO THE YOUNG MAN WHO was splitting logs by the side of his house.

His steed blew a cloud of steam from its nostrils.

"I'm seeking Kwercus Strongheart. Do you know where he can be found?"

Behind him, a dozen mounted men waited.

"And for what purpose do you seek him?" The young man drove the blade of the ax into an oak log, with a resounding thud.

The horse reared on its hind legs.

"I have a message for him— message from the king."

"Well, you've found him." Kwercus tossed his head.

His long blond hair was heavy with sweat and clung to his forehead.

The horseman patted his steed's neck to calm it before sliding out of the saddle. He tucked his gloved hand inside his tunic and retrieved the scroll.

Walking toward Kwercus, he extended the scroll. "For you, then."

As soon as Kwercus took the scroll, the man gave a small salute, spun on his heel, mounted his horse, and galloped back to the waiting men, who turned as one and rode away.

Kwercus examined the small parchment scroll and saw the King's seal. A mixture of excitement and fear pulsed through his body as he broke the seal with his thumbnail and unrolled the scroll.

Kwercus Strongheart, greetings.

You are hereby summoned to an audience with the King.

Please present yourself as soon as is convenient.

Kwercus flattened the scroll on the floor of his cart and read it a second time. He looked across the field toward his parents' cottage. Smoke was rising from the chimney. Blue-painted shutters hung against whitewashed walls, and their cow mooed from the barn. All seemed peaceful. Then he moved his gaze up the flanks of Mount Jinee, to its cloud-shrouded peak, and shuddered.

Kwercus threw the rest of the split logs into the cart, wiped off the head of his ax, and pulled the load to the barn. The cow's mooing became louder and more urgent.

"I'll be out smartly to milk you." He strode to the door of the cottage.

His mother was seated at her spinning wheel when he walked into the house. Without a word he walked to her side and handed her the parchment scroll. Her eyes widened as she read the invitation.

"But Kwercus, why you?"

"I know not, but I must answer the call of my king." He turned to the basin to wash his hands. "Just as my father did." He poured water over his hands. "Tsalix was called, too." He wiped his face with the damp cloth. "I must go."

His mother nodded. "Aye, you must." Tears overflowed and ran down her cheeks. "When will you be going?"

"I'll need to make sure everything is ready for you in this early spring. Another load of wood, I'm thinking. I'll do it tomorrow and fix that broken rail in the fence. Then on the next morn, I'll be leaving."

She rose from her spinning and moved to her son. "You be careful. You're all that I have left." She threw her arms around him and hugged him.

"Aye." He hugged her back. "I'll take the foot path along the foot of the high plateau so I don't have to cross the Plain of Wonadsi until the very end of the journey. It may add a day to my travel, but I think it is much safer. Abadon seems to have concentrated his strength on the plains, and I intend to skirt his forces." He wiped the sweat from his face. "But first things first. I need to milk the cow."

His mother watched his broad shoulders as he moved to the barn. She sobbed quietly as she thought of his eminent departure.

She traipsed to the cupboard and removed a volume from the shelf. After turning the fragile leaves, she stopped at a page where a turned down corner marked the spot.

Dear is the day ax, sword, and plowshare meet.

Though fraught with peril and deadened in defeat,

all may join in jubilation if faithful the carriers pursue the prize without guile or pride, with strength imbued.

And joined with friends through coincidence or design,

they reach fulfillment of the promise—a faithful nine.

From the barn came a tuneful cadence as the stream of milk hit the side of the pail. Inside the cottage, a mother wept.

CHAPTER 5

T SALIX FILLED HIS WATER SKIN FROM THE SPRING, DIPPED HIS head, and drank the frigid water until his thirst was slaked. The sun was rising over the swampland to the southeast, causing the wisps of fog that danced from its surface to glow as if on fire. He had decided the night before, when he'd escaped his tomb, to travel further to the east and move along the margin of the swamp, rather than try to evade capture on the plain of Wonadsi.

After catching a couple hours sleep, he was eyeing the foot path that led out of the forest and along the edge of the Swamp of Miasma. Buttonwood, alder, and dogwood grew in clumps where patches of land emerged through the water. The sounds of swamp-dwelling reptiles echoed across the foul-smelling sludge.

Tsalix shaded his eyes from the low rays of the sun and surveyed the trail that clung to the edge of the swamp. It weaved in and out like a drunken man. He knew it would add an extra day to the travel, but seemed a more prudent path. Making sure his sword was sheathed, his shield hung on his back, and his breastplate in place, he stepped out of the woods and began his journey. The ground felt spongy under his feet, and he had taken less than a score of steps before a dark-toned lizard, more than a yard long, scurried across his path. It reared its head and emitted a sound much like a fingernail rubbing down a washboard.

Tsalix's hand flew to the hilt of his sword, and he shuddered. "At least the dragons have been destroyed." His heart beat like a trip hammer in his chest.

Behind him the lizard watched him go, then emitted a burst of flame from its mouth.

Tsalix jogged down the trail, trying to keep close to the scrub. At first the sun flitted between the trees and the temperature was comfortable. But as the day wore on, the sun burst above the canopy, and with the added humidity from the swamp, caused sweat to pour down Tsalix's face and body. He stopped to catch his breath, and looked back at Mount Jinee. It seemed as if he had made little progress. Clouds still surrounded the summit and defied the sun to reach the top of the mountain.

Tsalix found a clump of dogwood and hid himself. He drank from the skin he carried, and ate the last of the food he'd packed before leaving home. He closed his eyes for a moment, before the lack of sleep the previous night caught up with him and he drifted off. He dreamed he was back in the cave, despairing of dying and never being found. Panic seized him as forcefully as if the dream was real, and he awoke with a start.

Standing at his feet was a man clothed in shepherd's garb. His silver hair was drawn back into a ponytail, and his beard divided into two points, each encircled with a leather band. He poked Tsalix's foot with his staff.

"Ye'r alive, then," he said.

Tsalix tried to spring to his feet, but he was tangled in the branches of the bushes. The shepherd took a step backward and raised his staff as if to strike.

"I mean you no harm," Tsalix sputtered.

The shepherd held the staff in front of him. "So you say. But how do I know you speak the truth?"

Tsalix finally regained his footing, and turned to pick up his pack. The shield on his back caught the shepherd's eye.

"You be one of Johona's men? I see the crest on yer shield."

Tsalix nodded, slipped the shield in front of him, and stroked the diamond-shaped crest. It was divided horizontally and vertically, and each quadrant was painted a different color—black, white, yellow, and blue. A ruby-red circle covered their central meeting point. The shield itself had been rubbed with coarse sand to dull its finish so the sun would not reflect.

Tsalix stepped out of the thicket and onto the trail. The shepherd drew back a few more steps while still holding his crook in front of him. Tsalix's hand rested on the hilt of his sword.

"Where are your sheep?" Tsalix eyed the older man.

"In the hollow." He kept his gaze on Tsalix. "I was going to lead them to water when I saw your body in the gorse. You looked dead to me."

"Just half-dead from lack of sleep." Tsalix yawned before he shouldered his pack and replaced his shield. "I best be on my way."

"Not so fast. Where are the rest of your troops?"

Tsalix shook his head. "I am alone. I have been summoned to meet with the king."

"It is foolish to travel these wastelands alone."

"I have no choice." Tsalix bowed his head. "Now I must be going."

The shepherd stepped off the trail and looked over his shoulder. Apparently he was satisfied that Tsalix meant him no harm.

In the distance, the faint bleating of sheep could be heard.

"How long will you stay next to these foul waters?" the shepherd said.

"Until I can safely leave them and ascend the slopes of Mount Deschee."

The old man stroked the points of his gray beard. "There may be a safer way."

"And what would that be?"

"The plain looks flat, but it is braided with gullies from the winter floods. A man who knows his way might be able to avoid Abadon's men. It is a thought."

"And I suppose you are such a man?"

The old man nodded. "I am."

"And why would you do this?"

The shepherd shielded his eyes and looked across the wasteland. "I suppose each man makes a choice." He pulled his cloak around him and started marching across the plain.

Tsalix watched him until he took fifty steps and then began to disappear as he traveled down the side of a shallow ravine. The volume of the sheep's bleating increased. Indecision held Tsalix in check for another minute, before he followed the man's trail, found the edge of the slope, and hurried after the shepherd.

"Wise choice," the old man said, when he felt Tsalix's hand on his shoulder. "We'll move slowly until sunset. Then we'll pen the sheep for the night, and I'll lead you through the labyrinth."

"But who will tend the sheep tomorrow?"

"My brother. He will add my sheep to his."

"How will he know where they are?"

"He'll know." The old man began to lead the sheep down the defile. "But now it's best to be quiet. If someone spies us, you do not look much like a shepherd."

The sheep drifted along, and Tsalix found himself growing impatient at the pace.

At last the evening shadows drew around them. The shepherd climbed out of the gully and gathered thorn bushes, which he tumbled down the ravine to Tsalix, who piled them up to create a barrier for the sheep.

Covered with sweat, and sore from being pricked by many thorns, finally he and the old man provided a sheep fold that would keep the animals from wandering off during the night.

"Let us sleep a few hours. Then we will begin our journey." The old shepherd lay down and pulled his cloak over his body.

Tsalix sat and rested his head against the wall of the gully. Weary beyond belief, it took but a moment before he fell asleep. It seemed as if he had just closed his eyes when the shepherd prodded him with his staff.

"Time to begin."

The night was dark, and a sliver of moon barely provided any light. In the bottom of the chasm, Tsalix couldn't see his hand in front of his face.

The old shepherd turned to him. "Hold onto my staff, young warrior. I am used to the twists and turns."

He held the crook of his staff behind him, and Tsalix grasped it. They hurried along until the old man stopped, reached back, and put his hand over Tsalix's lips. Above them, they could hear the faint whistling breath of wolacs. The two men tiptoed, trying not to make a sound. After a few minutes, Tsalix could see the red glow of campfires casting shadows into their pathway, and he could hear the sounds of men moving around the camp above them on the plain. The two of them pressed themselves against the wall of the ravine and strove to remain in the shadows.

Step by careful step, they continued their journey until the campfires dimmed behind them.

"There will be more," the old man whispered.

As if to confirm the shepherd's prediction, a wolac keened a baleful cry that echoed down the chasm.

Less than an hour later, they spotted the campfires of another band of soldiers. The floor of the gully had risen until Tsalix and the shepherd had to bend at the waist to keep their heads below the rim. A gentle west wind was blowing toward the camp.

A wolac became agitated and strained against its restraining tether.

"He has caught our scent," the shepherd whispered. "Continue down the furrow until you reach a place where the chasm branches. On the left side is a cave of sorts that has been scoured by the spring runoff. Hide there until I can rejoin you." He straightened and began climbing the shallow wall. "If I do not join you by sunset, continue down the right branch. It leads to a shallow pool at the base of Mount Deschee." He used his staff to push himself over the lip of the gully, and began striding towards the campfires.

Tsalix continued to bend and crept down the path at the bottom of the ravine. He had made it no more than a hundred yards when he heard a voice above him.

"Who goes there?" Accompanied by the sound of a sword being drawn from its scabbard.

"A shepherd in search of his lost sheep."

"Stop where you are and put your hands away from your body."

Tsalix heard the crunch of footsteps on cheat grass as the sentry marched toward the shepherd. "There are no sheep here, old man." After a search, the soldier led the shepherd away.

With the sentry gone, Tsalix moved faster down the gully. More than two hours later, he came to the fork in the trail and found the washed-out cavern under the east lip. Wearily and fearfully he forced himself into the shallow pocket. The sun was rising behind him and cast shadows on the opposite wall. He removed his shield and pack, drank the last of his water, and fell into a troubled sleep.

CHAPTER 6

Asur adjusted his pack, picked up his walking stick, and turned toward the road that girdled Mount Jinee. His father had embraced him from his bed and wished him safety and speed. His mother had tried to be brave, but she finally turned her face from him to hide the tears.

"I'll be fine, Mum. I'm sure a farmer doesn't pose a threat. The seeds are sown, and I should be back long before harvest."

There was still an hour till sunrise, and the air was crisp and cool. There was little traffic on the road, and he had passed only two carts that were going toward Aravah. He saw no one traveling his direction.

Asur had mixed emotions about leaving his home. He hated to leave his father with his injured leg. A month ago, their cart had lost a wheel, rolled over and caught his father beneath the bed of the wagon, snapping his leg like a matchstick. It would be at least another month before he was able to help with the farming. Even though Asur had sown the seed yesterday, he knew there would be hours of weeding and irrigating the fields that would fall on his mother. Still, he had to admit that he was both excited and perplexed at being summoned to meet with the king. Asur had understood when his friend Tsalix had been ordered to appear—after all, he was a warrior who had proven himself in battle. But why he had been directed to meet with the king surprised him.

The pack on his back contained a change of clothing, strips of smoked meat, two loaves of bread, a wedge of hard cheese, and a bag of dried fruit. He carried no weapon besides a small knife he had tucked under his waistband. He was dressed as most of the farmers of his village were, in soft leather leggings and a fringed tunic that was secured around his waist with a strip of cloth. His feet were covered with knee-length buckskin boots. On his head was the traditional wide-brimmed hat with a crown shaped like a gum drop. He had a traveler's cloak that furled behind him as he walked.

Asur had traveled along the road until the sun and his stomach told him it was time for lunch. He began looking for a spring where he could stop to eat. Less than a half-mile further, he found a shady spot blessed with water and he stopped for a rest. Across the plain of Wonadsi, he could see the tip of Mount Deschee shimmering in the heatwaves that rose from the ground.

He broke the end off one of the loaves of bread, added a slice of cheese, and nibbled as he gazed across the plain. Realizing there would be two, or possibly three days without a source of water, he drank deeply from the spring and made sure his water skin was full. A narrow road branched from the one he was on, and traveled in a straight line to his destination nearly two hundred miles away. He ate the last crumb of bread and stepped onto the road to Mount Deschee.

The temperature began to rise as he left the shaded flanks of Mount Jinee. After an hour on the road, he was drenched in sweat. Still, he traveled on, taking sips of water from his flask. The sun continued its relentless arc through the sky until it settled beneath the flat top of Mount Litso's highest peak in the southwest. Rays of gold and purple streamed into the scattered clouds that crossed the dome above him. The air was noticeably cooler as the night approached.

In the gathering darkness, Asur spotted a flicker of firelight off the trail to his left. He left the road and crept toward what appeared to be a campsite. As his eyes adjusted to the darkness, he made out a dozen tents pitched around a cooking fire. A single figure turned a spit on which a whole carcass was skewered. Flames shot up as driblets of fat fell into the pit. Asur sniffed, and the aroma of cooking meat made his mouth water.

He sat on his haunches and surveyed the encampment for several minutes. There was no movement except for the cook, yet it was clear that the meal was being prepared for a large number of people.

When no one else appeared, Asur rose to his feet and approached the encampment. He reached the rear of the circle of tents and stood as still as a statue in the shadow until he was certain the only person in camp was the cook. Staying in the shadows, he slipped down the side of the tent until he was no more than a dozen feet from the fire. Then he saw that the cook had only one leg—the other was a wooden peg. And around his ankle was a shackle attached to a long chain. Asur could not see where the other end of the chain ended, but it snaked into the shadows on the other side of the circle of tents.

Asur took a deep breath and crept into the firelight. The man who was tending the spit jerked upright.

"Who goes there," he quavered.

"Aye, I am Asur, born to the clan of Longtooth, and for the Bitterroot clan. Who might you be?"

The man grasped the handle of his butcher knife. "I am called Cedrus. I was born to the clan of Water Running Blue, and for the Rushing Wind clan." He eyed Asur. "What are you doing here on the Plain of Wonadsi?" He stepped back to place himself on the opposite side of the fire from Asur.

Asur spread his hands, showing that he bore no sword. "I have been summoned to Hayeli on Mount Deschee," he whispered. "I know not why, but I am responding to the call of the king." He pointed at Cedrus's shackle. "And what means this?"

Cedrus dropped his head in shame. "I was the last of Johona's men standing at the Battle of Sandhill. It would have been better had I been numbered among the dead. But instead I was seized by Abadon's forces." He wiped his arm across his face. "Now I am forced to tend the camp while they run their nightly forays across the countryside."

"How long until they return?"

"Near midnight." Cedrus turned the spit, and more fat dropped into the fire, creating a wall of flame. "And I must have food ready for them."

"Or?"

Cedrus looked across the fire, into Asur's eyes. The man paused before he slid his tunic over his head and turned so his back faced the fire. Asur could see the welts that covered Cedrus's back, some so new they were still oozing blood.

"Or this. Or worse." Cedrus looked down at the wooden peg that served for his left leg. "They let a wolac bite my leg with its pincers. The acid ate into my leg until I fainted from the pain. When I awoke, my leg was gone."

They two stood silently for several moments.

"Where do you get wood for the fire?" Asur said.

Cedrus pointed into the shadows between two of the tents. "There is a wagon load of wood, one of provisions, and next to it a water gully. The wolacs drag them here from the slopes of Jinee."

"I see." Asur looked at the thin sliver of moon that had risen over the eastern rim. "I wish there was something I could do to help, but I am a simple farmer without a weapon to even defend myself."

"I understand," Cedrus whispered. "I pray for help, but I know it will be a long time coming." He turned the spit again. "And while there is little help you can offer me, I can offer you at least your fill of meat and a chance to refill your waterskin. But I fear you must hasten and be on your way before they return."

"I thank you, Cedrus."

Asur made his way into the shadows and found the water cart. The other end of Cedrus' tethering chain was locked around the axle. He filled his skin, and when he returned to the fire the cook had sliced off a healthy piece of meat, which he offered to Asur on the tip of his knife. Asur found the offering too hot to handle, and waited until it cooled before taking it and sinking his teeth into the meal. When he had finished, he wiped his hands on his tunic and clasped Cedrus's hand in his own.

"Thank you again, my friend. I will tell others of your plight."

Cedrus bowed his head. "Now go, Asur Longtooth. And may goodness go with you."

Asur walked between the tents and waited for his eyes to adjust to the darkness before he returned to the road. He traveled another hour before he left the road again, found a shallow depression in the ground, lay down and covered himself with his cloak. Drenched in weariness, it took but a few seconds before he drifted off to sleep.

CHAPTER 7

K WERCUS SLIPPED THE HAFT OF HIS AX INTO HIS BROAD waistband and adjusted it so it did not hinder his step. The sun had not yet breached the eastern skyline, and a hint of frost was in the air. He had left home an hour before in the grayness of pre-dawn, and headed to the faint trail that skirted the base of the high plateau. His mother had risen with him and had filled his rucksack with food for his trip. It was all she could do to part with him as he left her embrace and responded to the call of his king. His heart ached for her.

A half-day's journey ahead of him, he knew he would reach the hamlet of Hagade that was built on the headwaters of the Tohkal River. Unlike most of the villages that subsisted on farming, the slopes west of Hagade harbored the entrance to the depths of Nanish, a gold mine that supplied the entire kingdom with precious metal. Abadon had spent an enormous amount of resources in trying to gain control of Nanish.

Kwercus wondered what kind of reception he would receive. Even with this potential problem, he felt he was safer than marching across the Plain of Wonadsi.

The sun rose, sending shafts of golden light into the eastern sky and making the crest of the plateau glow in the crystal morning air. Kwercus beamed and continued his journey down the faded trail. Years of lumber-jacking had toughened his body, and the thought of walking two hundred miles was no major obstacle. His mind wandered as he walked, and he could not help but think of his mother, home alone, with no one to look after her. He wavered, wondering where his allegiance lay, before striding down the pathway toward the king.

Mother will be all right. She's raised me without any help, and she can certainly take care of herself.

The sun was nearly overhead when Kwercus reached a stone bridge that spanned the Tohkal River. He stopped before crossing the bridge, and studied the village on the other side. There were few people in the street, but he could see no evidence of Abadon's forces. Still, he wanted to be sure before he crossed over the bridge.

He moved to the side of the road and sat on a large, flat stone. While he was drinking from his flask, a tall figure dressed in pale buckskin leggings and a fringed coverlet crossed over the bridge. Kwercus acknowledged the man with a nod \ as he wiped his lips with the back of his hand.

"Welcome, stranger," the man said, in a flowing dialect different from the harsher sounds of Aravah.

"Thank you." Kwercus as he rose to his feet and extended his hand.

The stranger clasped Kwercus forearm, a greeting common among the people.

"What brings you to Hagade?" the man said.

"I'm just passing through, on my way to meet with King Elosha."

"Indeed! And may I ask, what is your business with the king?"

"I know not. I am responding to his call." Kwercus lifted his rucksack to his shoulder. "May I pass?"

The stranger stared at him for a short time. "Of course." He waved his hand toward the bridge.

Kwercus nodded at the man, then continued across the bridge. When he reached the other side, he looked back at the stranger, only to find him striding away down the road.

Hagade was a small village of perhaps five dozen thatched-roof cottages. There was but a single road running through the town. On the east side, the river coursed by. While to the west, higher on the hill, the opening of the mine gaped. The trail to the mine was worn. In the middle of town was an inn with three separate rooms. One side provided a few rooms where travelers might sleep. In the middle was the eating room, and on the other side a small general store where a visitor might purchase necessities. There were none of the usual tourist items, and Kwercus surmised there were few who took this longer route.

He considered stopping at the inn and eating his midday meal, but he had brought little money with him and realized it would be prudent to keep his coins until he was sure he no longer needed them.

The people of the town stared at him as he passed through, but none spoke until he reached the far end of town. There, the only child he viewed in the entire hamlet, a small girl perhaps five years of age, said, "Mister, where are you from?"

Kwercus stopped and bent toward the little maid. "I'm from Aravah." He pointed back up the trail.

"I don't know where that is." She ran to her mother and buried her face in the woman's skirt.

Kwercus waited for someone else to speak, but when none did, he nodded and continued his trek. While he thought it was strange that no one had spoken to him or offered him a hand of friendship—which was common throughout the kingdom—he hoped he'd be able to reach the next town, Bitahkiz, by nightfall. Bitahkiz had been founded on the middle branch of the Tohkal River and was renowned for its broad pastures and healthy herds of cattle. The foothills of the plateau spread out for several miles until they merged with the cheat grass and scrub of Wonadsi. He hoped he might find a place to sleep, out of the chill of the night.

Kwercus lengthened his stride and pushed forward toward Bitahkiz. The sun was setting behind the high plateau as he rounded a corner and saw the wooden bridge that spanned the middle fork of Tohkal. Again he stopped before crossing the span. The trail had climbed higher on the hillside, and he was surrounded by lush green grass that extended down into the valley. Herds of cattle feasted in the meadow. The town of Bitahkiz was much larger than Hagade, and there were many people strolling down the main street. It appeared peaceful, and Kwercus could see no evidence of soldiers near the bridge.

He crossed the span with echoing footsteps that mingled with the rushing river below. A small shed sat to the side of the bridge on the far end, and as Kwercus approached it, a man stepped out of it. Although he was barely five-feet tall, he appeared to be in charge. He was dressed in black leather and wore a helm with a violet crest on his head. His hand rested on the hilt of his sword.

"Who goes there?" he said.

"Kwercus Strongheart of Aravah."

"And what is your business, Kwercus Strongheart of Aravah?"

Kwercus thought for a moment whether he should reveal his quest or not.

He swiveled his head and threw the hair out of his eyes. "I have been summoned to see the king."

"But what is your business with Bitahkiz?"

"None. I am just passing through."

"See that you do." The little man stepped back into the shed.

Trying to keep from laughing, Kwercus gave a faint salute toward the gatekeeper and walked into town. Just as in Hagade, no one spoke to him. He found a larger inn than in the previous town, and pushed the heavy oak door open and stepped into the tavern. A dozen tables were scattered around the room, while a long, stained bar curved around the far side of the chamber. Most of the tables were occupied by men who had tankards in front of them.

As Kwercus entered the room, every head swiveled his way and the noisy conversations in the room stopped. Except for a couple of throats being cleared and the scuffle of feet on the roughhewn floor, there was no sound. Kwercus wound through the seated patrons, to the bar, where a large, florid man stood behind it.

"Is there a place I can spend the night?"

The man snorted. "Not likely."

Kwercus could feel the tension in the room. He turned slowly and looked at the assembled crowd. Every eye was on him.

"You're sure?" he said.

The bartender nodded. "We're all full up."

"Then I guess I'll be moving on." Kwercus hurried to the doorway. "Good evening."

The door swung shut behind him.

What is going on? We'd certainly entertain a visitor in Aravah. It's as if everyone is frightened to death of a stranger.

He walked through the rest of the town until he reached a fence that ran down the hillside, onto the plain. The green grass ended on this side of the fence, and on the other side was a barren hillside. He stepped through a gate in the fence and looked over his shoulder at the townspeople. It was if a collective breath had been exhaled, and the people were coming back to life.

A few miles further down the trail, he came to a stream that was fed by a waterfall that feathered from the top of the plateau to the valley below. Kwercus traveled toward the base of the waterfall and found a valley about a half-mile in diameter. Wild berries grew on bushes surrounding the shallow pond, and they were sweet and refreshing.

Darkness was fast approaching, so he used some vines to bend over willows and fashion a leafy roof to protect him. He ate a meager dinner from his rucksack before lying back on the moss-covered ground and preparing to sleep.

"Tomorrow I'll reach Atsanh. Perhaps they'll be a little friendlier."

CHAPTER 8

"WELL?" ABADON SAID. "I DON'T SEE SILVERTHORN'S BODY."
Nash Doitsoh shook his mane. "It is not there, your majesty. Somehow the slab of rock we placed over his tomb has been moved." He growled. "I have failed you, your majesty." The huge warrior sank to his knees in front of Abadon.

Abadon screamed, "Find him! Bring him to me. Do not fail me again, or you'll pay." He pointed toward the doorway of the chamber. "Go!"

Captain Doitsoh pushed himself up and sprang for the door. "I'll not fail you again, sire." He disappeared down the hallway.

Abadon turned to the map and his list of twelve selected men. He could see the small mark where he'd begun to draw a line through Tsalix Silverthorn's name. He screamed again.

Nash Doitsoh gathered six of his most trusted men and started descending from Abadon's palace, toward the base of Mount Jinee. The obsidian steps curled down the side of the mountain. Although they provided great protection to the palace—only wide enough for one man to climb—they inhibited Nash and his men from moving downward as quickly as they'd have liked.

Once they reached the base of the mountain, he gathered his men around him.

"You four, go back to the cavern and see if you can follow the trail of that worthless worm. If you find him, bring him back, but do not kill him. Master Abadon must see him perish for himself." He beckoned to the other two men. "You come with me. I think we will visit his home in

Aravah and see if he has returned there. Perhaps some persuasion will help us find him."

Four of the men sprinted down the trail, while Doitsoh and his two soldiers began tracking backward to the northwest, around the foothills of Mount Jinee. They hurried, and in slightly more than an hour, they reached the quiet village. The three of them, clad in black mail and carrying a staff with the black and scarlet emblem of Abadon, strode down the main street. Doors slammed behind them.

Nash Doitsoh spotted an old woman scrubbing clothes in a washtub behind her cottage. A spotless white picket fence surrounded the house. He pushed open the gate, and in five steps was beside the woman.

"Where does Tsalix Silverthorn live," he said.

The woman dropped her clothes into the tub and raised her hands to cover her mouth.

Doitsoh drew his sword from its scabbard. "I asked you a question," he snarled.

The woman pointed at a home three doors down the street. "There," she squeaked.

Nash slammed his sword back into its sheath, spun on his heel, and beckoned to his men. A few second later, he pounded on the Silverthorn's door with his mailed fist.

"Open up!"

Tsalix's mother opened the door."

In one step Nash was inside the room. "Where is your son?" He put his hand on her shoulder and pushed her into a chair.

"He went to see the king?" she burst into tears.

"When?"

"Four days ago." She tried to escape the hand that was clamped on her shoulder. "He was summoned."

"Where is your husband?"

"He's tending the herd."

"Are you lying to me, woman?"

She shook her head.

Nash shook his mane and said to his men, "Search the house. Leave nothing unturned."

The two men immediately began their search.

"If I find out you are lying, I will cut your tongue out and stuff it down your throat."

She sobbed even harder. "I am telling you the truth," she sputtered, between sobs.

"For your sake, I hope so."

While Doitsoh held the woman with his steel grip, his two henchmen destroyed the cottage.

"Nothing," they said. "He's not here."

"Unless he escaped while we were searching the house. Perhaps he is hiding somewhere in the village."

"I'm telling you the truth," Tsalix's mother moaned. "He left four days ago to see the king."

Nash Doitsoh ran his hand through his beard. "Perhaps." He turned to his men. "Burn the village."

CHAPTER 9

Tsalix had slept fitfully in the little cavern cut into the wall of the gully. When the sun reached its zenith, light had flooded into the pocket and awakened him. He was parched and wished he had not drunk all his water. Knowing that Abadon's troops loomed near, and afraid to be discovered, he shrank back into the cavern and remained hidden from the nearby plain.

Throughout the day he heard the movement of wolacs and men above him. It seemed an eternity before the sun set behind the high plateau to the west. Tsalix wondered what had become of the shepherd and whether he'd ever see him again.

When, at last, the final gray shadows of dusk sank into darkness, Tsalix emerged from his den and stretched. His body ached from being bent and confined throughout the day. He replaced his breastplate and flexed his shoulders under the burden. His mouth felt as dry as powdered pemmican. He bent to retrieve his sword when he heard a sound behind him in the darkness. He drew his sword from its sheath as silently as he could, and positioned himself against the wall of the gully.

He strained to hear another sound, but only the moaning of the wind greeted his ears. Last night's sliver of moon was gone, and the darkness was even more oppressive. Tsalix's heart was pounding like a kettle drum in his chest.

A hand shot out of the darkness and covered Tsalix's mouth.

"Be still, young warrior," the shepherd whispered.

Tsalix nearly dropped to his knees.

"It is time for us to move on. Here, have a drink."

Tsalix guzzled. As he had done the night before, the shepherd held his staff so Tsalix could grasp the crook as they moved down the channel. Just like the previous night, twice more they passed campfires. The two men moved as silent as shadows until they were well past the encampments.

When the sky began to lighten, Tsalix realized the day was about to break.

"We must find a place to hide," he whispered.

"I think we are safe." The old man climbed out of the defile and looked around. "Yes. You can come up."

In the distance, sunlight shimmered off the surface of a shallow pond.

Tsalix scrambled up the side of the furrow until he stood next to the old man. Instead of dry cheat grass, there were clumps of green surrounding him. Mount Deschee loomed high above him, although he still had several miles to travel before he'd reach its base.

"I believe you will be safe now, my young friend. My sheep need me." The shepherd saluted with his staff and began to walk away.

"How can I thank you?" Tsalix took a few steps toward him. "And how did you escape?"

"You can thank me by following the king. As to my escape...well, I was just a shepherd looking for his lost sheep. I was no threat to anyone."

"You mean, they just let you go?"

"I spent the morning with them, listening to their chatter. When they were convinced I meant no harm, they released me."

Tsalix looked at the old man. He certainly didn't seem a threat to anyone, but it was still hard to believe that Abadon's men had let him go so easily.

"Go in peace, my friend," Tsalix said.

"And you." The old man turned and began walking back across the plain.

Tsalix watched him go until he was but a small figure on the landscape. Then he turned toward the mountain. It rose like a broad cone from the plain. The top was truncated, and on that flat surface was the town of Hayeli, which housed the palace of King Elosha. The sandstone peak glowed scarlet in the early morning sunlight. Tsalix knew the sides were not smooth. They were deeply seamed from erosion. But at this distance, the mountain looked like a smooth pyramid.

He adjusted his scabbard so that it hung comfortably on his left hip. He moved his water skin to his right hip. Somehow the old shepherd had managed to bring sufficient water to refill it. He waved one last time toward the shepherd before continuing his trek toward the mountain.

Before noon, he was walking through ankle-high grass. Cattle were grazing in the lush meadows. Tsalix could not believe the difference a few miles made. Having never traveled to Mount Deschee before, he had not expected to see what he was seeing.

An hour later, he came upon a small village. There was no sign giving its name, but as he entered, the people greeted him with smiles.

"Welcome, stranger," an elderly woman said, from the barn at the side of her house.

She was tending a thriving garden plot.

"Thank you," Tsalix replied. "Where am I? If I might ask?"

"It is called Teless. What brings you across the great plain?"

Tsalix approached the woman. "I am Tsalix Silverthorn of Aravah. I am responding to a call from the king."

She smiled. "It is good to have you cross our path." She bent to tug a weed from the garden. "You have come a long way. I suspect you might be hungry. May I offer you food?"

"With pleasure." He heard his stomach rumble. "If it is not too much trouble."

The woman removed her gloves, dusted off her smock, and bade Tsalix to follow her toward her cottage.

"I am called Tonya. Please, I have prepared a simple stew for supper. It is nothing fancy, but I think it is filling."

She opened the door to the cottage and let Tsalix into the cool interior of her home. The aroma of the bubbling stew made his mouth water.

"I am indebted to you." He bowed. "This is more than I could have hoped for."

"You flatter me, Tsalix."

She ladled stew into an earthen bowl and placed it before him on the table. As he began to eat, she studied.

When he had finished and had drunk two glasses of foaming milk, she said, "Are you one of the twelve?"

"Twelve?" His brow furrowed. "I know not what you mean."

Tonya took a step backward. "Perhaps I have said too much."

"All I know is that I was summoned by King Elosha, and I am here to obey his command."

The woman smiled. "Then I shan't delay you. There is still a long and wearisome climb to Hayeli, where the king resides."

She walked toward the doorway, and Tsalix realized she was dismissing him.

"Thank you for your kindness." He bowed. "You have made my day brighter." He waved over his shoulder as he continued his trek.

Many people smiled and acknowledged him either with a wave or a nod as he continued through Teless. The ground began to rise, almost imperceptibly at first. But after a couple miles, the slope increased dramatically. A narrow road spiraled around Mount Deschee, and Tsalix's legs began to tire. He realized he had traveled nearly halfway around the mountain, and decided it was time to stop and rest for a few minutes.

A large slab of sandstone had fallen to the side of the trail, and he sat in its shade. He drank deeply from his waterskin and gazed out over the view to the south. The green sward he had crossed on the north side of the peak extended a short distance to the south, where it was met with the borders of Shayeksten, the Desert of Desolation.

As difficult as his journey had been over the Plain of Wonadsi, he was glad he had not had to cross Shayeksten. The air was shimmering with heat, even though it was early spring. Occasional dust devils swirled across the sand. To the far south, the tip of Mount Tsood was visible through the dancing heat waves—a blue oasis in a sea of unbroken tan.

Tsalix stood and gauged the time of day from where the sun stood in the western sky. He knew he had only a couple more hours before darkness set in. He began striding as fast as his weary legs permitted.

As he predicted, the sun set before he crested the peak. He stepped to the edge of the trail and looked up. The top of the mountain seemed miles above him, and he realized he would not finish his quest this day. He looked for a spot where he could sleep with comfort, and found a place where erosion had created a bed of sand. He took the last of his food from his pack and drank the warm water from his skin. With pinpricks of stars shining down on him, he pulled his cloak around him and sank into a dreamless sleep.

CHAPTER 10

A SUR ROSE BEFORE DAWN AND RUBBED THE SLEEP FROM HIS eyes. The skyline to the east was just beginning to change from obsidian black to somber gray. He surveyed the countryside in all directions, and seeing no movement, he returned to the road that led to Mount Deschee. A stiff wind was blowing from the west, and tumbleweeds were racing across the ground like huge cockleburs, bouncing and spinning in the breeze.

He pulled his cloak around him and began striding toward the peak in the distance. After an hour the sun peeked above the horizon and the wind began to die down. Asur found a stunted tree near the side of the trail, sat beneath it, and munched on some of the food in his pack. He sipped, not knowing if there was any water ahead of him. After his brief break, he continued on his trek.

He had walked for nearly four hours when he saw something reflecting a flash of sunlight ahead of him on the trail. He looked for somewhere he could hide, but found none. Steeling himself for what might lie ahead, he continued down the road. Nearly an hour passed before he could see a convoy approaching him. He knew he could not hide, and his heart began racing.

A lone rider on horseback left the mass of men and cantered down the trail to intercept him. Asur found the hilt of the knife at his waist as he waited for the rider to approach. The sun reflected from the horseman's mail as he reined his horse to a halt and lowered his spear so the point was aimed at Asur's chest.

"Who goes there?"

Asur spread his arms to show he bore no weapons. "I am Asur Long-tooth of Aravah."

"What seek ye here?"

"I am summoned to Mount Deschee by King Elosha." Asur tried to keep his voice from trembling.

He began to reach inside his tunic to retrieve the scroll, but as he did the horseman pushed the spear even closer to his chest.

"Stop!"

"I meant no harm. I would like to show you the scroll."

The horseman pondered for a moment. "All right. Use one hand and keep the other above your head."

Asur withdrew the scroll and wrapped it around the handle of the spear behind the iron head. The horseman raised it and let the scroll slide down to his hand. After he examined it, he placed the butt of the spear in its socket and beckoned for Asur to approach him. He handed Asur the scroll, and Asur took a deep breath and tried to calm his shaking knees.

"Be careful, Asur of Aravah. There are those who would not like you to respond to the king.

He wheeled his horse and returned to the troops who had halted a quarter-mile down the road. As he turned, Asur saw the four-colored crest of Johona on the man's shield. He nearly fell to the ground in relief.

When he could finally trust himself to walk again, he continued his trek. The armed men parted as he approached them, and let him through.

"We would go with you and provide protection," the lead horseman said, as Asur passed him, "but we are on a mission that cannot be ignored."

The troops began marching past Asur.

"May peace go with you," the captain said.

"And with you," Asur replied.

He paused and watched as nearly five hundred men passed by, then resumed his course. He saw no one else for the remainder of the day.

As night approached he saw the first vestiges of greenery, and in the distance the glimmer of the lights of a village. He hoped he could refill his waterskin—it was nearly empty after a day of marching across the plain. His feet were sore and his legs were weary, but he continued until he saw a small farm house. There were lights shining in the barn, where a man was milking a herd of cows.

Asur turned from the path and walked into the barn. The sound of milk squirting into a pail was a familiar one. The farmer was intent on his task, with his head against the flank of the cow, and did not see Asur at first. When he caught sight of him, he jumped to his feet.

"You startled me."

Asur bowed his head. "I am sorry, sir. I meant no harm." He patted the rump of a black-and-white-spotted cow. "I have just crossed the great plain and am hoping I can fill my flask from your well."

"You crossed Wonadsi? You are made of stern stuff, young man."

Asur counted the cows in the barn. "You have a fine herd here, good sir. Would you like help milking them?"

The farmer looked uncertain. "Aye, if you'd like to help, I won't turn it down. My son who usually helps me has gone on an assignment with his sister."

Asur nodded again, slipped off his cloak, and took position at the side of one of the cows. He patted her side before milking her. The cow shifted, and Asur spoke to her in soft tones.

An hour later the two of them had milked the cows and poured the milk through a strainer, into huge earthen pots.

"Just like home." Asur smiled.

The farmer put out his hand. "Who are you and where are you from, young man?"

"I am Asur Longtooth of Aravah."

The man smiled broadly. "I am your kin. I am Sambucus, born to the Bitterroot clan. I left Aravah nearly twenty years ago when the fighting threatened our village. Welcome, Asur. Come into the house, eat with us, and tell us why you have crossed the great plain."

After washing the dust from their hands and faces, the two men entered the cozy cottage. The heady aroma of beef stew enveloped them. Sambucus led him into the kitchen, where a woman stirred the stew with a wooden spoon.

"Tonya, this is Asur, my cousin who has crossed the Plain of Wonadsi to visit us."

Asur bowed. "I am honored."

"And I." She reached for another bowl and began ladling the stew. "It is good I prepared extra today. You are the second man to grace our home."

"Oh?" Sambucus seated himself at the table and signaled for Asur to sit. "I did not know of another."

"He came earlier while you were out herding the cattle. He is traveling to see the king."

"As am I," Asur said. "Did he tell you his name?"

"Tsalix Silverthorn," she said.

Asur dropped his spoon. "How long ago was he here?"

"Half a day, I suppose. He was in a hurry to reach Hayeli."

"Then I must go."

"Eat first, my cousin," Sambucus said. "It is a full day's climb to the summit."

"And even if he gets there before you," Tonya said, "there is only one way. At the worst, you will pass him as you ascend and he comes down the road."

"Stay and sleep here where it is comfortable. You can leave first thing in the morning."

Asur rubbed his throbbing legs. "If I am no trouble."

"None at all," Sambucus said. "With our son and daughter gone, it is a comfort to have someone with which to share a meal."

"Where have they gone?"

Tonya glanced at her husband and saw the nearly imperceptible shake of his head.

"On an errand," she said.

CHAPTER 11

KWERCUS APPROACHED THE BRIDGE THAT CROSSED THE south fork of the Tohkal River. The town of Atsanh lay on the other side. This branch of the river was much broader than the previous two, and the bridge was supported on stone pillars that extended up from the midst of the rushing river. Heavy wooden planks made up the bridge's bed.

Kwercus stepped onto the bridge and heard a hollow echo from below. After the lack of greeting he had received in Hagade and Bitahkiz, he hoped for a friendlier welcome in Atsanh.

It was mid-morning, and the sun shone brightly from the eastern sky. A few sheep-fleece clouds scudded above the high plateau. Kwercus crossed the bridge without meeting anyone and continued around the bend that led him into the town. Atsanh was built within a fold in the hills created by two huge ribs of rock that thrust toward the plain below. As he turned the corner, the blast of a horn well above him rang out through the valley. Kwercus looked up to see a man high upon the hillside, with a long-barreled trumpet to his lips. He sounded a second and third blast before disappearing from view.

In a trice, the doors and windows of the village slammed shut. The few people who were outside their homes and shops scurried inside and closed their doors. Kwercus walked down the main street of the town without seeing a single soul.

He recognized the sign of an inn swinging in the mild morning breeze, turned in on its short path, and knocked on the door. No answer.

Bemused, he returned to the main road and continued walking toward the south end of town, where cattle grazed in the meadows. Herds of sheep were above the town on the grassy slopes and a few stray dogs sniffed at his boots as he passed them. Even they did not bark.

In less than a half-hour, he traversed the entire valley and followed the road around the rock rib that marked the end of Atsanh. Curious to see what would happen, he waited a few minutes then furtively stuck his head around the pile of rock. The town had come to life once he passed through. Although he thought the action was peculiar, he did not wish to create a scene, so he continued down the road.

He had almost reached the point where the road branched—the west branch continued on south, to the Sea of Tabass and eventually Mount Litso. The other branch turned to the southeast and crossed the toe of the Plain of Wonadsi, to Mount Deschee.

Kwercus stopped at the fork in the path, climbed a short distance up the foothill until he found a source of water, and sat to enjoy a brief stop for lunch. The shade beneath the trees was welcome, the spring water cold, and the view spectacular. He could see across the plain to the slopes of Deschee, forty miles away. The air was crystal clear, and it seemed as if, for once, the world was at peace.

He finished the last of the dried fruit his mother had packed for him, drank from the pool, and began the final leg of his sojourn. A bridge spanned Tohkal and sent him on the road to Mount Deschee.

He had traveled less than a half-mile down the trail when he heard the thunder of hoofbeats behind him. He spun around to see a warrior astride a wolac, bearing down on him. The rider had his tsenil, the double-bladed ax, drawn back as if to strike. Fear rose in Kwercus's throat and almost paralyzed him. At the last second, he side-stepped the racing beast and drew his ax from his belt. The wolac skidded to a halt, spun as quickly as its six legs would permit, and charged again. This time Kwercus was ready. Instead of side-stepping the charge, he dropped to one knee and stooped beneath the wolac. With a swift strike of his ax, he severed the left front leg. The wolac squealed and staggered to the left. Kwercus struck the left middle leg, and the steed toppled on its side. The rider was thrown off the back of the animal.

Although wolacs were armored with a thick exoskeleton on their backs and flanks, there was a soft spot between the head and thorax.

Kwercus's next blow nearly severed the beast's head from its body. He jumped backward to escape the viscous green fluid that spurted from the wound.

Kwercus drew a deep breath and tried to still his heart, which was threatening to burst from his chest. He crept around the tail end of the wolac and saw the rider lying a dozen feet away. He lay unmoving. His tsenil had slipped from his grasp and was laying a couple of paces away.

As Kwercus moved slowly toward the fallen man, sweat drenched his shaggy blond hair and ran down his neck. He approached the rider, remaining between the man and his weapon. Keeping his ax at the ready, he watched to see if the man's chest rose and fell. No movement. He picked up the tsenil and carried it back to the fallen wolac, where he stuck the blood-red head of the ax in the fluid that continued to pour from the fatal wound. The head of the tsenil sizzled and gave off noxious fumes as it began to dissolve.

Kwercus' knees shook. *Where there is one, there are more.*

He washed the head of his ax with water from his flask before trotting down the trail toward Deschee. When he had jogged for nearly an hour and had not seen any pursuers, he slowed down to catch his breath. Sweat was pouring off him, and his mouth felt as dry as a pussy willow. He fought the urge to drink all his water, and forced himself to stop when the skin was half-empty.

Once he had rested for but a moment, he began striding toward his destination. The encounter with the wolac and its rider had unnerved him, and he continually looked back over his shoulder to see if he was being pursued.

The wolacs were ridden without saddle or reins. Once a wolac hatched, it was assigned to a rider who raised it until it was full-sized. The beast responded to the thoughts of its master and needed no bridle to control its direction. The narrow spot between head and thorax created a comfortable spot for a rider. A full-grown wolac stood nearly ten-feet high at its shoulder, and with six legs, it provided a stable platform for a warrior.

Night was approaching, but Kwercus continued on the pathway. He had decided he would not be safe until he reached the slopes of Deschee. It was nearly midnight before he spotted a few blinking lights in the distance. At the side of the road was a sign that read, *Welcome to Chushka.*

He hoped the welcome there would be warmer than he had received in the three towns he'd already passed through.

Only a few of the houses had candles or lanterns lit, but enough that he could find his way down the main street. Laughter trickled as he crept down the road. It grew louder as he approached a building with an open door. Inside, a dozen men sat at round oak tables.

Kwercus took a deep breath and walked through the doorway.

"Hale, good fellow." One of the men raised his mug.

"And to you," Kwercus replied.

"You look weary. Have you traveled far?"

"Aye, from Aravah."

"You don't say. You have come a long way, my son. What brings you here to Chushka?"

Everyone seemed interested in his reply, but there was no malice in their faces.

"I have been summoned to the king."

"Have you now."

"Aye."

"Well, it's too late to see him tonight. Besides, you still have a long climb up the mountain." The innkeeper clapped a hand on Kwercus' shoulder. "Stay with us tonight, young traveler. You'll find your climb tomorrow much easier after a good night's sleep and with a full stomach."

"Hear, hear." The rest of the men raised their mugs.

Kwercus beamed. "How could I refuse such a kind invitation?"

He sank down on one of the benches and relaxed for the first time since his encounter with the warrior. *What a difference there is between the people of Chushka and the rest of the villages I've passed through.* He fought to keep his eyes open.

CHAPTER 12

THE VILLAGE LAY SMOLDERING IN THE LAST SLANTING RAYS OF sunlight. Not one cottage or barn had been spared. Nash Doitsoh sat astride his wolac and surveyed the scene before him. Most of the villagers had fled. He'd had them rounded up and each one inspected by his men before they led them up the mountain to Abadon's dungeons.

A few had perished in the fires. *Stupid souls trying to free their animals.* They had identified each of the burned bodies—Tsalix Silverthorn was not among them. It appeared that his mother had told the truth. *Well, that's the problem with war. One never knows who to believe.*

His wolac dropped to its knees at his master's mental request, and Nash sprang to the ground. With the toe of his boot, he brushed ash out of the way as he looked at the remains of an outbuilding that was now nothing more than a pile of burned wood. Wisps of smoke twisted upward and danced a macabre waltz through the fresh evening breeze. The air was thick with the acrid smell of fire and roasting flesh. Nash pondered the situation. He knew if he did not bring evidence of the death of Tsalix Silverthorn to Abadon, he was likely to lose his head. Where the boy was, no one knew. It seemed inconceivable that he could evade all the warriors that roamed the Plain of Wonadsi. He had troops scouring the plain during the day, and a second watch patrolling at night. It was a rare soul who escaped his grasp. Still, he had no idea where Tsalix might be hiding.

"Captain?" One of his men approached him.

"Speak."

"There is no one left alive in the town. All is destroyed, as you requested. We have rounded up and begun removing most of the villagers."

"How many are dead?"

The soldier rubbed his cheek with his mailed hand. "Perhaps twenty or so. But all were warned before we torched the town."

"Aye, they were warned." He dismissed the man with a wave of his hand. "Fools!"

Nash Doitsoh walked through the ash, to the remaining stone foundation of a barn. Inside were the carcasses of a dozen animals. He shook his head in disgust.

The body of a man lay near what had probably been a small calf. He was barely recognizable as a human being. Not only had his clothing burned away, but most of his skin was charred as well. Nash shook his head. His mane smelled of smoke, and as he tossed his head, bits of debris fell from it. He turned to leave the barn, then stopped and looked at the charred corpse again. He smiled and let out a hoarse laugh.

"Lieutenant Legai, I need your cloak."

Without hesitation, Legai removed it and handed it to his captain.

Nash wrapped the body in the cloak and secured it to the back of his wolac. The three of them returned to the stables at the base of the stairway that led to Abadon's palace. Ahead of them, the captives climbed the ten-thousand steps. While Captain Doitsoh led the way, two of his men carried the cloak-wrapped corpse.

Eventually they reached the gateway to the palace. Nash greeted the guardians at the gate with a salute, and the three men were admitted to the courtyard.

"Place the body there." Nash gestured to the spot.

His men placed the body on a stone bench. On the way back from Aravah, he had told his men that if anyone asked, the remains were those of Tsalix Silverthorn. When Private Chindi began to protest, he silenced him with a threat of death if he did not comply.

"There is one danger," Lieutenant Legai whispered. "What if the four men you sent onto Wonadsi find the boy? How can we explain that?"

"I will deal with that, if it happens. It would be easy for him to disappear."

After dismissing his two men, Captain Doitsoh approached the ebony

47

doors that guarded the approach to the throne room. Two tall guards bracketed the entrance.

"I have come with word for our master," he said.

"What word?" replied one of the guards.

"Of the death of Tsalix Silverthorn. Now stand aside."

The guards crossed the entrance with two gleaming tsenils, barring Doitsoh's entrance.

"Do not think to order us. We stand to protect the future king."

Nash tried to hide his irritation. "I meant no harm. Please send word to Prince Abadon. I am sure he will want to greet me." He stepped back from the entrance. *These palace guards annoy me. The day will come when they will answer to me.*

The guard who had questioned him tapped on one door with the haft of his tsenil, then waited. Eventually the door opened and one of Abadon's footmen stepped out. The guard relayed Nash Doitsoh's message. The footman nodded, turned, and disappeared back into the castle.

Nash looked over his shoulder at the cloak-wrapped body lying on the bench across the courtyard. Flies were already beginning to bother the shroud. He could hear their buzzing from where he stood. Ten minutes passed before the footman reappeared and spoke with the guards.

"Follow me," he said to Nash.

The two of them walked down the long hall that led to Abadon's throne room, where he was standing at the window, gazing down the side of the mountain. When Nash entered, Abadon waved the footman away and turned to the captain of his guard.

"You have found him, then?"

Nash nodded. "His body is in the courtyard."

"You are sure it is he?"

"As sure as one can be when the body is burned so badly." Nash stroked his mane. "There was a fire. Aravah is no more."

Abadon stared into his captain's eyes. "Place his head on a pike like the others."

Nash bowed, turned on his heel, and left the throne room to complete his grisly deed.

Abadon went to the map on the wall, picked up the quill pen that lay on the desk, dipped it in the ink well, and drew a line through Tsalix Silverthorn's name. A smile creased his lips. If Aravah has been destroyed, then the next two names could be crossed off as well. He drew a line through Asur Longtooth and Kwercus Strongheart's names. The final three names on the chart were being pursued and would soon no longer pose a threat.

Victory is near!

CHAPTER 13

K WERCUS STOPPED HIS CLIMB AND RESTED IN THE SHADE OF A finger of rock that pointed upward at the side of the trail. His journey had begun that morning when the people of Chushka had fed him a hearty breakfast, then sent him on his climb to the top of Mount Deschee. The trail continued through a second town, Teless, before it wound up the mountain, but he felt he had nearly reached the top as the sun approached its zenith.

His thatch of blond hair was drenched in sweat. He reached down, grabbed the free end of his sash, and wiped his forehead. He leaned back against the rock and looked up the side of the mountain, trying to judge how much further he had to climb. Satisfied he could reach it without further delay, he shouldered his pack and continued up the trail.

He had not traveled more than an hour before he heard sounds from above. At first he could not make out what he was hearing, until a bright peal of laughter cascaded down the hillside. It lifted his heart and made him climb even faster. He crested the hill and was amazed at the sight spread out before him.

Streets were laid out in straight lines across the valley on top of the mountain. In the center of the city stood Elosha's castle. Its turrets of shining alabaster glowed in the early afternoon sunlight. Every cottage in the city appeared to be well-maintained, with trees and shrubs surrounding them. Early spring flowers bloomed and gave color to the sparkling city. More impressive was the number of people he could see—some chatting with neighbors, others walking down the streets, and still others involved with chores. A broad wrought-iron arch painted gleaming white spanned the main road leading toward the castle. Kwercus was stunned by the beauty of the place.

Hanging from the top of the arch was a sign—WELCOME TO HAYELI.

He had not taken a dozen steps before a young boy trotted over to him with a grin on his face.

"You're new here."

"Yes, I am."

"Whatcher name?"

"Kwercus Strongheart of Aravah."

"You've come a long, long way."

"Aye, I have. I've come to see the king."

The boy took his hand and led him down the street toward the castle. Everyone they passed waved a greeting. Kwercus was amazed at how friendly everyone seemed to be.

After traveling several blocks, the boy let go of Kwercus's hand.

"You can find your way from here, can't you?"

"Aye, young lad. Thank you for your kind concern."

The boy skipped back up the path. He looked back over his shoulder and waved at Kwercus, who waved back. Less than ten minutes later, he approached the castle. A white iron fence protected the magnificent building. He stepped up to the gate and was greeted by a man dressed in a white robe.

"Well, my son, what can I do for you?"

Kwercus dusted off his clothing.

"I've come to see the king."

The gatekeeper smiled. "May I ask why?"

Kwercus shrugged. "I know not. I was summoned by King Elosha." He thrust his hand inside his tunic and removed the scroll, which he handed to the man.

The gatekeeper unrolled the scroll and read it. "Welcome, Master Strongheart." He bowed and opened the gate. "Please show this at the castle door." He handed the scroll back to Kwercus before closing the gate behind him.

Kwercus thanked the man and proceeded to the castle. Two gold-clad arched doors opened as he approached, revealing two men inside. He handed the scroll to one of them, who smiled and beckoned him follow.

The walls inside the castle were gleaming white. Substantial pillars supported the domed ceilings. Beautiful paintings hung on the walls. The carpet beneath his feet was woven with an intricate pattern of blue, gold, black, and white threads. Crystal chandeliers dangled from the ceilings, each with dozens of candles burning brightly. Refracted rainbows of color painted the walls. The faint perfume of lavender engulfed him.

The hallway ended at another pair of arched doors.

"Please, remove your boots." The guide smiled.

Kwercus noticed several other pairs of boots on a low shelf to the left of the doorway. He removed his and placed them on the shelf. The guide handed him a pair of white doe skin moccasins.

"I believe these will be more comfortable."

Kwercus slipped them on, and the guide opened the doors to the throne room. Sunlight streamed in through windows placed high on the walls. Inside, the great King Elosha sat on his throne, with his queen, Nadlee, at his right. Before them, two men knelt with their backs to him. Kwercus was unsure what to do so he stood observing from the doorway.

Elosha looked up from the two men and smiled. "Kwercus Strongheart, welcome. Please join us." He beckoned with his hand.

The two kneeling men rose and turned to face Elosha. Kwercus recognized Tsalix Silverthorn and Asur Longtooth, his lifelong friends. In three strides, he was embracing the two of them.

"As I told you, he would soon arrive," Elosha said.

The three of them faced the King and sank to their knees.

"Please be seated, my sons. You will be much more comfortable."

Tsalix, Asur, and Kwercus settled on a long, low bench before the king.

"I am sure you are wondering why I summoned you here."

The three young men nodded.

Elosha ran his hand through his long white beard. "I am faced with a problem that the three of you can solve for me."

"Anything," Tsalix replied, while the other two nodded.

"As you can see, I am growing old. The day is not far in the future when I will pass on to the next place." He looked at his wife and patted the back of her hand. "I am sure you know of the conflict between my two sons—Johona and Abadon." He closed his eyes for a few seconds, and then seemed to focus on a spot far outside the walls of the throne room.

The queen said, "They are twins. Not identical, of course. But twins, nevertheless. Johona is the elder by less than fifteen minutes, and Abadon has struggled with that." She wiped the corner of her eye with a lace handkerchief.

"*Struggled* is perhaps too gentle a word," Elosha said. "In order for a kingdom to exist, there must be laws, and those laws must be consistent with each other. That is why the king is the only one who can make a royal decree. Johona understands that and does everything in his power to uphold my law. Abadon is a different story. He seems to think he is wiser than anyone else, and he wants to make the laws suit him." Elosha took a deep breath. "Unfortunately he has persuaded a large number that he is right."

Tsalix summoned his courage. "May I ask, my liege, how many he has won over?"

Elosha nibbled on his lower lip. "He is very persuasive. And of course, he promises security. He has won the hearts of nearly a third of the people."

"That many?"

"I fear so. Of course, that is only part of the problem. Any who follow Abadon must swear allegiance to him and be willing to bear arms. There is no compromise. While those who follow Johona do so because they wish to. There is no compulsion. Hence, Abadon has more men in armor, ready to fight, than does his older brother."

"But what can we do, your Majesty?" said Asur. "We are but three, and only one of us a warrior."

Elosha tugged on his beard again. "That is true. But you are three without guile, who follow without complaint." He took the queen's hand in his. "There is, on Mount Destiny, a wand sealed in a crystal sphere. It is the Scepter of Power, and he who holds it holds control over all the land. It has been locked away for generations. My grandfather's grandfather placed it there to protect it from unrighteous use." He and the queen stood from their thrones. "Abadon desperately wants that scepter."

"He has tried more than once to free it from the crystal sphere," the queen said. "Of course, he has failed."

"He does not know the secret," whispered the king. He cleared his throat and looked at the three young men. "There are three talismans that must be gathered in order to open the sphere. One of them is on each of the other three sacred mountains. They have been spread as far apart as possible to protect them and the Scepter." He stepped down from the dais and bade the three men arise. "If you will accept this task, you will face mortal danger. Abadon will try everything in his power to ensure your failure and his success."

The three young men looked at each other while the impact of Elosha's words sank in.

Kwercus nodded. "Whatever it takes. Whatever you wish." A shiver ran down his spine.

Elosha smiled. "And the other two?"

Tsalix and Asur nodded.

"Then kneel, Kwercus Strongheart." Elosha placed his hands on Kwercus's head. "Kwercus Strongheart of Aravah, I give you wisdom beyond your ken, strength beyond your belief, and peace in your soul. Go forward, my young son, and complete the task before you." He removed his hands from his head and held them out to the kneeling boy.

Kwercus took the king's outstretched hands and rose to his feet. Tears streamed down his face.

"We will not fail, your majesty."

Elosha nodded, then beckoned to Asur, who knelt before him.

"Asur Longtooth of Aravah, to you I give the ability to judge without being judgmental, the composure to see without anger, and the knowledge of the ages." He likewise raised Asur to his feet. "Now, Tsalix. Elosha placed his hands on the kneeling warrior's head. "Tsalix Silverthorn of Aravah, you of your own volition have already served your king on the field of battle. To you I give the knowledge that no task given you will be too great—there will always be a way to succeed. I give you quick wit, with the ability to solve the puzzles that will befall you. Most of all I give you a compassionate heart. Now rise." The king embraced the three young men. "Tonight you will rest, and tomorrow you will begin your quest."

Tsalix took the king's outstretched arm and grasped it as the king grasped his. "Sire, what are these talismans? What are we looking for?"

The king furrowed his brow. "I cannot tell you more, lest if you are captured you reveal what you seek."

The queen reached forth her hand. "They are on the tops of the mountains. You will know them when you see them. It is as if they will float before your eyes."

Asur took his friend's arm. "We'll figure it out, Tsalix."

"There is one other piece of the puzzle you need to know," said Elosha. "You must gather each talisman in the proper order—first the black, then the blue, and finally the yellow."

All three men turned to the king with consternation was on their faces.

"That means we have to go back to Mount Jinee."

"Yes. I wish there had been some other way to prevent you from having to take that journey twice, but as you can see, I had to meet with you face to face."

"So be it." Tsalix sighed. "We'll return home and find the first talisman."

"There is one last gift I will give you," said Elosha.

The queen extended a small box to him. He opened it with reverence. Inside were four small sealed vials, each wound by a silk cord. The king picked up the first and held it in front of his face. Although it was black as night, it had a glowing aura.

"Earth." Elosha handed it to Tsalix.

Tsalix cradled the warm vial, then placed the silk cord around his neck and put the vial beneath his tunic.

"What does it hold, your majesty?"

"You will know when it is time to break the seal. Then you will fully understand." Elosha lifted a second vial from the box. "Wind." He handed it to Asur, who held it gingerly.

It was snow white, and like its black brother, glowed brightly. Asur put the silk cord around his neck and tucked the vial away.

"Fire." The king held the shining gold vial before passing to Kwercus.

Elosha lifted the fourth small container from the box. It shone brilliant turquoise blue.

"Water." He pressed it against his brow before extending it to Tsalix. "Guard these well. Be careful. Once they are opened, they cannot be closed again. He smiled. "But you will know when to break their seals." He closed the empty box and handed it to the queen. "Before you go, there are two others who would like to wish you well." He nodded, and a small silver chime sounded.

The door behind the thrones opened, and a tall, blond man dressed in silver entered the room. Behind him was a young woman, stunningly beautiful.

"This is my son Johona, and my daughter, Angelica."

The three men dropped to one knee and bent their heads before them.

Johona smiled broadly at them. "Rise, my friends, my brothers. I'm sure father explained the importance of your odyssey. My men and I will help anyway we can. But for much of this journey, you will be on your own. If you succeed—nay, once you succeed—the rewards will be greater than you can imagine." He shook hands with each of the three before leaving the room.

The three men's eyes filled with tears. "Anything he commands, we will obey."

Angelica turned to follow her brother. then she paused and took several steps toward Tsalix and his friends.

"My father's fate is in your hands." She gave a wan smile. "But I know you will not fail." She put her hand on Tsalix's shoulder and looked into his eyes.

He felt his cheeks heat as he returned her smile.

"I, along with my father, will await your return." She smiled at Tsalix before turning leaving the room.

Elosha and Nadlee returned to their thrones.

"You have had a difficult trip to arrive here," Elosha said. "Have a pleasant evening, and rest. We would like to break bread with you before you leave."

Tsalix, Asur, and Kwercus realized they had been dismissed, so they rose to their feet and moved toward the door that opened into the hallway.

"I think she fancies you," said Asur.

Tsalix's cheeks flamed. "I don't think so."

Kwercus and Asur chuckled. "We shall see."

CHAPTER 14

Breakfast had been delicious, and now the three of them were striding across the mountaintop, on the road that led to the trail down the flanks of Mount Deschee. They had not slept much the night before, as the importance and danger of their task sank in. There had been much discussion as to which route to take to return to Aravah. Kwercus had told the other two of his encounters with the lone wolac and its rider, which implied there might be more of Abadon's men on the trail beside the Tohkal River. On the other hand, Tsalix had told of the close encounters he'd had as he traversed the Plain of Wonadsi. He admitted that, without guidance he'd have a difficult time choosing the right gullies to get them home.

They finally decided to retrace Kwercus's path along the foothills of the high plateau, and keep a sharp eye for Abadon's troops.

The descent from Hayeli went much quicker than the climb to the city. As they passed through Teless, Asur saw that Sambucus's barn was empty. It was just past noon when they entered the town of Chushka. The fields around the village were lush and green. A waterfall down the side of Mount Deschee had carved a deep bowl in the rock at its base. Water had been diverted into the fields to irrigate the crops. Cattle grazed in the knee-high grass.

The three of them were welcomed at the local inn and were fed a hearty joint of meat and loaves of crusty black bread. When they had eaten their fill, they continued on their way.

"This is the worst part of the journey," Kwercus said. "We have to cross forty miles of the plain before we reach the foothill path. "This is where I battled with the wolac." He placed his hand on the head of his ax. "There is no water, either, and it will take us most of a day."

Although the path was narrow, it was marked. The three men traveled in single file, Kwercus in the lead, followed by Asur, then Tsalix. They watched as the sun sank behind the western rim of the plateau before them and sent flames of gold from the tops of the hills.

"Maybe two more hours." Kwercus scanned both sides of the trail for the remnants of the wolac and the warrior.

After another hour of travel, the sun had set, and they were traveling by the light of a thin slice of moon.

"We have to reach the main trail before we stop for the night," Kwercus whispered.

They traveled on in silence, until in the distance, an animal howled.

"Maii the coyote." A shiver ran up Tsalix's spine. "How much further?"

"Not long now," Kwercus replied."

He stopped and raised his hand to halt the others. To the right of the trail was the spot where the wolac had died. All that was left was a crude black circle on the ground, and a putrid odor. Nothing was to be seen of the rider.

"This is where I was attacked. Someone has done a fair job of cleaning up the mess."

They had been silent on their journey, but now they tried to avoid even the sound of footsteps on the path. It did not take long until they reached the bridge across the Tohkal River and the intersection with the main trail. Kwercus led them into the cleft he had discovered on his previous journey. They settled into the protective undergrowth and gulped from the spring.

"I think it would be wise to spend the night here rather than trying to find lodging in Atsanh," Kwercus said. "They seemed less than friendly when I passed through on my way to Deschee."

They agreed, and a few minutes later, they curled up in their cloaks and fell asleep.

At midnight, Tsalix awoke. Something wasn't right.

Lying still, he tried to see down the mouth of their small canyon, to the trail below. In the pale moonlight, a large form plodded down the path. Tsalix sniffed and thought he could detect the acrid odor of a wolac on the faint breeze that blew up the canyon. He watched as the form continued down the trail and out of his sight. But shortly afterward, another passed by. This one raised its head and squealed. Tsalix slid his sword from its scabbard and prepared for battle, but the beast moved on.

He was about to awaken his companions when a third wolac moved past the cleft. Tsalix strained his eyes to see if he could spot a rider on the huge beast, but the light was too dim to tell. Eventually three more of the armored animals passed by and headed toward the bridge. When he was sure no more were coming, he slipped from his resting place and stepped down to the footpath. On the trail, the wolacs had left droppings whose odor was overpowering.

Tsalix scanned the scene before him until he caught a movement past the bridge on the trail that led to Mount Deschee. *It is good we did not stop on the trail. I wonder how far they will range?* Confident they had escaped detection, Tsalix returned to the shallow canyon and struggled to fall back to sleep. *This journey may be more difficult than we believed.*

Sunlight from the east moved into their resting place and awakened the three men. They drank from the spring and filled their water bags before rejoining the trail. When Kwercus and Asur spotted the wolac spore, Tsalix told them of the beasts that had passed the night before.

"I think that means Abadon is patrolling at night as well as during the day."

"We'll have to keep a sharp eye," Asur said, as they marched on toward Atsanh. They reached the rib of rock that protected the south flank of the village, and as before, the sound of a horn warned the people of the town. The three of them watched in amazement as everyone scurried into their homes and closed their shutters.

"What's that all about?" Asur said.

"I don't know," Kwercus replied. "The same thing happened a few days ago when I passed through. They obviously have a watchman on the mountainside, who warns the people of approaching travelers." He pointed across the town at the man perched high on the hill.

"But we mean them no harm," Tsalix said.

"We know that, but they may not," Kwercus replied. "I suspect this reaction is toward the kinds of men who passed on their wolacs last night."

When they reached the inn with the swinging sign, Tsalix knocked on the door. No answer. He tried opening the door, but it was locked. Tsalix shrugged, and the three men continued their march through the town.

They had almost reached the other side of the village when Asur spotted a small girl peeking her head around the corner of a cottage. He smiled at her and winked. She tried to wink back, but closed both eyes. Asur dropped to his knee and beckoned to the child.

She inched around the corner of the house, then stopped. Asur reached into his pack and took out a piece of the cake Queen Nadlee had insisted they take with them. The little girl's eyes widened, and she took a half-dozen more steps toward him. The door to the cottage flew open and a woman screamed, ran to the child and picked her up, then hurried back into the house. Before she could close the door, Asur sprang to his feet and jammed his foot into the opening. The woman let out another shriek of terror. The little girl began to cry.

Asur pushed the door open. "We mean you no harm, good lady. Nor you, young miss."

The woman was gripping the child's hand, as the girl hid behind her mother's skirts. Both continued to cry.

Asur raised his hands. "Forgive us for intruding. We are curious about the people of your town."

At last the woman calmed down enough to speak, and wiped her eyes and nose with her apron. The little girl continued to burrow into her mother's skirt.

"What do you want with me?" the woman pleaded.

"Nothing," replied Asur. "Why is there such fear among the people?" He kept his hands spread in front of him. "My friends and I do not wish to frighten you. We are just passing through."

"Whom do you serve?" she managed to gasp.

"The king," Asur replied. "Why?"

"Then go."

"I still don't understand?"

"Don't you? If Abadon discovers we have helped any of Elosha's men, he will destroy this village. We live under his protection and must obey his commands."

Asur dropped his hands to his sides. "Is there no freedom?"

The woman shook her head. "Go. Please, go. If anyone in Atsanh knows I have been talking to you, I will be reported and face consequences."

"And what would they be?"

The woman shook her head violently. "Leave. I've already lost my husband, and if I am punished, who will take care of my daughter?"

Tsalix looked up on the cliff and saw the watchman looking down on them. *He will report the woman. She is not safe.*

"Asur," he whispered. "Tell the woman to grab her broom and force you out of her house."

"What?"

"I'll explain later. Tell her to drive you out."

A moment later Asur fell backward, covering his face with his hands, while the woman beat him with her broom. Tsalix pulled his friend from the ground, and the woman retreated inside.

Tsalix yelled, "A fine hostess you are, refusing us aid and driving us out of your cottage."

He shook his fist in the air, and the three of them strode up the trail, around the rib of rock, and out of sight of the watchman.

"What was that all about," Asur growled.

"If the watchman thought she was giving you aid, he would have reported her and she'd have been punished. I hope our ruse protected the woman and her child."

Asur smiled and clapped Tsalix on the shoulder. "Quick thinking, my brother."

Kwercus said, "Things are worse than I thought. No wonder I was given no welcome at any of these villages. The people are frightened to death of Abadon's rule. And apparently with good reason."

The bridge across the south branch of Tohkal lay ahead of them. With measured steps they crossed it and continued their course up the trail. Before they had traveled much further, Kwercus called for a halt.

"I have been wondering if we will put the people of Bitahkiz and Hagade at risk if we pass through their towns," he said.

"You make a good point," Tsalix replied.

"Especially with you dressed like a soldier. It is hard to miss Johona's crest on your shield."

"When we reach Aravah, I will dress like the two of you."

"Aye, but until then I wonder if we should ford the river and make our way on its marge." Kwercus looked at the water rushing by.

"It looks deep," Asur said. "And I am not much of a swimmer."

"Let us look for a safer place to cross." Tsalix replied. "Then let us put your plan into action."

They traveled for over an hour, before Tsalix spotted a log that lay across the stream. Although some water spilled over the log, most of the current had been diverted to the gap between the end of the log and the far bank of the river. There, the water shot with explosive force, churning and spewing plumes into the air.

Tsalix measured the distance from the end of the tree trunk to the river bank. "I think we can cross here. With any luck, we can jump from the log to the shore."

The other two men eyed the crossing with concern.

"I'll go first," said Tsalix. "It shouldn't be that difficult." He took small steps along the log, arms extended at his sides to give him better balance.

The log was jammed in place, but the surface was slippery. He reached the end without incident, took his shield from his back, and threw it onto the grassy slope of the river bank. Then he tossed his breastplate, sword, and rucksack. He took a few steps back on the log, ran toward the end, and launched himself across the gap. He landed in a crouch, on the other side. After rising to his feet, he waved the other two across.

Kwercus was the next on the log. Mimicking Tsalix, he tiptoed across the log. Twice, a foot slipped and he dropped into a crouch to regain his balance. At the end of the log, he threw his pack to Tsalix, then slipped his ax from his belt and threw it onto the slope. After a quick run, he leapt across and landed on the river bank.

"Come on," he yelled, through cupped hands.

Asur stepped onto the log. He took tiny steps, struggling to keep his balance, until he reached the gap. To him it seemed enormous. Trembling, he stepped back.

"You can do it," Tsalix yelled above the crashing sound of the water.

Asur's legs were trembling as he ran to the end of the log. As he pushed off, his foot slipped, and with a scream he fell into the churning water. He struggled to keep his head above the surging current as he was swept downstream. He gulped a mouthful of water before thrashing his arms and reaching the surface. The river was frigid, fed by the melting snows of the spring runoff.

Asur was dragged beneath the waves, and the current roiled and frothed. He landed on his shoulders against the bed of the river, and was dragged several yards before he was able to get his feet beneath him and push toward the surface. He thrust his head out of the water and gulped a lungful of air before being somersaulted to the bed of the river again. He fought to regain his footing when a submerged branch hit his head. He saw stars before his world turned black.

Tsalix and Kwercus broke sprinted along the bank to keep up with Asur as he was carried away. They saw his frenzied gasps for air as he broke the surface of the raging river, then watched him disappear again.

Freed from the log jam, the river began to spread and flow slower. Asur floated to the surface, and his back broke through the water. After a hundred-yard chase, Tsalix grabbed the back of Asur's collar and pulled him onto the river bank. No movement.

Tsalix and Kwercus rolled him onto his back and began pushing on his stomach. After what seemed to be an eternity, Asur spewed water from his mouth and began coughing and gasping for breath.

"You gave us a scare." Tsalix wheezed.

"Aye, I gave myself one," Asur said.

The three of them lay on their backs while the adrenalin pumped out of their systems. Once they'd caught their breaths, the three men returned to their packs and ate a meager lunch while they waited for Asur's clothing to dry.

"I hope that is the least of our problems," Tsalix said.

The sun was warm, and just over an hour passed before they were able to continue their journey home.

CHAPTER 15

T SALIX TAMPED THE SOIL OVER THE FINAL GRAVE WITH THE
  back of his shovel. Asur and Kwercus stood with bowed heads. Their
faces were covered with ash and dirt, and rivulets of sweat cut channels
through the filth.

They had searched through the scorched remains of Aravah and found
the bodies left moldering where they'd fallen. With mixed emotions
they'd realized none of the charred bodies were those of their families, but
still there were neighbors with whom they'd lived all of their lives.

"Well, that's done," Tsalix said.

"Aye," the other two said.

Tsalix shaded his eyes and looked back toward where his home had
stood. "I wonder if there is anything left?"

He trudged into the village and knelt in the ashes of his family's cottage. Tears streamed down his cheeks. The stone chimney stood like a
tombstone. The rest of his home was destroyed. His mother's only silver
candelabrum—her prized possession—had melted to an undistinguish-
able lump beside the hearth.

After struggling to his feet, Tsalix surveyed the rest of what had been
Aravah. Asur and Kwercus stood together in the street, with their heads
hung down. There was no doubt who had caused the carnage, but why it
had happened was unknown.

With dragging feet, Tsalix joined his companions. Their gazes moved
up the slopes of Mt. Jinee. Abadon's palace was out of their view, on the

other side of the mountain, but it was as if they could feel its malevolence cloaking the remains of their home.

Tsalix stuck the point of his sword into the pile of ash at the side of the road.

"Where did they all go?" he said.

Asur shrugged. Kwercus shook his head.

Tsalix returned to the remains of his home and leaned against the chimney. He could see no evidence that either his father or mother had perished in the inferno, but where they had gone escaped him. There seemed to be no place nearby where they could have found refuge.

He rested his head against one of the chimney stones and felt it give slightly. Afraid that the chimney would disintegrate and collapse upon him, he pulled back a step and noticed that only one of the rocks appeared to be loose, while the rest seemed solid. He grabbed the stone and pulled it from its place. Tucked away in the cavity was a small piece of folded parchment about an inch square. Tsalix dropped the stone and retrieved the piece of paper. With trembling hands, he unfolded it, revealing a piece of parchment as large as his hand. Written on it were two peculiar lines:

Clean and pure the unicorns remained eternal.
Drawn by yon albatross before another dawn or noon.

Asur and Kwercus gazed at the message, over Tsalix's shoulders.

"What does that mean?" Asur said. "It seems to be gibberish. Unicorns and albatross?"

Tsalix dropped his hands to his sides. "It is a simple code my brother and I used before he died. My father must have remembered it." A tear ran down his cheek.

"What code?" Kwercus said. "All I see is some nonsense."

Tsalix wiped the tears away. "It's simple. You just read the initial letters of the words."

Asur scanned the message. "Captured by Abadon." His head drooped. "Where has he taken them?"

"I know not, but it is as we suspected," Kwercus spat. "So now what is our mission? Do we search for a talisman, or do we try to find and rescue our families?"

"Three of us against all of Abadon's men. What chance do we have?" Asur sank to one knee. "I say we redouble our efforts to claim the talisman. Somehow, deep inside I feel that it will be of more value to our families than rushing pell-mell into a conflict that will likely cost us our lives."

Tsalix nodded. "The question is how do we get to the top of Mount Jinee without being captured? From this wanton destruction, it is clear Abadon's men are all about, and the only way to the summit is to climb the obsidian staircase and pass through Abadon's lair." He looked at the crown of clouds that covered the top of the black mountain.

"Perhaps not," said Kwercus. "Before his death, my father spoke of another trail—steep, difficult, and ill-marked—that ascended the back side of Jinee. Even though it will be difficult, I believe it will be preferable to fighting our foe, outnumbered as we are."

"But can you find it?" said Asur.

Kwercus shrugged. "I think so. At least, it may be worth a try."

With heavy sighs, the three men lifted their packs to their shoulders and began skirting the base of Mount Jinee. The trail led through pine trees and scree that had fallen from crags high on the mountainside, the same trail Tsalix had traversed a short time before.

They had traveled most of the day when Kwercus raised his hand.

"Are we near?" said Asur.

"Perhaps," Kwercus whispered. "There are sounds ahead that sound more like the clattering of feet on stones than wind in the trees." He pointed to the trees above them, on the hillside.

They left the trail and hid in the shrubs and trees above the path. Tsalix caught a stench. The further they traveled, the stronger it became, until the odor of decay was thick around them. A few steps later, at the side of their pathway, they discovered the bloated body of a deer laying on its back, with its feet sticking into the air. A black shafted arrow with red fletching was lodged in its side. It was obvious the deer had been wounded and had run onto the hillside before it lost enough blood to collapse.

The three men gagged as they passed by. Kwercus put his finger to his lips before sliding along the mountainside. Keeping hidden, they continued for another hundred yards before Kwercus dropped to the ground. The other two followed.

Tsalix peeked his head up and peered through the white flowered branches of a dogwood tree. He spotted about a dozen of Abadon's men a hundred yards ahead of them on the trail below, sitting around a fire pit. A spit had been placed across the fire, and the carcasses of two small animals were being roasted. There was no sight of a bedroll, so apparently they were encamped somewhere nearby.

Tsalix drew back, signaled for his friends to wait, and started scaling the mountainside until he was well-above the encamped soldiers. He took step by careful step, making sure he dislodged no stones he crossed above them, until he could see past the bend in the trail below, where he stopped. He had barely sunk to his haunches when the whistling squeal of a wolac pierced the air. He crept behind a wild persimmon and hid. The wolac called out again. One of the soldiers stood, rounded the shoulder of the mountain, and shouted at the beast to be quiet.

"There's nothing to be excited about," he growled, and the wolac ceased its squealing.

The man disappeared from view as he returned to the fire.

Tsalix crept down the hillside until he grasped the narrow trunk of an aspen, and leaned over the edge of a small gorge. Twenty feet below him, a dozen wolacs were tethered. Tsalix began backtracking to where he'd left his friends when he noticed a mark scratched into a black obsidian boulder behind him. There was a faint arrow pointed straight up the flank of the hill. He stopped his descent and scaled the hill until he found the faded markings of a path. Then he surveyed the hillside before returning to Kwercus and Asur.

"I believe I've found the trail," he whispered. "But there's no way we can reach it without alerting Abadon's men."

"It will be difficult to remain secret throughout the night," Asur said. "Perhaps we should retreat. The steep slope is too dangerous for us to try to sleep. We may lose our footing and roll down onto the trail."

Tsalix thought for a moment. "Unless we could direct them away from us. A diversion would give us time to reach the trail."

"Aye, but what kind of diversion?" said Kwercus.

Tsalix pulled his companions close. "Remember the deer carcass we passed?"

"How could I forget," Kwercus said. "It stinks to high heaven. It made my gorge rise."

"If we threw that to the wolacs, I think it would cause a great commotion."

"No doubt," Kwercus replied.

Tsalix started back along the path they'd taken, leading his friends to the rotting corpse. The three tied their sashes around their faces, covering their mouths and noses, while lifting the lifeless deer. After struggling to carry the carrion without making noise, they eventually reached the spot above the wolacs. Already the beasts had caught the scent of the dead deer. They were whimpering and straining at their tethers.

With a mighty shove, they dropped the carcass among the wolacs, who began slicing off pieces of putrid flesh with their pincers and stuffing it into their maws.

Tsalix climbed to the obsidian marker, followed by his mates. The noise of their scramble up the hillside was covered by the sounds of the wolacs as they fought each other over the proffered food. Before the clamoring ceased, the three men had found the faint markings of the trail that seemed to climb up the southeast slope of the mountain.

"I hope we can find water so we can wash the stink from our hands," said Asur. "It still makes me sick to smell it."

They all sniffed their hands and shuddered.

"We should have removed the arrow," Kwercus whispered. "I fear it will alert them that someone was here. It is clear that the deer did not launch itself over the cliff."

"You are probably right," said Tsalix. "We'd better put as much distance between them and us as we can."

A crescent moon rose in the east, over the low hills that defined the edge of the kingdom. By its faint light, they sought to follow the trail. They had traveled for at least a half-dozen hours when the markings disappeared.

"Let us see if we can find some place to spend the rest of the night," Tsalix said. "My legs feel like they can go no further. And I fear that without seeing the trail, we'll wander into danger." He motioned to his friends.

They sought a level place to rest, and after another fifteen minutes of scouting they discovered what appeared to be a shallow cave. The mouth was hidden by a massive thicket of wild raspberry bushes growing from a broad pocket of soil, just beginning to leaf out. Their thorns presented a challenge, but by holding the plants down with Tsalix's shield, the three young men were able to climb over it, into the cave.

The temperature inside was cooler, and while they shivered, they knew they could not risk a fire, so they wrapped themselves in their cloaks and tried to sleep.

Asur and Kwercus drifted off immediately. Tsalix lay on his back and tried to make out the roof of the cavern. He could not help but think of his entombment not many days before, and shuddered.

Eventually fatigue overwhelmed him, and he joined his friends in sleep.

CHAPTER 16

TSALIX FELT THE SUN ON HIS FACE AND OPENED A WEARY EYE. His companions were also beginning to stir. Yesterday's march had left them stiff and sore, and the floor of the cave had been unforgiving.

He pushed himself to his feet. In the dawn's light, Tsalix could see more of the cavern in which they'd spent the night. Although the mouth of the cave was narrow, the roof rose a dozen feet. Roots from trees and shrubs above them penetrated the ceiling and hung like braided ropes. Obsidian glistened the walls, and a half-inch of black sand and pebbles covered the floor.

Asur moved further back into the cave and discovered it veered to the right, where, after a dozen steps, he was plunged into darkness again. He placed a hand against one wall and extended the other in front of him. He continued deeper into the recess, and his heart raced as he slid further into the blackness. After he'd stepped a hundred feet up the passage, his hand contacted a rough wooden surface. He turned and looked back the way he had come. The sunlight streaming through the cave cast a golden glow into the mouth of the tunnel.

I need light. He turned back to the wooden barrier in the tunnel and felt the surface with the both hands. After some exploration, he found hinges on one side of the slab. He then examined the other edge until he found a padlocked hasp which resisted his attempts to open it. Knowing he'd need help, he retraced his steps to the cave where Tsalix and Kwercus were readjusting their packs.

"I've found a door!"

"Where?" said Kwercus.

Asur pointed toward the back of the cavern. "It turns to the right, and a few score yards down the passage is a locked door." He started back toward the tunnel. "We need light and perhaps your ax," he said to Kwercus.

"Patience, my brother," Tsalix said. "Let us see if there is anything we can use as a torch."

The three of them scoured the cave, but found nothing that would burn.

"Perhaps we are not meant to find our way past the door," Tsalix said. "I see nothing that would give us light."

Kwercus reached inside his tunic and removed the vial Elosha had given him.

He slipped the silk cord over his head. "I know not what might happen, but I have this gift from the king. The golden vial pulsed in his hand. "Shall we see what comes from opening *Fire*?"

Tsalix chewed on his lower lip. "Perhaps there is somewhere in our future that we might need it more than now."

"We don't even know what it will do," Kwercus said. "At least this will give us a clue to the other vials."

"That is true," Tsalix replied.

After ten minutes of discussion, Kwercus won the argument, walked to the back of the cavern, and turned into the tunnel. He pried the stopper from the golden vial. When the stopper popped from the vial's neck, a blinding flash of light erupted and illuminated the cave more brightly than sunlight. A finger of fire shot down the tunnel and ignited the door, which burned for a few moments before turning into a charred portal. The fire continued down the passageway behind the door.

Kwercus dropped the vial to the ground, where it gave off a few more flashes of light before turning to ash. The three men were blinded by the intense light from the vial, and it took them some time before their sight was restored.

Kwercus was still trembling from the experience. When Tsalix and Asur could see again, they moved to Kwercus' side.

"I-I had no idea," Kwercus stammered.

"None of us did," replied Tsalix. "It behooves us to be careful before opening any of the other three vials."

As they knelt at the top of the tunnel, a wave of hot air flowed over them. It was strong enough that it blew Tsalix's mop of dark hair away from his face.

"I wonder where this tunnel leads," he said.

Asur peered down the tunnel and realized he could see barely where the door had been. The portal was outlined with a pale light from beyond. He beckoned to his companions and pointed at the feeble glow.

"There may be enough light to tell," he said. "The question is, do we explore, or do we continue on our quest?"

"Might this not be part of the quest?" Tsalix replied. "I have had the feeling since we left Hayeli that we are part of a bigger tapestry woven by unseen hands. This strand may be part of the larger pattern we cannot see from our vantage point, but it is important in the overall picture." He rose to his feet and began making his way up the tunnel. "Besides, after using the power of the vial it would seem prudent to see what has been uncovered."

He was joined by the other two young men. The floor of the tunnel sloped upward. They passed through what remained of the door that had guarded the way, and continued for another several minutes before the path leveled out. Ahead of them, the channel turned left. For some time, they had heard what appeared to be the sounds of metal on metal, and as they approached the twist in the path, the sounds became louder. Tsalix signaled to the other two to keep back as he peered around the corner. A blast of hot, malodorous wind streamed past him. Before him was a pit several hundred feet deep, and at the bottom appeared a legion of black-smiths working over bellow-driven fire pits. Sweat poured from their bodies as they struck hammers to steel forming double-headed tsenils, arrow points, and armor. They were girted only in loin cloths, and wearing sandals.

Tsalix beckoned his brothers forward so they could see. A stairway had been cut into the sides of the shaft leading from their vantage point, to the floor of the pit. Standing on a raised platform in the middle of the circle of smiths were a half-dozen men clad in black mail. They carried bull whips at their sides and used them to keep the smithies working. On the far side of the abyss, a wolac was harnessed to a four-wheeled wagon on which the finished armaments were placed. As frenzied as the men worked, no one spoke. There were no cries of pain, even when the lash creased a shoulder or back.

"Their tongues have been cut out," Tsalix whispered. "They've been silenced."

A gong sounded, and the men put down their hammers, turned away from the forges, and approached the circular wall of the pit. Buckets of water were splashed over them to cool their overheated bodies while they guzzled from flasks that hung on the wall. A canvas cover was thrown over the finished weapons, and the wolac dragged the heavy-laden wagon up a tunnel that led from the hellish pit below.

Asur tapped Tsalix on the shoulder and pointed up the shaft. The flue continued upward another hundred or so feet before it was capped with a heavy metal grill.

"An exhaust chimney," said Asur. "I wonder where it ends?"

"At the top of the mountain, I suspect," Tsalix whispered, and motioned for them to return the way they had come.

When they had reached the cave where they'd spent the night, he said, "It will do us well to remember what we have seen." He shouldered his pack. "Now I think we have spent too much time here. The flash of fire must certainly have been noticed. Let us continue on our way."

CHAPTER 17

A BADON ROSE FROM HIS THRONE. "ARISE."

The two soldiers clad in black staggered to their feet.

"And what have you found?"

"Carpinus was captured on the trail between Miasma and Deschee. He fought bravely and he died bravely."

Abadon smiled. "And the other two?"

"Juglan and Corylus were traveling together. They were on the edge of the Sea of Tabass, making their way toward Chushka when they were intercepted. Juglan died trying to protect Corylus, but in the end both were taken."

"Excellent!" Abadon clapped as he strode to the map of the kingdom. "Place their heads on pikes outside the castle door." He dipped the tip of his quill in the ink well and drew lines through the names of the last three men on the list of twelve. "Elosha's twelve chosen ones are no more. It will not be long before we crush Johona's forces and restore order to the land." He removed a leather purse from his belt, took out ten gold pieces and placed five of them in each of the men's outstretched hands. "Thank you for such excellent service."

He waved his hand, and the two soldiers saluted, turned on their heels, and left the throne room. Abadon walked to the window that overlooked the ten thousand steps to the plain below, and ran his hands down his long locks. Victory seemed so near, yet he had not been able to eradicate Johona's forces. Once he'd begun his nighttime patrols, he had been able to locate many of his brother's camps. But they were always guarded with sentries. The few skirmishes his men had engaged with the enemy had seen mixed results—sometimes his troops won, sometimes they were forced to retreat.

He returned to the map and focused on Mount Destiny, which anchored the east point of the kingdom. There lay the Scepter of Power, encased in its crystal sphere. Three times he had traveled to the summit of Mount Destiny to try to free the scepter, and three times he had failed. The crystal globe deflected blows of sword, tsenil, and spear. It was impervious to fire. The sphere itself was anchored to the bed rock of the mountain.

"If only I had that cursed scepter." He moaned. "I'd control this kingdom without a shadow of a doubt."

Pinned to the map were scraps of red cloth representing the locations of his troops, while scraps of white represented Johona's forces. Abadon stroked his pointed beard as he contemplated how he could relocate his men to achieve a quicker victory. The majority of his troops were placed in a sweeping arc that ranged from Mount Litso in the west, to Mount Destiny in the east, across the Plain of Wonadsi. A scattered few bands of soldiers patrolled the Desert of Desolation—Shayeksten—that stretched from the south side of Mount Deschee to Mount Tsood, where it defined the south side of the kingdom. Even fewer men kept vigil along the shores of the Tabass Sea in the southwest, and the Swamp of Miasma in the northeast margin of Wonadsi.

"Perhaps that is where Johona's soldiers are evading my men. I may need to move more men to the swamp and the sea. And yet the patrol on the shore of the Tabass Sea located and eliminated Juglan and Corylus." Abadon stroked his beard again as he returned to the throne to ponder his next move.

Then he raised one eyebrow and struck the gong next to the throne. His vizier appeared and prostrated in front of the throne.

"Rise," Abadon barked.

The servant rose to his feet. "What is your wish, your majesty?"

"Bring me the priests and the Book of Prophecy." Abadon waved a hand in dismissal.

"As you wish." The vizier backed out of the room.

Abadon tapped his fingers on the arm of the throne. "Perhaps I have been going after this the wrong way. There may be an answer in the ancient writings that will show me how to acquire the scepter."

The vizier approached the throne, with three long-bearded men behind him. Each was dressed in a flowing scarlet robe with a black waistband. On their heads were black miters emblazoned with three red stripes.

"Your Majesty, the priests." The vizier bowed and moved into the shadows behind the throne.

The three holy men approached Abadon. The one in the middle held a large leather-bound book in his hands. Burnished on the cover were words in the ancient tongue.

"You are learned men," Abadon said. "Tell me what the Book says of the Scepter of Power."

The priests nodded and began turning the age-stiffened pages of the ancient book. After several minutes one of them spoke.

"In it is power," he said, with a high-pitched voice. "He who holds it will be honored by all. In that honor is the true power." He closed the book.

"I know that!" Abadon jumped up from the throne. But how does one acquire the scepter?"

Another of the priests held up his hand, with his finger extended. "Ah, that is a different story." He began searching in the fragile pages of the book until he located the passage he sought. "The scepter can be freed from its crystal tomb by one who holds the three sacred talismans." He closed the book.

"That's all? There is no other mention of it in the book?"

"None, Master."

"And what are these three talismans?" Abadon growled.

The three men shook their heads.

"We know not," a priest decreed. "What they are is not defined, nor does it describe them in any way. All we know is they are to be found on three of the sacred mountains and must be restored to the fourth...and they must be acquired in a certain order."

"Order?"

"Yes, Master," the priest continued, "beginning here on Mount Jinee. Then they must be brought to the cavern on the top of Mount Destiny where the blessed scepter lies."

"It starts here?" Abadon paced. "Here on Mount Jinee?" He took a few more steps. "Is there anything more?"

"No, your majesty. We have told you all that the book reveals."

"Then go, while I ponder these things."

The three wise men bowed their heads and left the throne room with the ancient tome.

Abadon sank back onto his throne. "Perhaps I was too quick in eliminating Elosha's men. If any of them were still alive, they could lead me to the talisman on top of my own peak. Then he could be eliminated. Here on Jinee, it begins. What is the talisman? What does it mean?"

The vizier stepped out of the shadows. "Will there be anything else, Master?"

Abadon looked at his servant with hooded eyes. "Yes, send for Captain Doitsoh. I have a new task for him."

"Yes, Master. I believe he is with his men in the stables at the base of the mountain. It may take him some time to arrive."

"So be it. With the twelve chosen ones eliminated, we have all the time in the world." Abadon sent his servant away. "But let's not use too much of it."

CHAPTER 18

Tsalix bent to retrieve his shield from the floor of the cavern when he heard the sounds of men scrambling up the trail that he, Asur, and Kwercus had followed the previous night.

"Listen," Tsalix said to his comrades. "I fear we have been discovered."

He looked around the mouth of the cave, toward the faint path. A half-dozen black-clad soldiers were less than a quarter-mile below.

"Quickly!" He placed his shield on top of the raspberry bushes, and the three young men scampered across them.

They climbed the side of the hill until they were high enough on the mountain that only a few scrubby trees existed. Tsalix scanned the hillside for any hiding place, but could see none other than the trees. Praying that the warriors below would not look up, they flattened themselves against the mountain, in the shade of the stunted pines.

Abadon's men reached the mouth of the cave and were stopped by the wicked thorns of the raspberries. One soldier removed his cape and threw it on top of the bushes, but the thorns penetrated the cloth. A second cloak, a third, and a fourth were spread over the bushes, and still the thorns tortured the men as they crawled across them, into the open maw of the cave.

"Now!" Tsalix said, when the last soldier disappeared from view.

The three sprang to their feet and began traversing the mountain side.

"While they explore the cave, we may gain on them," Tsalix said.

They hurried across the steep slope of the hillside. Before long, the rock was scored by a waterfall-carved canyon. Tsalix led them to the edge of the coursing water, which plunged to a pool a hundred feet below. A hundred feet above the water sprang from the side of the cliff. There seemed to be no way to cross the torrent.

While Asur and Kwercus anchored him, Tsalix placed one foot on a rock shelf that extended behind the waterfall. It was barely four inches wide, and covered with filamentous algae that made it as slippery as a liar's tongue. He experimented by putting his weight on the rock, but his foot slipped, nearly pulling the three of them into the cascading water.

Tsalix shook his head. "We cannot cross here." He stepped back a few feet and looked up the side of the mountain. "But perhaps we can make our pursuers think we did." He drew his sword and lay next to the waterfall. "Hold my feet."

Asur grasped an ankle, Kwercus the other, and they leaned back as Tsalix edged along the narrow ledge. He extended his sword and scraped the algae from the rocks. Then he began to inch backward as his friends pulled him to safety.

"I hope that fools them into thinking we tried crossing on the slippery stones." He removed his cloak, wrapped a boulder-sized piece of obsidian in it, and dropped it to the rocks at the base of the waterfall. "And I hope they think we failed."

Asur wiped the sweat from his forehead. "I'm not sure that will be enough, my friend. What else can we do to make it appear that we lost our footing and did not succeed in crossing?"

Kwercus pulled his ax from his waistband, and with a mighty swing, cut down one of the stunted trees.

"Perhaps this will help." He wrapped the tree in his cloak, fastened it around the branches, and sent it falling into the pool at the bottom of the fall.

It landed with a splash and floated to the surface, where it moved in slow circles.

"From here I think it might fool them into thinking someone has fallen and drowned," Kwercus said.

"At least it may give them pause and us a few minutes more to escape," said Asur. "Let us be gone." He used his staff to rise to his feet.

The three adventurers backtracked out of the canyon and started scaling up the mountain at a nearly ninety-degree incline. A half-hour later, out of breath, they reached the shelf of rock from which the waterfall began its plunge to the pool below. The cloak-wrapped tree looked more like a body from their perch than it had below. It had snagged on something on one side of the pond and waved back and forth as if it were alive.

The shelf on which they rested extended back several feet to a cleft in the rock from which the water poured forth. The three of them moved into the shadow of the hill, hidden from the trail below.

They had not rested but ten minutes when they heard shouts from below. Tsalix slid forward on his stomach until he could gaze over the ledge. Abadon's six men were gathered at the edge of the waterfall. Although Tsalix could not hear them clearly, it appeared they were arguing. One of them pointed his spear at the cloak floating in the pool below. Another put his foot on the shelf of rock behind the waterfall. The man took one step and slipped, and fell screaming into the abyss. He hit the pile of rock at the edge of the pool, bounced into the water, and weighted down by his armor, disappeared beneath the surface.

The rest of the men withdrew from the side of the waterfall. The leader of the troops gestured to another of his men, who approached the narrow ledge. He stuck his spear behind the water and tried to determine how he could safely cross. After a few moments, he pulled his spear back and shook his head. The leader ordered him to cross, and when the man refused to go, the chief withdrew his sword, and with one thrust, sent the man cascading over the edge. He, too, disappeared beneath the waves.

After a third man tried the ledge and joined his companions in the pool, the remaining three men realized the futility in trying to cross behind the falling water. The leader gestured down the hill, to the base of the waterfall, and soon the three were slipping and sliding down the hillside.

"We need to move, now!" Tsalix slid back to his friends as soon as the men abandoned their attempts.

They gathered their belongings and began scaling the mountain again. Not far above them, clouds ringed the peak. The lightning and thunder that had been with them since they began their quest grew brighter and louder as they approached the mist. They kept glancing over their shoulders to see if their pursuers could be seen.

The clouds became thick enough to hide them, and again they felt they could rest their legs. The three sank down on water-slicked rocks.

"How long do you think before they are back on our trail?" Asur said.

"There are but three," Tsalix replied, "but they will have discovered our ruse when they reach the pool. Will that spur them on? I know not. But I do know they will certainly pursue us." He took a deep breath. "What lies ahead? How will we find ourselves in this fog? What is above the fog? Is there any place for us to hide?" He shook his head.

A bolt of lightning flashed above them, followed by an ear-shattering peel of thunder.

"I wish I knew more about what we still face before we crest this infernal hill." Tsalix held his head in his hands. "We cannot fail. Even with my training as a soldier, I cannot contend with three hardened troops. And the two of you are brave enough, but untutored in battle."

They sat in silence, each deep in thought.

"Tsalix, do you not remember that you were promised that no task given you would be too great?" said Asur.

"Aye, but I'm not sure Elosha knew what we'd face."

"And I'm equally sure he did," Asur replied. "Now let us put off this despair and carry on. We are but three. But we are three, and we will succeed."

"I wish I were as sure as you." Tsalix got to his feet.

"Tsalix, I think it would be wise to remove your armor," said Asur. "The lightning above us is thick, and the metal will draw it to you."

Another bolt of lightning sparked through the clouds.

Tsalix removed his breastplate and shield and stuck them behind one of the dwarf pines. The clouds closed around them, and soon they were climbing through mists as thick as steel wool. Periodically, lightning illuminated the clouds and thunder crashed. Not only could they not see a foot in front of them, they could not see any evidence of a trail at their feet. The rocks were bathed with moisture from the clouds and were as slippery as a frog's back.

The soft leather soles of their boots gave little grip to the stones, and they fell often, struggling to keep from sliding back through the girdle of clouds. There was nothing growing in this perpetual mist, nothing to hold onto. Their clothing was soaked, and rivulets of icy water coursed down their backs as they inched up the mountainside.

"I can't go any further without a rest," Kwercus said. "My legs feel like rubber."

"Find somewhere to dig in your toes," Tsalix replied. "We don't want to slide down and have to climb this accursed mountain again." He wiggled his toes into a crack in the rock.

He sensed Asur was on his right, and Kwercus on his left, but the mist was so thick he could see neither of them.

"Courage. This can't go on forever."

CHAPTER 19

LIEUTENANT LEGAI STUCK THE TIP OF HIS SPEAR INTO THE
pool, fishing for the bodies of his men. The water was deeper than he
expected, and his probing was unsuccessful. He knew he had been tricked,
and he was furious at himself for having fallen for this hoax. But he was
even more furious at the men who had perpetrated it.

He lifted his spear and drove the tip of it through Kwercus's tree-filled
cloak, which had snagged on a shard of rock at the edge of the pool.

"The next thrust will be through your heart!" he screamed up the side
of the mountain, and shook his fist.

"What is your command?" said the younger of the two remaining
troops.

"Are there just two of them? We have two cloaks." Legai paced at the
edge of the pond. "If there are only two, we can easily subdue them." He
continued to pace. "But what if this is part of a greater deceit? What if
there is a legion above us and this is but bait to draw us into their trap?"

He leaned against a tree and searched the hillside above him. Peered
at the band of clouds, willing it to part and reveal what might be hidden
above him, but the mist refused to reveal its secrets. All that greeted him
was a flash of lightning and a rumble of thunder.

Legai rubbed the back of his neck with his mailed hand as he stared
into the pool. *I was too hasty. I should not have sent these three to their
deaths. I need every man I can muster.*

He knew the remaining soldiers were assessing him, wondering how
long it would be before he made a decision.

"Let us go," he said. "We will pursue them and cut out their evil, conniving hearts."

Lieutenant Legai dug the shaft of his spear into the pebbles at the side of the pool, and steadied himself as he began the torturous ascent. *Had I not fallen for their little trick, we would not have these two hundred feet to climb again.* The fury built up within his heart.

The three of them reclaimed fifty feet before they had to stop and rest. Thunder rumbled down the hillside. Leaning on their spears, they drew great drafts of air into their tortured lungs.

A half-hour passed before they found themselves at the place near the waterfall where their three companions had fallen. Legai flailed himself mentally again for reducing the strength of his forces. The anger boiled like molten lead in his chest.

He cast one last glance at the pool below before continuing his climb up the mountain. Instead of continuing straight up the slope, he led his men on a less steep incline along the face of the peak. After moving nearly a mile, they had gained barely another hundred feet of elevation.

Legai reversed, still keeping on an upward slope. Although switching back and forth on the mountain took longer, it was not as tiring.

Late afternoon they encountered the bottom of the cloud bank and paused to rest. Thunder clap made them flinch.

"What lies ahead, sir?" said one of his men.

Lieutenant Legai hated to admit that he did not know, and he was not aware of anyone who had climbed through the mists to the top of the peak.

He leaned over and supported himself on his spear. "More of the same."

They were perched on the eastern side of Mount Jinee, and already the shadows of night were encroaching. Legai craned his neck, looking for a flat spot where they could spend the night, but he could see none. They were barely able to stand on the slope, let alone lie down. He was reluctant to enter the cloud bank until daylight, but there seemed to be no alternative. He hated indecision, but he feared the unknown even more.

With one more look at the mists above, he said, "We will continue around the mountain until we find a place where we can rest for the night."

"What if we do not find one," said one of the men.

"We will," Legai snapped.

He lifted his spear, and the three of them moved around the peak, toward the south. There was no trail to follow, and the way was treacherous. Behind them, the moon rose and gave scant light as they continued their trek. Even the lightning and thunder seemed to have taken refuge for the night.

A couple of hours passed before they reached a place where a huge boulder had split from the hillside, leaving a flat spot about eight feet square behind it. The three men sank down, opened their packs, and ate their rations.

"We will spend the night here," Legai said. "Tomorrow we will finish scaling the peak and succeed in our mission."

After removing their mail and wrapping themselves in cloaks, the three men tried to find a comfortable spot on the sloping, slick rock floor. It was not easy, but eventually they all fell asleep.

CHAPTER 20

J OHONA ENTERED THE THRONE ROOM, HAVING BEEN SUMMONED
by his father moments before.

"Father, I am here." He nodded at his mother.

"Where are our three young disciples?" Elosha stroked his beard.

"According to Neahsja, the owl, they have reached Mount Jinee and are scaling the peak."

"That is good." The king smiled.

"Yes, but they are pursued. They opened the vial of fire, and the ensuing flame was seen by my brother's overseers."

"Ah. Did they use the vial wisely?"

"That remains to be seen, Father. Sometimes time must pass before we see the impact of our decisions." Johona looked into his father's deep blue eyes. "But I am not telling you anything you do not know."

Elosha nodded. "What is done is done."

He rose from the throne and moved to one of the windows that overlooked the streets of Hayeli. The twinkling of a thousand lamps lit the homes below.

"Are they in need of help?"

Johona walked to his father's side. "Perhaps. They have entered the mists that surround Jinee, and darkness has fallen upon them. They are tired, but not discouraged."

The queen said, "Perhaps we can offer help."

Elosha put his hand on his son's shoulder. "Send Atsah, the eagle, and his brothers to offer aid."

"As you wish." Johona turned and left the room.

He hurried up the polished steps, to the aerie, where he found Atsah gazing out a window to the north.

"Atsah, my friend."

"My liege. What brings you here?"

"There are three young men perched on east side of Mount Jinee, hidden in the clouds. They are on a mission, sent by my father. They cannot fail."

"I understand. What would you have me do?"

Johona smiled. "You have great wisdom, my friend. These men are being pursued by my brother's troops, and my father wishes you to help."

Atsah nodded. "But my prince gives me no more instruction than this?"

Johona shook his head. "In your wisdom, you will know what to do."

"Then I'll go, and I will take my brothers with me." Atsah furled his great wings and sent out a call that echoed across the top of the mountain.

A dozen responding calls echoed as the great eagle launched into the pale moonlit night.

Johona watched as the huge birds blotted out the lights of the village below and flew north.

CHAPTER 21

ATSAH LED THE HUGE BIRDS OVER THE PLAIN OF WONADSI. Below, he spotted a hundred campfires dotting the plain. They crossed the wasteland below, until Jinee's black and ominous peak rose before them. Atsah led his flight to the east side of the mountain and climbed through the air until they were above the clouds. He strove to see through the mists, but they were too dense for even his keen eyes. He called to his brothers, who followed him to the rim of the caldera at the top of the peak. Once they had all landed, he began to formulate a plan.

He turned to the giant eagle on his right. "Fly below the clouds, and then fly up through them until you rejoin us here."

With a dip of its head, the massive bird launched into the air and flew outside the ring of clouds until it turned downward, drew its wings to its side, and plummeted through the air. A few moments later, he reappeared in a swirl of mist that created an open channel in the clouds, and rejoined his brothers on the edge of the abyss. Behind him, the tunnel he had created in the clouds began to fill in.

Atsah nodded. "Brothers, if we all fly wingtip to wingtip through the clouds, we will sweep them away for a moment. We must do that until we locate the three chosen ones. Follow me."

The eagles screamed through the air until they were below the clouds. They spread their wings to break the fall, then turned upward. Stroke by powerful stroke, they pushed through the dense fog. On the fourth such trip, Atsah spotted Tsalix clinging to the side of the cliff.

With a call to the other birds, he slowed his ascent and beat the mists with his outstretched wings. Joined by his brothers, it was not long before Atsah discovered Asur and Kwercus.

"Climb, my young friends," Atsah called. "We will clear the way."

In a few minutes Tsalix, Asur, and Kwercus had reached the dry mountain side above the clouds.

"Can you reach the top of the peak by yourselves?" Atsah said, as the eagles hovered above them. "We dare not pick you up with our talons for fear we will cause damage."

Tsalix saluted Atsah. "We can reach our goal. "But without your help, we might have failed."

Atsah dipped his head. "Then Godspeed, my friend."

With a final spiral above them, the birds whirled around the peak to the south and disappeared in the faint moonlight.

Hours passed until Atsah and his brothers returned to Hayeli to find Johona waiting for them.

"What did you discover?"

"They are safe," Atsah said. "Weary and wet, but safe."

"Thank you, my friend. As always, we have been able to count on you."

"It is nothing." Atsah settled on his perch and tucked his head under his wing.

"One more thing," Johona said, as he left the room. "As you take your daily flights, please keep an eye on the three of them, and bring me word of what you find."

"Of course." Atsah buried his head deeper beneath his wing.

CHAPTER 22

L IEUTENANT LEGAI WOKE FROM A TROUBLED SLEEP. THE DAWN
was perhaps an hour away, and the sky to the east had turned slate
gray. His two companions were still snoring.

He struggled to his feet and looked up at the cloud bank above his
head and shuddered. The mountain was steep enough and hard enough
to climb without entering the foggy shroud above. Once the sun struck
the clouds and warmed them, the lightning would begin. Legai knew the
stones would be slippery with dew, and the way hard to see.

He sat back down on the narrow shelf of rock and considered his
options. The obvious one was to lead his men through the bank of clouds
and pursue their prey—whoever and however many there were. Another
was to give up the chase and return to their base. He could report that
they had found no one. The flaw in this second plan was that the two soldiers might talk of what had happened to their companions, which meant
he'd have to dispose of them as well and return to camp alone. While this
meant no one would tell of their failure, he'd have a difficult time explain-
ing what had happened to the five other men in his patrol. Besides, after
sending three men to their deaths, he had little stomach to kill the other
two. But who was to say they would not report his actions at the waterfall? And his survival was what counted most.

He sat with his head in his hands, trying to think of a third option.

One of his men stirred. The sun was nearly on the horizon, and Legai
would have to decide soon. He grabbed the staff of his spear and pushed
to his feet.

It's too bad my men did not die in battle. Then we could have returned without scorn.

His eyes brightened as he considered a third alternative. Both of his men were still sleeping. As much as he deplored doing it, it would take little to dispatch them.

With a quick thrust, he drove his spear through the heart of one of the men, who awoke with a scream as he grasped the head of the spear. Legai jerked the spear free and turned toward his other soldier. The man was struggling to get to his feet when Legai's second thrust of the spear sent him falling backward over the edge of the cliff.

Blood was bubbling from the mouth of the dying man at his feet. Legai lifted him to his shoulder and sent him plummeting after his companion. He wiped the blood from the tip of the spear, and without a backward glance, began retracing his steps down the mountain side.

Above him, a clap of thunder announced the beginning of a new day. Legai sat, opened his pack, and ate breakfast. The sun warmed him, and he dozed for some time before shaking himself awake. He shouldered his pack and took one last look at the clouds before trekking down the hillside.

During the descent, he formulated the story he'd report to Captain Doitsoh. He had nearly reached the trail that girded the foothills when he realized he bore no sign of battle. He stepped onto the trail and pulled his cloak around him. A short double-bladed knife was in a sheath on his belt. He drew it from its scabbard and slashed the cloak until it was a mere rag around his neck.

He steeled himself and closed his eyes as he drew the razor-sharp blade across his bicep. Blood ran down his arm and dropped from his fingertips. He gritted his teeth and drew the blade across his calf, above his greave. Soon his sandal was sticky with blood. After replacing his knife in its scabbard, he began limping down the pathway, leaving a crimson trail. He considered stopping so his wounds would stop bleeding, but it was late enough in the day that he forced himself to carry on.

The moon was rising when he reached the encampment of Nash Doitsoh. A sentry challenged him, but once he recognized the wan face of Lieutenant Legai, he bade him pass. In the center of the camp, a whole pig turned on a spit above glowing coals. Torches in front of the circled tents lit the campground. Legai crossed the open ground to Nash Doitsoh's tent, which rose higher than the others in the circle. The door flaps were rolled open and secured with leather thongs. A guard stood on each side of the opening. The black and scarlet banner of Abadon flew on a staff above the tent. Legai fell to the ground in front of the door. The guards crossed their tsenils across the opening.

"Who is it that disturbs me," Nash Doitsoh growled.

"Legai, my captain."

Nash rose from his bed and crossed the floor of the tent in two strides. He waved the guard to their posts.

"You are injured." He knelt beside his lieutenant.

"Aye. Nothing that won't heal with time."

Doitsoh helped Legai to his feet and seated him upon a stool covered with lambskin.

"Bring me wine and water," he called to one of the guards.

The man returned a few minutes later with a flagon of wine and a basin of water. Nash Doitsoh uncorked the flagon and handed it to Lieutenant Legai.

"Drink. Then wash the blood from your body." He placed the basin at Legai's feet.

Legai drank deeply before he wiped his lips with the back of his hand. Then he dipped a linen cloth into the basin and began wiping the blood and dirt from his body. When he'd finished he struggled to his feet and saluted.

"What happened?" Doitsoh said.

"We were ambushed, and were severely outnumbered. My men fought bravely, but there was no way we could win. I was wounded, but continued to fight until I wearied from loss of blood, and fell and hit my head on a stone. When I awoke, I was alone. Apparently they thought me dead and left me." He bowed his head. "I failed you, my captain."

"Sit." Doitsoh stroked his mane. "You alone were left?"

Legai nodded.

"Interesting. I wonder why?" Nash rose to his feet and paced the length of his tent. "How many were there, Lieutenant?"

Legai looked at the top of the tent as if he were counting. "Perhaps three dozen men."

"All armed?"

"Yes, Captain."

"Where exactly did this battle take place?"

Legai began to sweat. He realized the corner he had forced himself into. If the battle had taken place on the mountain trail, there would be little room for a force of any size to organize itself. Yet Captain Doitsoh knew they had been sent up the mountain side to find their foe after having been alerted to the flash of fire that had burst above the forge room. Moreover, there was not room in the cave from which the fire had erupted for that many men to assemble.

His captain stood waiting for an answer.

"Certainly you remember the spot." Doitsoh raised a brow.

"Near the head of the waterfall," Legai spat out. "They encircled us, and as you know, the terrain is steep and treacherous. There was little ground on which to stand and fight." He blew out a breath.

"I see." Doitsoh stroked his mane. "When you have healed sufficiently, I will have you lead me to the spot. Then we will decide whether to pursue this...force."

"They have probably fled."

"I think not. There are not many ways up and down Mount Jinee, and I have men guarding all of them. I do not think that three dozen men can escape without being seen." Doitsoh glared at his lieutenant. "Not even a single man."

Legai shuddered. "As you wish."

CHAPTER 23

EXHAUSTED AND SHIVERING, THE THREE FRIENDS RESTED ON an outcropping of rock. Their clothes were soaked, and a steady breeze curled around the mountain from the west, chilling them even more. Although they were freezing, their spirits were light.

"Well, my brothers," Tsalix said, "do we climb the rest of the way tonight, or do we wait until morning?" He looked at his two friends.

"Give me a moment to gather some strength, and let's push on," Asur said. "I'm too wet to sleep. And besides, there doesn't seem to be any place to lie down. We might as well try to reach the summit."

"Aye" Kwercus replied. "We've come this far. And with Atsah's help, I can see the end to our quest."

"Perhaps," said Tsalix. "Rest then, my brothers. And when we're able, we'll crest the hill."

Only a few minutes later, they realized it was impossible to get any rest on the steep hillside.

"Let's reach the top." Kwercus gasped. "It is not that far away."

An hour later, Tsalix dug his fingers into the shallow crack that ran horizontally along the rock face, and struggled to pull himself up the cliff. With his toes he sought for a ridge of rock, but all he felt were pebbles sliding away and cascading down the mountainside. Kwercus was to his left, and Asur to his right. They were within a yard of reaching the rim of the caldera. It had been a harder climb than any of them had suspected. They had done so by using small protrusions and fissures, but it had been slow progress. Now there seemed to be nothing that offered a hand or foot hold.

Sweat coursed down their backs.

"Tsalix, if you can raise your foot to my shoulder," Kwercus said, "I think I can hold both of us while you lift yourself over the lip." He flexed his shoulders made strong by years as a woodsman.

"Are you sure? I would not want to send you down this cliff again."

"Aye. I've got a good grip, and I've hoisted more than your weight, my friend."

Tsalix dug his fingers into the crack and lifted his left leg until he could place his foot on his friend's shoulder.

"Ready?"

When Kwercus nodded, Tsalix began to shift his weight onto his foot. Slowly he raised himself until he slid his left hand out of the crevice and grasped the rim of the caldera. Pulling with all his strength, he moved his other hand until it slid over the edge of the crater. He felt as if his arms would pull out of their sockets as he heaved himself over the brink of the mountain top. He locked his legs against the rocks and extended his arms until Kwercus could reach his hands. Kwercus freed his hand from the crevice and grabbed for Tsalix's outstretched hand. Their fingers met, but not securely enough, and Kwercus let loose and struggled to find the crack in the rock again. He hung by one arm until, with Herculean effort, pulled himself high enough to thrust the fingers back into the fissure.

"Lift Asur first," Kwercus wheezed, "while I regain some strength."

Tsalix readjusted himself so that his arms hung to where Asur dangled on the side of the hill. Asur took a deep breath, pulled his fingers from the crack and grabbed Tsalix's welcoming hand. Tsalix struggled to keep his balance atop the crater.

"Now!" he shouted.

Asur's grabbed Tsalix's other hand and nearly pulled Tsalix over the edge of the caldera. Inch by inch Tsalix pulled up until Asur was able to throw his leg over the rim. Both fell to the ground, panting.

"Thank you, my brother." Asur gasped. "Now let us both help Kwercus.

Tsalix lay down and extended himself over the edge of the crater, while Asur wrapped his arms around Tsalix's legs. With the added anchor, Tsalix was able to reach down and grab the back of Kwercus's tunic with both hands. Kwercus wrapped his hands around Tsalix's wrists, and Asur helped pull the two of them to safety. The three of them lay exhausted on the ground.

"That was more difficult than I had imagined." Kwercus panted. "But again, we found a solution to the problem."

Once their breathing returned to normal, they sat up and surveyed the top of Mount Jinee. Before them lay the shallow crater of an ancient volcano about a half-mile wide. Near the center was a raised cone that signaled the top of the vent that extended from the forge room more than a thousand feet below. The floor of the caldera was covered with millions of polished black and obsidian pebbles—some the size of a pea, others the size of an egg.

Tsalix wrinkled his brow. "Where is the talisman? I thought we could end our odyssey, but I see nothing that makes me think of a talisman. As I feared, our problem is not yet solved."

He began walking across the rock-strewn field. As he approached the center vent, the heat of the air rose through the conduit from far below. In less than ten minutes, he had crossed to the other side of the shallow valley, where he peered over the edge and saw the ring of clouds that hid Abadon's palace from view.

Tsalix traveled back to his friends, who were sitting on a stone ridge that ran partway around the rim.

"Nothing." He sat beside them.

The sun was nearing its zenith and beaming on the three young men.

"Perhaps if we have something to eat, an idea will enter our minds," Tsalix said, as they emptied their remaining food from their packs. "We had better find a solution soon, because we have little food left."

As they ate, Asur stirred the pebbles with the toe of his boot. "Is there nothing on this mountain top but stones?"

"Nothing I can see," replied Tsalix.

"Then the talisman must be a stone," Asur said.

"But there are millions of them." Tsalix shook his head. "How will we know which one is the one we seek?"

"I know not. But I know just sitting here will not answer the quest." Asur knelt and began lifting each stone at his feet and inspecting it. "I'll start here."

Tsalix moved to the right and began turning over the obsidian pebbles, while Kwercus moved to the left. They had picked up thousands of pieces of rubble when the sun began to sink beneath the horizon.

"How will we know?" Kwercus said. "Look at how little we've done and how much more there is to explore."

The three of them sank to the ground. The moon rose in the east and cast its wan light over them.

"Were you not promised that no task given would be too great?" Asur said.

Tsalix nodded.

"And were you not blessed that you would have a quick wit that would allow you to solve puzzles?"

Again Tsalix nodded.

"Then why such despair? I know not the answer to our problem, but I have great faith we will find the answer."

Tsalix pondered their situation. "If indeed the talisman is one of these stones, it must be different from all the others."

"Different? How?" Asur said.

"I'm not sure, but it must be different in some way."

"They all look the same to me," Kwercus said. "Except for their size."

"But there are many of the same size, regardless of which measurement you use. It must be something else." Tsalix rubbed his hand through his thick black hair. "What else could it be?"

"Not color," Kwercus replied. "They're all black as a moonless night."

The moon drew overhead as they thought about the problem that lay before them. Tsalix tried to remember exactly what the king had told them about the talismans, but all he could recall was that the king would not tell them what they were, in case they were captured. Elosha had said nothing else.

Then it struck him like lightning—the queen had said that the answer would float before them.

"Asur, Kwercus, I think I know the answer."

"Oh?" said Kwercus.

"What would that be?" Asur replied.

"Do you recall what the queen said?"

Both men shook their heads.

"She said the answer would float before our eyes. One of these stones is lighter than the rest."

"If you are right," said Asur, "it still means we must lift each of these millions of pebbles. It could take a very long time. More time than we have."

Tsalix rose to his feet and reached inside his tunic. He withdrew the Water vial and removed the silk cord from around his neck.

"Come stand with me. I do not know what will be the result, but we saw what happened when we opened Fire."

The three young men retreated to the stone ridge and stood atop it, while Tsalix unstopped the vial. A torrent of water gushed out of the tiny container until the caldera was filled at least two feet deep. It took several minutes for the water to settle. And then on the peaceful surface, a single stone the size of a hen's egg floated, moonlight reflecting from its surface.

Tsalix stepped off the stone bench on which they waited, and waded through the newly formed pool until he reached the floating talisman. He lifted it and returned to his friends' side. By the wan light of the moon, they examined the stone. Engraved in gold on one side were the letters *TS*. The rock pulsed in Tsalix's hand.

"TS. Tsalix Silverthorn!" said Asur. "They are your initials."

"Aye. We have found the first talisman." Tsalix smiled, turned it over in his hands, and then slid it into the purse that hung from his belt.

The light of the moon was extinguished. Kwercus turned and shrank back. Emerging from the vent in the center of the caldera was an enormous spider—large enough that it cast a shadow that reached across the top of the peak. It dipped its front legs into the water, then jerked them out.

The three young men slid next to each other.

"It's huge," Kwercus whispered. "But it seems afraid of the water."

"I wonder how long it will be before the water recedes?" said Asur.

"I don't know," Tsalix said. "But we might want to leave before it does."

CHAPTER 24

Lieutenant Legai had slept fitfully, his dreams filled with the shrieks of demons reaching up to claw him from the bottom of a bottomless pool. He had awakened several times, drenched in sweat. After Captain Doitsoh's questioning the previous night, he had felt less and less sure that his story would hold up to scrutiny.

He struggled from his cot and inspected his cuts. Both had scabbed over. He bent to retrieve his armor when a shadow filled the tent.

Nash Doitsoh stood in the open doorway. "Feeling up to a hike?"

"Of course, Captain."

"We will take thirty men with us, unless you think that will be too few."

Legai shook his head. "I'm sure that will be sufficient." He fashioned the greaves around his calves, stood upright, and slipped his breastplate into place. "Whenever you are ready, Captain."

Doitsoh shook his mane. "After breakfast, then." He turned on his heel and marched away from the tent, leaving Legai trembling.

Legai headed to the mess tent and struggled to force a few bites of food into his queasy stomach.

An hour later, the platoon began its journey. Before noon they reached the spot where the upward trail began.

Captain Doitsoh called a halt. "It will be a hard climb from this point on. One we may not be able to achieve before sunset. And once we are on the side of the mountain, there may be nowhere to rest."

He turned to Lieutenant Legai. "Am I not correct?"

"It is a brutal climb, Captain." Legai nodded.

"Let us be on our way. The day is passing as we speak."

Legai nodded again as Doitsoh led his men up the side of the hill. Often he stopped to inspect the trail before continuing on.

Late afternoon they reached the pool at the base of the waterfall. The bodies of the three dead men had bloated and floated face down on the surface. Nash Doitsoh reached out with a mailed hand, grasped the shoulder strap of one of the corpses, and dragged it out of the pond. Much of the face was missing.

"I see no wound."

Legai pointed at the skull of the ghastly visage. "He took a blow to the head."

"Perhaps." Doitsoh stuck out his spear and dragged another of the corpses to the edge of the pond, where he pulled it out. "This one has a wound to the heart." He looked at Lieutenant Legai. "What weapons did your foe have? This appears to be a thrust from a sword, one such as we carry, with two serrated edges."

"They were so armed," Legai said.

"Interesting," Captain Doitsoh murmured.

After he dragged the third body from the pool, the men began their climb up the side of the waterfall. The way was steep and made more difficult as men dislodged stones and sent them cascading on the men below. Eventually all reached the small flat ledge at the top of the torrent.

"It was here you fought them?" said Doitsoh.

"A-aye," Legai replied. "You can see how little ground there was to stand and fight."

"Yes, I can see." Doitsoh. He surveyed the site. "Hardly room to fight. And an amazing lack of blood."

He ordered his men to fill their waterskins, and when they had finished he led them up the side of the mountain. The sun set before they reached the bottom of the clouds.

"Lieutenant, is there anywhere where we can spend the night?" Doitsoh said.

Legai shrugged. "A few small pockets where slabs of stone have peeled from the mountain side. But other than that, nowhere."

Doitsoh drove the shaft of his spear into the loose gravel at his feet.

He examine the slope. "We cannot enter the mist tonight. Scatter along the hillside and find some place where you can sleep. We will assemble here at daybreak. Now go."

The troops began searching along the slope for some place they could weather the night. The moon had risen high in the sky before all of them had found somewhere to settle.

"We will reach our destination before noon," Doitsoh said. "Then we shall see how many of the enemy we must face."

CHAPTER 25

THE WATER BEGAN RECEDING AFTER THE SPIDER EMERGED from the vent. Tsalix, Asur, and Kwercus backed up to the edge of the pool until they felt the ridge of the caldera at their backs. The spider kept testing the ground with her hairy front legs. Each time she touched water, she drew her legs back against her body.

"Why does she fear the water?" said Asur. "It is only a foot deep and would pose no threat to her."

"I know not, Tsalix replied. "But it will not be long before the water has drained away and she can touch the pebbles beneath it."

Even as he spoke, the monster reached out her front legs and felt the stones beneath an inch or two of water. She stepped away from the vent and moved toward the three young men, who shrank back against the low wall of the crater. When she was a dozen feet from them, she halted and waved her palps in the air.

Tsalix noticed the chain extending from her left hind leg, into the opening from which she'd appeared.

"She can come no further," he whispered, pointing toward the chain.

She turned her massive head and searched for Tsalix with eight eyes.

"Who has ascended the peak?" she said.

Her voice reminded Tsalix of the willow flutes he and his father had made when he was but a wee lad.

"I am Tsalix Silverthorn," he replied, with as much courage as he could muster.

"And what is your mission?"

Tsalix began to relax, but he was still not sure what the spider's role was.

"We have fulfilled our mission," he said, "and now we must retreat down the mountain."

The spider rubbed her palps together. "I am Nashjie." She bowed her head. "I hoped you might have come to free me."

"Why are you captive? Who enslaved you?" Tsalix sat on the narrow bench of rock that encircled the edge of the crater, staying a comfortable distance from her massive jaws.

Nashjie bowed her head again. "It is a long story, and one that may not interest you. Sufficient to say, I have been held captive here for decades."

"Indeed. Please tell us." He spread his arms to encompass Asur and Kwercus. "It may help us with the rest of our quest."

"Who are your companions?"

"Excuse me. This is Asur Longtooth and Kwercus Strongheart. All three of us are from Aravah, and we have been sent on an odyssey by King Elosha."

Nashjie's voice rose. "Then you are not sent by Abadon?"

"No," the three replied.

The huge spider settled her weight on the stones while extending her legs to the side.

"So be it," she said. "My grandmother, Dadihteh, was a renowned weaver. She wove cloth that shimmered like silver, was soft as a baby's breath, yet strong as forged armor. Everyone in the kingdom knew of her prowess, and she was sought regularly to create fabrics for royalty."

"I have seen her tapestries," Asur said.

"Then the obsidian wars began, and Abadon captured my grandmother. He wanted her to create armor for his soldiers, for with it they would have been able to withstand the cruelest blow from any sword or spear." Nashjie paused. "She refused. She knew how black was his heart and how oppressive his rule would be."

"Then what happened?" Tsalix said.

"At first he tried to convince her to weave her magic cloth. But after nearly a year, she still refused. So he turned to torture. He was afraid that if he damaged my grandmother, she would be unable to weave, so he did something unspeakable. He chained my grandmother to the wall of the forge chamber, brought in my mother and threatened to mutilate her in front of my grandmother's eyes."

"Certainly your grandmother couldn't bear to see that happen." Kwercus whispered.

"My mother knew what awaited her and what anguish my grandmother would suffer if the torture went on. Although she was heavily guarded and had chains around her body, she was able to reach out with one leg, grasp a spear from one of the guards, and thrust it into her own heart. Her last words were, 'Better to die free than live a slave.' Nashjie's voice had dropped to a whisper that floated like a zephyr across the caldron. "My grandmother nearly died of a broken heart, but her resolve was strengthened. She steadfastly refused to weave one inch of cloth for Abadon."

"She must have been exceedingly brave," said Tsalix.

"She was, she was." Nashjie lifted her head. "Then Abadon searched until he found me. I was dragged before my grandmother, and Abadon threatened to dismember my body in front of her eyes. My grandmother had seen her own daughter perish, and now her granddaughter was in peril. She had seen so much bloodshed and malice." Her voice trailed away.

"Surely your grandmother, Dadihteh, could not let that happen to you," said Tsalix. "What did she do?"

Nashjie sighed. "She agreed to weave cloth for Abadon. She had watched her daughter sacrifice her own life, and now her granddaughter's life was in peril." The spider sunk even lower on the ground. "I was brought here and chained as insurance so my grandmother would keep her word. That was nearly fifty years ago, when the obsidian wars began."

Kwercus leaned forward "What happened to Dadihteh?"

Nashjie raised her head. "She wove cloth from the silk she spun."

"But in battle I have pierced the armor of Abadon's troops," Tsalix said. "It offered no great resistance."

"There is a secret, one that Abadon has never learned. Not all spider silk is the same. We can control not only how tacky the strand is, but also how strong. It is a secret known only to my clan." She paused to look at the three young men, apparently deciding whether or not she could trust them. "My grandmother spun silk strands no stronger than any other threads, then wove it into fabrics for Abadon. In a rage, he killed her," she whispered. "And in revenge, left me chained."

Kwercus stood. "Perhaps we can take care of that." He drew his ax from his belt.

Nashjie drew back.

"I mean you no harm. My blade may sever your chain." He marched past the spider until he was standing beside her cuffed leg. "Do not move. I would not want to cause damage to you." He lifted his ax above his head and brought it down with a mighty blow.

Sparks flew, but the chain remained unscathed.

"It is enchanted," said the spider. "I fear you cannot help."

Kwercus rubbed his shoulder. "I've never felt such resistance to my ax. There must be some way." He lifted the link of chain and examined it. "There's nary a scar on it! But look, there's a heavy nick in the blade of my ax."

The sun sent its first feeble rays over the horizon, and Tsalix looked past the encircling clouds across the broad Plain of Wonadsi, to the tip of Mount Deschee, glowing red in the sunlight. He sighed deeply and started to sit back down on the stone bench. His purse, heavy with the stone talisman, slid backward on his belt and sat upon it. It seemed to vibrate.

Tsalix reached down and slipped the purse into place on his hip. It radiated heat. Slowly he removed the talisman from his purse. It glowed in the faint morning light.

Guided by some unseen force, Tsalix followed Kwercus's path to the back of the huge spider. He placed the glowing stone on the link of chain next to her foot. It took but a few seconds before the link dissolved and the talisman fell into the last inch of water that covered the mountaintop. A cloud of steam geysered into the air.

Nashjie let out a scream as she shook the shackle free from her leg. All that remained was a branded bright white band that encircled it where the shackle had been.

"Freedom won at a price." Tsalix retrieved the talisman and returned it to his purse.

Nashjie stretched her eight legs before moving to the edge of the crater. "Someone approaches. Many men." She raced around the rim of the crater. "They come from all sides."

"Then we are trapped!" said Tsalix.

CHAPTER 26

CAPTAIN DOITSOH URGED HIS MEN UP THE MOUNTAINSIDE. Tendrils of mist clung to them like strands of ivy. With the warmth of the sun, the crackle of lightning lit up the cloud with an accompanying kettle drum of thunder. Nash Doitsoh prepared to step into the fog when one of his men called to him.

"Captain, I've found a breastplate and shield," he called, through cupped hands.

"Indeed." Doitsoh waved the man to his side. "Just one?"

The soldier scampered across the precarious mountain side. "Aye, Captain. Wedged behind a scrawny pine."

"I wonder why? Why is there only one?" Doitsoh held the shield and sneered at the crest of Johona before flinging it down the mountain side, followed by the breastplate. "I'll not have my men without armor! Climb!"

His order was answered by a flash of lightning and a crash of thunder. He flinched before moving up into the tendrils of mist. He had not climbed a dozen feet into the cloud before another fork of lightning flashed. One of his men screamed when he was struck by the bolt, and fell from the mountain. Fear gripped the rest of the men as they scrambled up the steep hillside.

In the two hours before they emerged from the cloud, a dozen more men were struck by bolts of lightning and flung from the side of the peak.

At last the remaining men finished their ascent through the fog, soaking wet and shivering.

"The crest of the crater is not far above us," said Nash Doitsoh.

The mountain rose at a nearly ninety-degree incline. Nash pointed with the double-headed blade of his tsenil. Struggling to find toe holds, the men crept up the hill. The climb sapped their strength, and the thin air at this elevation caused them to struggle for breath. What had appeared to be a few minutes climb stretched on for nearly three hours.

"I can go no further without rest." Lieutenant Legai gasped.

"Very well," Captain Doitsoh snarled. "Rest for ten minutes. Then we finish our climb. The enemy waits above, and we must be ready for their treachery."

Beneath them, flashes of lightning illuminated the clouds, followed by bursts of thunder. Doitsoh shook the water from his mane and pressed against the side of the peak. As he rested he began reviewing his battle plans. At first he had thought Lieutenant Legai had spun a story about being attacked, and he thought there would be few, if any, forces to contend with. But with the discovery of the discarded armor, he reconsidered their position. If indeed a significant force had entrenched themselves on the top of this infernal peak, then his men might be in danger. The stronger defensive position is always from above, not to mention the difficulty of the last few yards of the climb, which would drain strength from his men.

He shook his head and thought of a stratagem of surprise attack.

"Lieutenant," Doitsoh barked. "How many men do we still have with us?"

"Seventeen men, plus the two of us, Captain," replied Legai.

"Send word to have all but two join us."

"And the other two?"

"Have them move to the opposite side of the cone, and upon our signal, finish their climb. Once atop the peak, have them call down the mountain as if they are encouraging the rest of the men to hurry to their aid. That will focus the foe on them. Meanwhile we will lead the rest of the men over this side of the crater and catch the enemy from behind."

"As you wish, Captain. It will take a few minutes for the men to move around the mountain to the positions you command."

Captain Doitsoh nodded. "As long as we are not discovered, there is time."

Lieutenant Legai trudged across the mountain. Within a few minutes, the word had been spread and all troops began moving to their appointed spots.

"We are ready," he called to his captain.

"Send the signal," Doitsoh growled.

"Aye, Captain."

Word was passed to the two decoys on the opposite side of the peak, who began their final assault on the mountain.

CHAPTER 27

"WE ARE TRAPPED." TSALIX SEARCHED FOR SOMEWHERE TO hide.

"Drag the chain back to the opening of the vent," Nashjie cried.

The three young men began dragging the heavy links behind them. When they reached the vent, they lifted the end of the chain, fed it over the edge, and listened as the links clanked against each other.

"I can help you as you helped me." The huge spider began spinning a web around Tsalix.

Once finished she reached back with one front leg and secured him to its hairy surface. A second web secured Kwercus to the opposite front leg. Asur was likewise attached to a third leg.

"Trust me, my young friends." Nashjie climbed up the side of the vent and attached a strand of silk to the links of the chain nearest the surface.

Once the strand was secured, she continued to secrete the silk from her spinnerets and descended head first down the chimney. Tsalix felt the heat of the forge below growing stronger and stronger the closer they came to the grate that blocked them. The sound of hammers on steel grew louder and louder as they dropped, and the sulfurous odor nearly choked them.

Soon they reached the last link of the chain and continued downward. The vent was shaped like an hour glass, and the chain ended before they reached the narrow throat of the passage. Although there was more than enough of an opening to permit Nashjie to pass through, Tsalix felt as if they would be stuck. He closed his eyes and tried to make himself small.

The huge spider slipped through the opening. Once through the narrow neck, the chimney widened again. The heat from the forge was intense and flowed up over them like a liquid bath. The sound of the forge was deafening. Tsalix could see the grate that blocked the opening another two hundred feet below them. The descent had been so rapid that his ears popped several times with the change in elevation. Strapped as he was to Nashjie's leg, he could see only what lay directly below them.

The enormous spider brought their fall to a halt and began swinging at the end of their long pendulum. Tsalix fought nausea, and just when he thought he could bear it no more, they reached the side of the funnel and Nashjie grasped an outcropping of rock.

"We will rest here a moment," she whispered. "We are out of sight of prying eyes from both above and below."

She secured the silk to a spine of rock and released the strand they had descended on so that it swung free. The updraft of heat from below caught it and blew it upward until it caught the rocks surrounding the narrow neck of the funnel, where it stuck.

"When we are sure we will not be observed," said Nashjie, "we'll continue our journey."

Tsalix peered down at the metal grate. It appeared to be constructed of steel bars woven into a mesh, and it blocked the tunnel.

"How will we get past the grate?" he said. "It is gigantic. It must weigh more than a ton."

"There are ways," Nashjie replied. "Do not fear. It is but a minor obstacle that you have to face. There will be others far more difficult." She checked the anchoring of the web strand. "We will go more slowly now. We must be quiet, for even with the sound of the hammers the overseers are always alert."

Nashjie descended the remaining distance to the edge of the grate. The closer they came, the larger it seemed to be. The spider reached a rock shelf that extended around the throat of the vent, and the grate rested upon the ledge. She freed each of her passengers from her legs. The silk fell from their bodies as if it were made of crystal. She stood them next to her on the eight-foot-wide rock shelf.

Tsalix stepped forward and examined the edge of the enormous grid. He felt around the flange that rested on the rock, and found it to be solid. The grating was made of steel bars placed at right angles to each other.

They were spaced about a foot apart. He grasped one of the rods and tried to move it at all. No success.

Shaking his head, he stepped back to his friends. "It is too heavy to move."

The three of them sank down onto their haunches, while Nashjie watched.

Kwercus rose to his feet, crept to the edge of the grate, and tried to force the bit of his ax under the flange.

He returned to the others. "It is too massive."

They sat staring at the obstacle before them. None of the young men had any idea how to move it, and despair seeped into their minds and bodies.

"We're trapped," Kwercus said.

With a shake of her head Nashjie whispered, "Did you not free me from the shackle that bound me?"

Tsalix rose to his feet. "Aye, but if I try to cut through the steel, the rod will surely fall to the floor of the forge and we will be discovered."

"Not if I secure it with my silk. If you were to cut through four of the bars, two in each direction, I believe it would leave a hole big enough for the three of you to pass through. I will keep the steel from alerting the men below." Nashjie readjusted herself on the shelf and cast a strand of silk onto the nearest bar. "I am ready."

Tsalix removed the talisman from his purse. The black stone pulsed, and his initials glowed. He held it against the end of the bar, and with a few sparks, the stone slid through the steel. He moved to the other end of the bar, while Kwercus knelt and reached for the cut end.

"It will be very hot," Nashjie said. "Wait a few minutes for it to cool."

Kwercus extended his hand and felt the heat from the steel. Five minutes later he tested the rod, and although it was still hot, he was able to hold it without pain.

Tsalix nodded at Nashjie. "Ready?"

"Yes," she whispered.

The talisman cut through the other end of the bar as easily as the first. Nashjie drew it up, while Kwercus steadied the rod. The spider swung the steel around and lowered it next to the wall.

"The next one will be more difficult," she said. "You will have to climb onto the grid to cut the bar loose."

Once Nashjie attached her silk to the next bar, Tsalix crept onto the woven web of steel. Again he pressed down the talisman and cut through the bar before slipping back onto the rock shelf. After enough time passed, Kwercus slid out to the end of the bar and grasped it. Tsalix knelt on the web work of steel and sliced through the other end of the rod. As before, Nashjie and Kwercus guided the rod next to its companion on the shelf. The steel bars they had removed provided an opening over two-feet wide, but it was still crisscrossed by two bars that would have to be removed. Nashjie attached her strand to one of these, and Tsalix prepared to cut its end when he slipped and sent a shower of pebbles into the forge room below. He scampered back onto the shelf.

The cascading rocks landed on the weapons cart with a clatter. The noise in the room was so intense that the only wolac harnessed to the cart wailed. A single flick of a bullwhip from one of the overseers quieted it.

Once Tsalix's racing heart slowed, he crept back to the end of the bar. This one was welded to the flange that circled the vent, but the talisman sliced through it. A few minutes later, he cut the other end and Nashjie swung it onto the stone ledge.

"One more to go," she whispered.

After ten minutes the final bar rested near its companions.

"We have an opening we can pass through, but what comes next?" Asur wiped his brow. "I see no way to descend into the forge room without being caught."

Tsalix ran his hands through his hair. "The hole is large enough for the three of us, but what about you, Nashjie? You cannot pass your bulk through that narrow window."

After a long silence, the giant spider said, "My place is not inside this cavern. I long to be free. For too long I have been fettered to this place. Now I wish to roam. You will go on, my young friends, but I will return to the top of Mount Jinee and seek my family beneath its slopes."

"As you wish," Tsalix said. "Yours may be the wiser choice anyway, for I see no way to escape."

He looked down into the hellish room below, while the sounds of the smithies striking steel resounded.

CHAPTER 28

NASH SENT WORD, AND THE HEAD OF THE DOUBLE-BITTED tsenil was thrust over the ridge of the crater, and Privates Hesh and Kut climbed over the edge. They fell to their knees and struggled to catch their breath.

When Hesh had regained enough strength to stand, he leaned over the edge of the caldera and called, "Hurry, men. We have a foe to fight!"

Eager to see if the ruse had worked and what, if any, chance they had of surviving the onslaught, he staggered around the lip of the crater. No one there.

The two men crossed the crater and peered over the opposite side. The rest of the force was within a yard or two, or cresting the summit.

"There is no need to hurry," Kut said. "There's no one here, Captain."

A few minutes later, all nineteen soldiers stood on the pebbled floor of the crater. Nash Doitsoh scanned the top of the mountain for any signs of life. The remnants of the flood were still seeping into the floor of the caldera, and the water had erased any signs that anyone had been there before them.

Captain Doitsoh divided his men into two groups, one of which he led, while Lieutenant Legai led the other.

"Walk carefully and search for anything that could tell us where they've gone," Doitsoh said.

His skepticism over Legai's report of a huge force was growing by the moment.

The men spread out and began combing the top of the peak. A half-hour later they reached the other side without discovering anything significant.

"Where have they gone?" Doitsoh walked to the edge of the small cone in the middle of the crater.

Warm air streamed out of the vent. With a practiced eye, Nash walked around the chimney and examined the edge of the cone until he saw a faint scar in the rock. He climbed up the side of the cone, where he saw the chain hanging into the abyss.

"Lieutenant," he growled over his shoulder. "Come here."

Legai scrambled up the cone. "Yes, sir."

"That chain should give you purchase. Climb down and see if you can find this foe you reported."

Legai gulped. "Captain, I'm not sure if I can—"

"That's an order, Lieutenant!"

"Yes, sir." Legai dropped to his stomach and grabbed the chain before sliding over the opening of the vent.

His fingers slipped into the links, and he wrapped his legs around the chain and began his descent. He had traveled barely a hundred feet of the thousand-foot chain before it felt as if his arms were being yanked from their sockets. He looked for some place on the side of the chimney where he could place his feet and rest, but he could see none.

The light from above was being swallowed up by the jet-black walls, and the faint light from below offered little illumination, although the heat was increasing with every foot. In a frantic effort, he tried to wrap the chain around his foot, but it was too heavy.

"Captain, I can go no further. Pull me up!" he cried.

Captain Doitsoh's head appeared in the spot of light at the top of the tunnel.

"Continue, Lieutenant. The links are too heavy to lift. Your life is in your hands. I am sure you are equal to the task."

Legai tried to squeeze the chain between his legs, but the links proved too slippery. He tried to pull himself up, but his arms lacked any strength. He looked down at the grate a thousand feet below and knew he would never make it. Tears flooded his eyes as he tried to climb further down the chain, but after another desperate minute, he had no strength and felt himself slipping. He grabbed, trying to wrap his fingers around one of the links, but to no avail. His scream died only after his lifeless body slammed into the grate at the bottom of the shaft.

On the top of the mountain, Captain Doitsoh moved down the side of the vent, to where his men stood in fear.

"They must not have gone that way," he said. "How could they have escaped us? We were on the only trail that leads up the mountain. They could not have passed without being discovered." He turned to his remaining men. "Perhaps they were just phantoms. Perhaps our dear lieutenant encountered no one when he first climbed this accursed peak." He paced in front of his troops. "It may have been that Legai was a traitor in our midst and that he led us here so that our camp below might be weakened. That would explain why a single breastplate was found on our ascent. If so, he has met his just reward. Quickly, we must return to our camp." He threw a leg over the edge of the caldera and gestured to his men.

The descent was as treacherous as the climb, and two hours passed before they entered the top of the cloud bank. Lightning flashed as they slipped and slid through the impenetrable fog. Before they emerged, two more men were struck by lightning and flung from the mountainside. Those who survived the adventure were dripping wet as they assembled in the frigid wind.

"The worst is behind us," Doitsoh said "Now let us haste down this mountain to our camp. Warm food and dry garments await us."

He led his men down the faint trail that embraced the mountain side.

CHAPTER 29

J UST AS THE BODY SLAMMED INTO THE GRATE, THE GONG FROM
the forge room sounded. The blacksmiths dropped their hammers and
dragged themselves to the walls of the chamber to have cool water poured
over them and to slake their thirst from the waterskins that hung from
pegs driven into the walls of the room. Two of the smiths acknowledged
the sound of Lieutenant Legai crashing onto the grate by glancing up, but
apparently none of the overseers heard it over the cacophony of the forge
room.

The gong sounded a second time, and the smiths retrieved their cloaks
and flagons before marching past the weapons wagon and up the tunnel.
The wolac dragged the wagon after them. The overseers stepped down
from their elevated central platform, gathered on the opposite side of the
room, and refreshed themselves with food and drink. A few minutes later,
the new shift of workers arrived and hung up their cloaks and water flasks.
An empty wagon was dragged into place by a wolac that turned it so the
tail of the cart faced the forges. The overseers climbed back into place, and
the sounds of steel on steel began again.

When Legai's body struck the grate, Tsalix's first thought was to race
onto the grid and try to help the man. But it was clear he was beyond sav-
ing, so he restrained himself. What would happen to the body remained
a mystery.

Tsalix, Asur, Kwercus, and Nashjie observed the shift-change in the pit
below.

"During this time, when they are distracted, one of us might be able to reach the floor of the pit," Tsalix said. "Nashjie, can you lower me on your silken strand?"

"Of course," she whispered. "What will you do then?"

Tsalix shrugged. "That remains to be seen. The exit tunnel is directly below us and may provide a way to escape."

"Perhaps," she said. "I wonder how long it will be until the next change of men?"

"We will have to be patient and see."

The four of them rested on the rocky shelf and waited. After each hour, the gong sounded and the men were able to drink from their flasks before they returned to work. Beneath Tsalix, the canvas tarpaulin was thrown to the side and the wagon filled with weapons of war.

Six hours passed before the gong sounded twice. Tsalix slid on his belly to the edge of the chasm and watched as the blacksmiths gathered their belongings and shuffled up the tunnel. Nashjie spun a loop in the end of a strand of silk, and Tsalix placed his foot in it. As soon as the overseers left their posts and began to eat and drink on the far side of the cavern, Tsalix slipped through the opening in the grill. With his foot in the stirrup, he grasped the strand with all his strength as Nashjie spun her silk and lowered him to the floor. Once he alighted, he signaled to her and she drew up the silken rope.

Tsalix crouched and crept toward the shadow of the tunnel, where he pressed his back against the wall and waited for his eyes to adjust to the gloom. Two dozen feet into the tunnel, a heavy iron-bound door closed the portal. He pressed himself into a nook in the wall and remained hidden. Above him, Kwercus and Asur lay on their stomachs, watching the scene below.

It seemed like merely a heartbeat before the door screeched open on heavy hinges, and the new shift of blacksmiths shuffled down the tunnel to their task. Behind them, an oversized wolac dragged the empty weapons wagon. Tsalix waited for the cart to pass before he fell in step behind it. Once the wagon was in place, he slipped beneath it until the canvas cover was thrown to the side. Then he rolled beneath it.

The wagon was crudely made. Two metal sleeves hung beneath and wooden box, the rear sleeve fixed in place, the front attached to a pivot. Through these sleeves the axels extended and the wheels were attached to their ends.

When the blacksmiths began to work, Tsalix slid back beneath the wagon and inspected the axle sleeves. Six inches of space between the axle and the bottom of the wagon box. The front wheel assembly was near the front of the wagon, allowing it to swivel and guide the cart. The back wheel assembly, however, hung about three feet from the back of the wagon.

Tsalix measured the distance between the two sleeves with his body. Although it would be uncomfortable, he felt he could lie face down, wedge his toes between the rear axle sleeve and the box, and grasp the front sleeve with his hands. Convinced he could hold himself up long enough to pass through the doorway, he slipped back underneath the tarpaulin and gathered his strength, awaiting shift-change. Eventually the gong struck twice. He lifted himself into position beneath the cart. It began to move.

Tsalix felt as if his hands were slipping from their grip on the forward axle sleeve as the cart crept forward. He wedged his toes above the aft sleeve, and his body hung an inch or two above the ground. His strength was failing, and he knew he could hold on no longer. With his flagging strength, he pulled his feet free, let go of with his hands, and flattened himself against the ground as the cart continued forward. He was nearly run over by the empty cart being hauled into place. Once it passed him, the door swung shut behind him. He crept into a crevice in the rock wall as he watched two men secure the door by dropping a wooden beam into iron brackets on the back of the heavy slab.

The passageway was lighted by a few widely spaced torches hanging in sconces on the wall. Tsalix melted further into the shadows as the two soldiers finished securing the door, turned, and marched up the tunnel. When he was sure they had gone, he slid out of the fissure, and keeping in the shadows, snuck up the passageway. He had not gone far when he came to a branch in the tunnel. He stuck his head into the branch on his right and saw nothing but a dark, empty corridor. The other branch disappeared in the distance, as poorly lighted as the passage through which he had come. But from the corner of his eye, he caught some movement in the dim torchlight far down the tunnel.

Tsalix leaned against the wall and considered his options. *What would my father do?*

It seemed strange that he would ponder that question. After all, he was nearly nineteen and he'd served two years in Johona's army.

A voice whispered to him, *"Choose the right branch."*

Tsalix blinked and searched the darkness. No one in sight.

The voice came again with the same message, this time stronger.

Tsalix pushed away from the wall and moved into the darkness of the tunnel on the right. The further he went down the passage, the darker it became. He stopped to let his eyes adjust to the gloom, and placed his hand against the wall. It was then that he felt the gentle breeze coming from up ahead.

"There must be an opening."

He kept one hand on the wall, with the other extended in front, and tiptoed down the passage.

CHAPTER 30

FROM THE LEDGE ABOVE, ASUR SEARCHED THE BOTTOM OF THE pit for any sign of Tsalix.

"Do you think he escaped?"

Kwercus shook his head. "I know not. But at least it seems he was not discovered in the room below." He slid back from the edge of the shelf. "Nashjie, I will follow at the next changing of the workers."

The spider whispered back, "Why not both of you, now that we know it is possible?"

"Can you bear that much weight?" Kwercus said.

"Of course. Did I not bear the weight of all four of us when we escaped from the peak?" She began spinning a strand with two loops, the first at the end of the silk, the second about six feet higher. "There is not enough room for both of you to pass through the grate together. One will have to go first. The second will follow."

Asur put his hand on the front leg of the gentle giant. "We will miss you, Nashjie. You have saved our lives, and we will not forget it."

"You, too, saved my life, else I would be tethered without hope of escape." She lifted the hind leg which bore the white brand. "You will not be forgotten, either."

They lay in silence, listening to the incessant hammering below, counting the number of times the gong rang. Eventually they heard it ring twice, and crept to the edge of the ledge. The blacksmiths shuffled up the tunnel, followed by the weapons wagon.

Kwercus and Asur stepped into the stirrups that Nashjie had woven in the end of her silken strand, and as the overseers left their platform and assembled to eat, slipped one after another through the opening in the grill. The spider lowered them to the floor of the pit, where they freed themselves from the web and glided into the shadowed niches in the sides of the tunnel. They searched for any sign of Tsalix, but seeing none, turned their attention to the heavy wooden door that blocked the passageway.

"Tsalix must have gotten past the door," Asur whispered. "Now we must figure out a way to get to the other side.

Kwercus nodded.

"It will open when the shift changes so the men and the wagon can pass," Asur said.

"Then our task is to wait for it to open. And we must find somewhere to hide that will keep us from being captured." Kwercus scanned the scene. "I see no where that we can secret ourselves that will not be observed once the smithies pass by. Nor do we know what we will find on the other side of the door."

The wolac attached to the weapons wagon sensed the two men and squealed. An overseer snapped a lash above its head, and the beast snuffled before stopping its plaintive cry.

Kwercus pointed to the wagon and motioned with his head. The two men left the shadow-filled niches and dropped beneath the wagon, where they waited for the hours to pass.

CHAPTER 31

Fᴙᴏᴍ ʜᴇʀ ᴘᴇʀᴄʜ ʜɪɢʜ ᴀʙᴏᴠᴇ, Nᴀsʜᴊɪᴇ ᴡᴀᴛᴄʜᴇᴅ Asᴜʀ ᴀɴᴅ Kwercus scamper beneath the wagon. Once she was confident they had found cover, she picked across the grating until she reached the crumpled body of Lieutenant Legai. After removing his armor, she lifted his head and shoulders with a pair of legs and spun a cocoon around him. Once finished, she lifted his legs and completed the web. Cradling him with two legs, she began her ascent up the vent, pausing only long enough at the narrow throat to gaze at the room below.

"Go on with courage, my young friends," she said, in her reedy voice.

After an arduous climb, Nashjie stuck her head through the opening and checked to make sure she was alone. Then she crested the cone and laid the body on the obsidian pebble-strewn summit. She freed Legai's face from its silken shroud and examined his features. As she gazed at his crumpled face, tears began to fall.

"Yours was a fool's errand," she whispered, and looked at the sky. "Why do so many young boys have to die." She brushed his blood-matted hair with her foreleg and sank to the ground.

The transformation began slowly as she, too, shrank in size. But once she reached her true height, the change accelerated until Queen Nadlee stood beside the fallen man, in her true state. She placed her hand upon Legai's forehead, closed her eyes, and began to chant. The wind picked up the melody, and soon the mountaintop resonated with the sound of her voice.

After removing a small knife from her belt, she cut through the cocoon and freed the broken man from its embrace. She continued chanting as his battered face began to correct itself. Legai's lungs expanded and his chest rose rhythmically. Queen Nadlee kept chanting for over an hour, until his eyes fluttered open and he struggled to sit up.

"I wish I could remove all the pain," the queen said, "but it may be a reminder of your foolishness in following my son Abadon."

"Who are you?" Legai said, through gritted teeth, as the pain was almost more than he could bear. "Why have you done this?"

"To save you. Now rest. The way down will be difficult, and you will need your full strength." Nadlee set down a woven bag. "Inside are food, drink, and herbs. The pain will subside, and you will be able to make your way home."

"But how can I ever repay you."

"That remains to be seen." She stepped away from him.

A mist began to gather around her, and within seconds she was obscured from his view. The cloud extended over the top of the mountain, and when it cleared, she was gone.

Legai opened the bag, drank from the flagon within, and once his thirst was slaked, lay back down and slept. The memory of the queen began to fade from his mind.

CHAPTER 32

K WERCUS AND ASUR POSITIONED THEMSELVES IN THE SHADOW of the wagon, waiting for the shift-change. Afraid to even whisper with the keen-eared wolac just in front of them, Kwercus signaled to Asur to hold onto the front axle sleeve before the wagon began to move. Asur nodded.

After what seemed an eternity, the double crash of the gong sounded. The two men reached up and grabbed the sleeves. Shortly they saw the feet of the blacksmiths passing by the side of the cart, and then the wolac began pulling the loaded weapons wagon up the ramp to the tunnel. As they were dragged up the pathway, Kwercus saw the double track of their heels furrowing the ground behind the wagon.

"As soon as we pass the doorway, let go," he whispered.

They had barely passed the door when the unloaded weapons cart rolled past them toward the forge. Kwercus and Asur let go of the sleeves, dropped flat on the ground, and lay there until the wagon moved over them. Then they stood and clung to the back of the wagon until it entered the shadowy passageway. Behind them, the door swung shut and the bar was lifted into place.

Asur spotted a shallow crevice on the right side of the tunnel, grabbed Kwercus's arm and dragged him into the darkness it provided. The two men who had secured the door marched past them up the ramp. When Kwercus and Asur were sure the soldiers had gone, they stepped out of the niche, into the poorly lighted tunnel.

"Where do you think Tsalix has gone?" said Asur.

Kwercus shrugged. "I know not. But I know we can't stay here." He placed his hand on the head of the ax that hung from his belt, and strode up the passage.

Asur followed closely until they reached the branch in the tunnel.

"Which way do we go?" said Kwercus.

Asur looked into the tunnel on the right. "It is dark. There are no torches lighting the way."

Kwercus stepped into the other branch. "I can see faint light in this channel, but where it goes, I cannot say." He rubbed his chin. "I suggest we split up and each reconnoiter one of these paths, then return here and decide which way to go."

Asur nodded. "Which route would you have me take?"

"It matters not to me." Kwercus shrugged. "You take the right. I'll take the left, and we return here in a half-hour."

"Aye, Kwercus." Asur placed a hand on his friend's shoulder. "Be careful."

They began their exploratory journeys.

CHAPTER 33

ELOSHA RESTED ON HIS THRONE, AWAITING THE ARRIVAL OF HIS wife from her long journey. Initially he had been against her plan to visit his three young disciples. But as usual, she had prevailed. He had no doubts about her capabilities, nor did he worry about her safety. But he was concerned about her return to the place where her mother had died. It always awakened dark memories.

Johona's forces had been victorious in battle along the marge of the Swamp of Miasma, and for the time being, there was clear passage on the road that led between Mount Destiny and Mount Jinee. How he wished the danger had been alleviated across the Plain of Wonadsi. But Abadon's forces still held sway over much of that desolate plain.

The doorway behind the throne led to their private chambers, and when King Elosha heard it open, his heart leapt. He rose from his throne and turned to see his queen, clothed in purple robes, enter the throne room. He stepped down from the dais and took her in his arms.

"Success?"

Queen Nadlee nodded. "Yes, but it could have turned out differently had I not gone to their aid." She kissed her husband. "More importantly, Tsalix has retrieved the first talisman."

"That is good news." The king led her to her throne. "And you return unscathed."

Beneath her flowing robes, Nadlee rubbed her left ankle with the other foot. "Almost. Nothing serious."

The king frowned. "Meaning?"

She lifted the hem of her robe and showed him the white, puckered skin that surrounded her ankle.

"It will be fine, given enough time."

Tears coursed down Elosha's cheeks. "Again you sacrifice yourself for the cause."

"It is but a trifle. It was a necessary thing to put everything needed in place." She rose from her throne. "You have given so much more. Do not scold me for such a minor affliction."

"Your courage is beyond my comprehension."

"As is the courage of these young men. They are resourceful, too."

"And you think they will now succeed?" Elosha rose and held her in his arms.

"Yes! They are stronger than you can imagine. You did well in choosing them to complete this odyssey."

Elosha sank back down on his throne. "Nine others perished. Nine other fine men whose families have been scarred forever." He held his head in his hands. "These three are the only hope for the kingdom."

"With their dedication to the cause, there is more than hope."

Outside the throne room, the low sound of a horn announced the arrival of someone seeking audience with the king. A page entered and approached the raised dais on which the thrones sat. He extended a rolled parchment scroll. The king nodded, took the scroll and unrolled it. He scanned the writing, and his countenance darkened.

"Admit him." He glowered.

The doors on the opposite side of the room opened, and a man dressed in black entered the chamber. He carried a helmet beneath his left arm, black with a scarlet crest. He crossed the room and stood before the king and queen. He did not kneel or bow his head.

"I bear a message from my master—"

Elosha raised his hand. "To whom am I listening? There are certain conventions we adhere to that make life so much more bearable. Telling us your name is among the simplest."

The man sneered. "I am Commander Moasi. The message I bring is simple—my master does not wish to continue the bloodshed until there are few men left to till the soil and carry out the other duties of trade. Thus he asks that you abdicate and let him take his rightful place as heir to the throne."

"That is absurd." Elosha's jaw hardened.

"Then you refuse?" Moasi said.

"Of course." The king glared at him until his anger subsided. "You may tell Abadon that if he wishes to surrender his troops and bow himself before the king, we will spare the lives of those pledged to him."

Moasi laughed. "I was told you would not acquiesce to this request, regardless of how kindly it was presented." He spun on his heel and marched toward the doors.

When he reached them, he turned, raised his mailed fist, and snarled.

"Let their blood be upon you! For you and your weakling son will soon be begging for mercy." He shoved through the doors.

Nadlee reached for her husband's hand. "Do not fear, my king. Your three chosen sons will succeed."

Elosha heaved a sigh. "I fear not for them. I weep for my son, who has let pride bind his heart with bands of steel. His arrogance and his longing for honor and power have blinded him to what is truly important. I fear his fall will be beyond belief."

CHAPTER 34

TSALIX FELT ALONG THE WALL UNTIL HE CAME TO A SLATTED door that blocked the end of the passage. Fresh air and faint light streamed through the openings in the panel. He pushed against it and it swung open, into an unoccupied hallway. He stepped through the doorway, looked for a place to hide, and listened for the sounds of anyone approaching.

Silence.

The hall extended at least a hundred yards in both directions. The walls were dark gray, with lighted torches affixed to them. The floor was polished obsidian.

Tsalix could see to both ends of the empty hallway. He moved down the hallway to his right. Every twenty feet, numbered doors were recessed into the walls on both sides of the passage. Tsalix paused at the first door and placed his ear against it.

Nothing.

He repeated his action at each of the remaining doors, with the same results. When he reached the end of the hall, he discovered that it veered and continued for some distance. Still no sound, other than the tapping of his heels against the polished floor. He rounded the corner and continued down the hall until it came to an end.

The final door was wider than the others he had passed by, and when he placed his ear against it, the door moved inward slightly. He pushed on it and found that it opened into a small room with a spiral staircase that ascended into the gloom above.

Tsalix backed out and retraced his steps to the slatted door through which he'd entered the hall. He heard sounds echoing down the hallway, from where he'd inspected. He struggled to identify the them—seemed to be a beast of some sort, whose squealing was growing louder with each second.

Tsalix was frozen to the spot, trying to decide what to do, before he pulled open the slatted door and stepped into the shadows behind them. He drew his sword and prepared to spring into action. He wished he still had his breastplate and shield, but they were nothing but a memory.

The squeal grew louder. Tsalix struggled to see through the slats. Just when he thought his heart would burst, he saw what was making the sound—a squeaking wheel on a cloth-covered heavily laden cart being pushed by a huge, misshapen man wearing a black tunic cinched at the waist, with a red sash. An immense ring of keys hung from his belt. His head was too large for his body, and only a few bristles of hair stuck out from his scalp. His lips hung like slabs of raw liver, and rivulets of drool dripped from the corners of his agape mouth, exposing a few yellow teeth. He grunted as he pushed the cart past Tsalix's hiding spot.

The creature waddled a few feet further down the hall, then stopped and reached for the ring of keys to unlock a door on the opposite side of the hall. Once the door was open, he dragged the cart inside and closed the door behind him. Tsalix sheathed his sword and waited in the shadows.

Several minutes ticked by before the door opened and the creature appeared with an empty cart. With its burden delivered, the cart made little noise as it was pushed down the hallway. Tsalix waited until the faint squealing faded before he stepped through the doorway. He crept crossed the passage and tried the door the creature had opened, but it was locked. He looked down the hallway to his left, where the man had gone, but it was empty.

Tsalix slipped down the corridor, trying each door as he went. He could hear nothing from behind any of the doors, and all were locked. He reached the end of the passageway, and as on the other end, found that it made an abrupt turn. There were fewer lighted torches at this end of the hall, and they cast flickering shadows on the walls.

Tsalix expected this hallway would be a duplicate of the one on the other end of the passage, but as he turned the corner, the cart that had passed by him was thrust into his stomach, pinning him against the wall.

"Who are you, little man?" The creature slobbered through liver lips.

Tsalix struggled to free his arm and reach his sword, but the cart was pushed too tight against him.

"Who are you?" the creature said again. "And what do you want here?"

"I am Tsalix Silverthorn." He gasped. "I am trying to return to Mount Deschee."

"Return? From where?"

"From the summit of Mount Jinee."

The creature chuckled, although it sounded like burst of thunder. "No one goes to the top of this mountain."

Tsalix struggled to push the cart away from him, but the man was too strong.

"I have been there," Tsalix said. "Please let me breathe."

The creature considered for a moment, then relaxed his pressure on the cart.

"Why would you go to the top of the mountain? There is nothing there, I am told."

Tsalix breathed deeply and tried to free his sword hand. He wondered how much he could or should reveal about the mission he'd been sent to complete.

"I was sent there," he said.

"By who?"

"The king."

The creature considered this for a moment. "Who is this king?"

"There is only one king—Elosha."

"I know only Prince Abadon. Who is this Elosha?" The words slithered from his lips.

"You do not know of Elosha? He is Abadon's father."

"I do not know of any king called Elosha. How do I know you do not lie?" The man rubbed his head. "And why are you here in the storerooms if not to steal from Shal?"

Tsalix was finally able to pull his arms free. He spread his arms to show he had nothing in them.

"I am just trying to return to Mount Deschee. I have not come to take anything. If you can lead me out of your storerooms, to the mountainside, I will bid you farewell."

Shal rubbed his head again. "This is a puzzle, and Shal does not like puzzles." He relaxed the pressure against Tsalix's stomach even more.

Tsalix realized he could now reach his sword, but something told him to bide his time.

"How do I know you will not come back and steal from Shal?"

"Shal, you must believe me. I have not come to take anything from you."

The man wiped his mouth with the back of his hand.

"Do you take care of all the storerooms?"

Shal shook his head. "My brother, Hashchid, helps me."

"What is it you store?"

Shal shrugged his massive shoulders. "Everything for the castle. Why do you want to know?"

"It must be quite a task." Tsalix looked down the length of the corridor. "You must be very good at what you do."

Shal broke into a hideous grin. "I have done it since I was a young boy. No one but Hashchid and me knows where everything is stored." Apparently satisfied that Tsalix was not a thief, he rolled the cart away from him. "Come. I will show you the way out of the castle." He beckoned with his hand and shuffled to the end of passageway.

There, as on the other end, a spiral staircase twisted up.

Shal placed his foot on the first step before he stopped and looked at the sword hanging from Tsalix's belt.

"I think you go first. I would not like to be stabbed from behind."

Tsalix moved past Shal and started climbing the staircase. They continued for nearly ten minutes.

Shal said, "Stop on the next landing."

When they stopped, Shal removed the ring of keys from his belt, selected a key, and unlocked the door.

"Where are we?" Tsalix said.

"On the floor below the throne room, where Prince Abadon lives."

Tsalix pulled it open gingerly, allowing Shal to pass by him. On the other side was a dressing room with shiny black armor hanging from pegs on the wall. Five men were sitting on stools, removing the greaves from their legs, and when the door opened, all of them turned.

Tsalix hid himself behind the door.

Shal waddled into the room and continued down a passageway, assuming Tsalix was following him. From his hiding spot, Tsalix peeked through the crack in the door to see where Shal was heading.

Once Tsalix was sure of Shal's destination, he wedged a scrap of fabric into the lock, let the door close, and waited.

CHAPTER 35

ASUR FELT HIS WAY BACK TO THE SPOT WHERE HE AND Kwercus had parted. He had found no end to the tunnel in his short exploration, nor had he found any sign that Tsalix had been there.

In the distance Asur heard the muffled sound of the gong behind the door that led to the forge room. He sank into the shadows in case anyone other than Kwercus should approach. Asur was not sure how long it had been since the two of them had parted, but when the gong sounded again, he realized it had been well past the appointed time to meet. He didn't know what to do. Kwercus would not desert him, he knew, and there had to be some reason he had not returned.

Asur rested on his heels and pondered the situation. Either something dire had happened and detained his friend, or he had found something that required further investigation. In either case, Asur decided he needed to find Kwercus. His eyes had adjusted to the dim light, and he could see down the fork Kwercus had taken. He crept up the tunnel and traveled for nearly a quarter-mile before the passageway made veered right. Tiptoed to the corner and peeked around a protrusion of rock. The way was blocked by another heavy wooden door bound in iron and blackened by the smoke from the torches. On either side of the door a guard stood at attention.

Asur slipped back around the corner and searched for somewhere to hide. Two monstrous boulders had fallen from the roof of the tunnel and lay against the wall. He wedged himself between them while he figured out a plan. Nothing came to mind.

From his hiding place, he could see around the corner to where one guard stood, armed with tsenil and sword. No way past him.

Asur tucked further behind the rocks. He had been there well over an hour when he saw the guard disappear from view, and heard the screech of hinges as the door was pulled open. A troop of men rounded the corner and shambled down the corridor. Asur shrank even deeper into the shadows as the men passed by. He waited to hear the sounds of the door closing, but all was silent.

Change of shift for the blacksmiths.

Another troop walked past him, toward the forges. Asur slid out of his hiding place and peered around the corner. The two guards had disappeared. Asur inched to the open doorway, keeping his back against the wall. He could see a dingy room on the other side of the portal, but no activity. He stepped into the room and was assailed by the odor of sweat and decay. He took two more steps into the room before someone grasped his shoulder and spun him around. Asur stared into the face of one of the men who had been guarding the door, sword drawn.

The man pointed across the room, turned Asur around, and marched him toward a shadowy portal, with the tip of his sword pressed between Asur's shoulder blades. They stopped only when they reached a closed door. The guard forced Asur to the side while he knocked with the pommel of his sword. The door swung open, revealing a large, well-lit room. The guard thrust Asur through the doorway, into the midst of a dozen armed men.

"Look what I found." His captor gave a raucous laugh.

"Another one?" said the leader of the group.

"Aye. Another worm."

"Bring him here."

One guard bound Asur's wrists behind him with strips of leather. Then two men grabbed his elbows and dragged him down a hallway lined with barred cells. They passed by a few when someone called out his name. Asur snapped his head to the side and recognized one of his old neighbors from Aravah.

"Castan."

"Silence, worm," one of his captors snarled, and slapped Asur on the side of his head.

Asur saw more and more of his imprisoned townspeople as he was dragged further down the cell block. Eventually they stopped, and he was thrust into an empty cell. The door slammed closed behind him. The cell had been carved out of the native rock, creating a pocket about eight-feet square. Iron bars were set in the stone across the front of the cell. The only furnishings were a straw pallet on the floor and a small basin of tepid water.

Asur sat on the pallet and struggled to get his hands in front of him. His wrists were still bound. After some effort he was able to draw his knees up to his chest and wiggle his arms past his feet. He began picking at the leather straps with his teeth, and after a frustrating hour was able to free his hands. He hid the thongs beneath the pallet before pushing up to his feet and grasping the cell bars.

He could see into three of the cells across the hall, but it appeared that only one was occupied. In that chamber someone was lying immobile on his pallet. Asur began to pace as he fought despair. If those who had survived the burning of Aravah were imprisoned and had not been able to escape, what hope had he? He had not seen his parents, which made him even more despondent. On top of that, the prison was eerily silent, as if all within had given up hope.

Asur continued to pace, until he heard a strange sound. He wondered what was happening, and steeled himself for the worst. The sound grew louder, until he was able to make out the sound of footfalls, mingled with the clash of metal on metal. A short muscular man pushed a large cart into sight, removed a metal tray, and shoved it through a slot in the bottom of the bars of his cage. On the tray was a small, hard lump of bread and a bowl of watery soup. A large black beetle floated on the surface of the liquid. Asur shuddered at the sight, but he was so hungry that he picked up the bug and dropped it on the floor. The cart disappeared from sight.

Asur sat on the floor and gnawed on the bread. It was so hard he could barely scratch a few flakes of crust from its surface. He dropped it into the bowl in hopes it would soften in the soup. While he waited, he glanced across the hallway and saw the person in the occupied cell struggle to his knees. In the faint light, a flicker of recognition crossed his face.

"Kwercus?" he whispered.

The man raised his head and stared across the passage. "Asur, is that you?"

"Aye. Are you all right?"

"Silence!" a voice rumbled down the corridor, followed by two guards who bore clubs in their hands.

Asur drew back from the barred opening of his cell as the two men passed by, occasionally running their clubs across the bars, creating a staccato beat that echoed down the hallway. After they passed, Asur scooted to the front of the cell and struggled to see Kwercus's face, but his friend had crept back to his pallet and was lying down.

Despair filled his soul like an inky cloud. There had been some semblance of hope that Kwercus was free and could come to his aid, but now it was clear that he, too, was trapped.

Asur stared at the floor, too despondent to even try to eat the meager meal before him. With Kwercus imprisoned and no word from Tsalix, there seemed to be no solution.

CHAPTER 36

Tsalix kept his ear to the door and waited for silence in the armory, which would signal that the room was empty. He had not seen Asur and Kwercus since he'd escaped from the forge room hours before, and having watched Shal waddle across the room and down a passage, he was certain the route led to escape, but he didn't want to leave without his friends.

Tsalix cracked the door open and peered into the room. He could see a number of men either removing armor or putting it on. Since his escape was blocked, he pulled the door closed. He withdrew to the landing at the top of the spiral staircase, and as he contemplated what to do, something thundered against the door. Tsalix jumped. The door was pushed open, and Tsalix raced down the stairway to the storage level. He could hear someone descending the stairs behind him. When he reached the bottom of the stairway, he sprinted down the passage to the slatted door, pulled it open and continued down the dark tunnel. He paused at the branch in the tunnel. He thought he'd see Asur or Kwercus somewhere in the tunnel, but there was no sign that they'd been there.

Tsalix listened for the sound of pursuit, but heard nothing. He sank to the floor and caught his breath while deciding his next move. In the darkness, his eyes adjusted to the dim light of the tunnel on the left, and while he searched the length of the tunnel, the muffled sound of a gong echoed twice. Then he heard the groan of the forge room door and the sounds of feet moving toward him.

He searched for a place to hide, and after finding none, took a few steps back up the tunnel to his right. *If they come this way, I'm trapped.*

The footsteps drew nearer until, at last, the blacksmiths appeared. Tsalix pressed himself against the wall. His heart pounded in his chest. Only after the men continued down the tunnel on the left did he realize he'd been holding his breath, and he exhaled through pursed lips. As the last man passed, Tsalix slipped from his hiding place and fell in step behind the retreating smiths. In the shadowy tunnel, he felt no one would notice him as long as he stayed close to the last man in the column. After a quarter-mile hike, they veered to the right, halted, and shifted to the left wall before the next shift of men shuffled past them, toward their duties at the forges.

Tsalix could see a dimly lighted room through the doorway ahead of them. The odor of decay washed over him as the men began moving forward again. As soon as he passed through the doorway, he looked for a place to hide. But before he had taken a half-dozen steps, he felt the point of a sword between his shoulder blades.

Tsalix reached for the hilt of his sword and spun to his left. Someone grasped his wrist to keep him from drawing his weapon, and slammed a club into the side of his head. Tsalix saw stars as he fell unconscious to the ground.

He awoke with a throbbing headache. He tried to sit up, but the pain almost caused him to vomit. He sank back down on the straw pallet and forced one eye open. Blackness. He closed his eye and fell asleep.

He had no idea how long he'd slept, but this time when he awoke he was able to open his eyes and push up into a sitting position. He felt the side of his head, where a huge lump had formed.

Tsalix raised to his feet and surveyed his cell. He shuffled across the cell and hung onto the bars. He was then seized by a wave of dizziness, forcing him to close his eyes and lean against the bars. When the room stopped spinning, he blinked his eyes open and tried to focus on the cells across from him. Someone or something was curled up in a ball on the floor of the cell across from him and to his right. The cell directly across was empty, as was the one on its left. He sensed there were more prisoners, but no one spoke. Except for the faint sounds of wheezing and the scuffle of feet on the floor, there was no sound.

Tsalix rubbed the side of his head again, which sent flashes of pain through his skull. He retreated to the pallet, sat and leaned against the obsidian wall. As his mind cleared, he began assessing his situation more closely. He was not surprised to find that his sword had been taken, but he was relieved that he still had his purse. He opened it and felt inside to see if the talisman was still there. *Yes!* The remaining vial still hung around his neck. He removed the stone and turned it over in his hands. Unlike before, his initials did not glow. Instead they appeared as flat, dark gray markings on one side of the jet-black stone.

Tsalix crawled back to the bars and touched one of them with the talisman. Nothing happened.

He sat cross legged on the floor and examined the stone before replacing it in his purse. The person in the cell across from him moaned.

"Are you all right?" Tsalix said.

"Silence!" rumbled down the corridor, followed by two guards who glared into every cell.

Tsalix scooted back away from the bars, sat on the pallet, and rested his head against the wall. The he heard a *click*. He pressed his ear against the wall and heard the sound again. *Click...click.*

What could that be?

Click, click, click, click...click, click, click, click.

He listened closer.

Click. Pause. *Click. Click. Click. Click. Click.* After a longer pause, it continued. *Click. Click. Click.* Pause. *Click. Click. Click. Click.*

The sounds stopped as if waiting for a reply. Tsalix mused over them, but could not finding a meaning. They began again and repeated the same pattern.

A memory of something flitted through his mind like a butterfly, but he couldn't bring it into focus. His head pounded.

The clicking repeated again. Tsalix remembered when he and his friends were small children and had used a five by five grid to send coded messages. They had drawn five rows intersected by five columns and written a letter of the alphabet in order, from left to right. The first row A through E, the second F through J, and so on. They found little use for Z, so it was ignored. They could send messages by writing the column and the row, like 5,1 for an E, or 4,2 for an I.

Tsalix struggled to construct the grid in his mind as he listened to the tapping sounds again. *Click.* Pause. *Click.* He thought about his grid—1, 1 would be the A.

Click. Click. Click. Click. Pause. *Click. Click. Click. Click.* Fourth column, fourth row—S.

The tapping continued. First column, fifth row—U. Third column, fourth row—R.

A-S-U-R.

Tsalix's heartbeat pounded. He removed the talisman from his purse and began tapping on the wall. *Tap. Tap. Tap. Tap. Tap.* Pause. *Tap. Tap. Tap. Tap.*

He had only sent the first three letters of his name when he heard a frantic tapping. Either Asur knew from those letters who he was, or there was danger.

After a silent moment, Asur began tapping again. After a half-hour of tapping, Tsalix understood that Kwercus was injured, in the cell across the hall. While he sat trying to figure what to do next, the sound of the food cart interrupted their tapping conversation. A hard roll and a bowl of watery soup were pushed through the slot in the bars.

Tsalix ate the meager rations before lying back on the pallet and falling asleep.

CHAPTER 37

TSALIX AWOKE TO THE SOUNDS OF SOMEONE RATTLING A KEY in the lock of his cell. His head still throbbed, although the lump was smaller. The guard unlocked the door, swung it open, and beckoned for Tsalix to come with him. Tsalix staggered to his feet and followed the man into the corridor between the cells. There were a few dozen men stumbling ahead of him.

"Where are we going?" Tsalix said.

The guard cuffed the side of his head. "Silence!"

Tsalix lurched to the side and nearly fell. The guard grabbed his arm and pushed him after the others. They left the cells behind and continued down a passageway cut into the living rock and lighted by widely spaced torches that gave off an oily smoke. They walked for nearly a half-hour before they came to a steel door that spanned the width of the passageway. A small peephole was set in the center of the door. The guard who had led the processions pounded on the door, then lifted a medallion hung around his neck to the peephole, which opened for a moment, then shut.

A moment later the door opened. Tsalix threw his hand in front of his eyes to shade them from the sunlight streaming through the open door. He took a deep breath of fresh air as he joined the rest of the captives in a courtyard cut into the mountainside bordered by a ten-foot high wrought iron picket fence with spear-like points jutting toward the sky. A hundred or more people were already assembled when Tsalix's group joined them. Scattered among them were fifteen or twenty armed guards maintaining silence.

Tsalix scanned the crowd looking for Asur and Kwercus, and as he searched his gaze fell upon his father and mother standing silently on the opposite side of the yard. Before he could call out to them, his mother shook her head and put her finger to her lips. Tears streamed down her cheeks, but were offset by a look of joy on her face. He winked at her before continuing his search for his friends. They were nowhere to be seen.

The crowd milled around under the watchful eyes of the guards, until above them a horn sounded. Everyone peered up the side of the hill to a balcony fifty feet above them. A lone page stood with the horn pressed to his lips. The trumpet's lead pipe extended five or six feet in a to the bell, and from it hung a black banner fringed in red, with a red bar extending diagonally across it. The page finished his fanfare, turned, and disappeared from the balcony. A moment later Abadon strode to the edge of the platform, leaned on the railing and looked down on the prisoners below.

"People of Aravah," he rumbled. "I hope you are enjoying your visit to my castle." He chuckled. "I do wish your accommodations were more comfortable." He flashed a malevolent smile. "There is a simple way to have a much more enjoyable time during your stay here." He leaned over the balcony rail. "All you have to do is swear allegiance to me." Another sinister smile. "And you will be able to join my other loyal subjects, rather than rotting in prison."

"Never!" shouted one of the men near the edge of the throng below.

A guard clubbed him and knocked him to his knees. The guard kicked him in the ribs, and the man fell on his face. The other guards drew their swords and held them at the ready. The rest of the crowd fidgeted for a few moments, before Abadon spoke again.

"Are there any of you who are wise enough to put aside your foolish traditions and join with me?"

No response.

"Very well. Perhaps another week in the dungeons will help you see the error of your ways." He pointed to the steel door with his gloved hand. "Until next week." He spun around and disappeared from the balcony.

The guards separated a fourth of the people from the rest of the crowd and drove them back past the portal into the tunnel that led to the cells, while the rest of them were pushed back against the wrought iron fence.

Tsalix watched his father and mother being herded into the passageway. His mother smiled as she disappeared into the maw of the tunnel. Tsalix's spirits sagged as he watched them leave. They were much thinner that he recalled.

He moved to the back of the crowd and looked through the fence over the edge of the parapet. Twenty feet below the courtyard was one of the many landings that offered rest from the insufferable climb up the ten thousand steps. Past that the mountain dropped off precipitously. His gaze traveled up the wrought iron to the arrow point before he sighed deeply. There seemed to be no way to escape.

Ten minutes passed before the second group of prisoners were led away. The remainder drifted about under the watchful of the remaining guards.

Tsalix leaned against the fence, closed his eyes, and tried to think of something he could do. He felt someone tug at his sash, but as he started to turn around, a hand was placed on his shoulder.

"Wait," someone whispered.

Tsalix waited for a few moments, then stretched his arms and yawned while he pivoted. Asur and Kwercus were standing a few yards away. Kwercus was leaning on Asur's shoulder, his face white and haggard. Tsalix smiled at his friends, who appeared to be looking past him, at the balcony. As the remaining people milled around, Tsalix was able to get to his friends' sides just as the third group of captives was led away. Five guards remained with the three dozen prisoners, and Tsalix realized it was foolish to try to talk to Asur or Kwercus. Still, his heart rejoiced now that they were all together again.

After a time they were led back to their cells. Tsalix noticed that only one key was used to lock all the doors.

If we can get that key, we can escape. But where would we go?

He sat on his pallet and leaned his ear against the wall. Asur's tapping had already begun.

CHAPTER 38

LIEUTENANT CHA LEGAI ATE THE LAST OF THE PROVISIONS HE had been supplied. The pain in his body had subsided over the past few days, and most of his strength had returned. Those days had been a time to reflect on the miracle that had happened to him. He had been faithful to Abadon, as had his father and grandfather before him—faithful since the beginning of the obsidian war. He had been schooled with the concept that Johona and his forces were evil. That they wished to usurp the rightful power of Abadon and rule with unrighteous dominion over the kingdom. He had been taught that Elosha had led the land into the dark paths of corruption, and that Johona wished only to continue the depraved tenants of his father.

Abadon had promised protection and security to all who followed him and demanded that they support and defend him with their lives. Legai had believed this doctrine from the time he was born. There was great comfort in knowing that you were being protected and nurtured by a wise, omnipotent ruler. There had never been a shred of doubt in his mind that he was doing the right things for the right reasons.

Then he had been ordered to certain death by his captain, who was the embodiment of a follower of Abadon, just as he had ordered others to death. And on the heels of that horrific experience, he had awakened to the kind ministrations of Queen Nadlee, who not only restored his life, but healed his wounds. If all that Abadon professed was true, why would Queen Nadlee extend such a gift to him?

During the days of recuperation, Legai pondered all that had happened, and realized he had been deceived, along with the masses that followed Abadon. He realized that he had been pledging blind obedience to a leader who demanded everything from him. He was racked with torment over the lives of the men he had sacrificed in his pursuit of an unknown and unseen enemy. He wept over the recognition of his own cowardice and duplicity.

Now that he was healed, and with his strength restored, he vowed that he would make amends for his past actions. How he would accomplish this, he was unsure, but he knew that through his harrowing experience he was a changed man.

Legai rose to his feet and walked to the edge of the crater. His armor and his sword lay far below, on the grid above the forge room, and he was clad only in a black tunic with a red sash. He looked down on the bank of clouds beneath him, took a deep breath, and swung his leg over the rim to begin his descent through the mists. The side of the peak was steep and peppered with small stones that slid like grease beneath his sandals. He flattened himself against the mountainside as he slipped down into the clouds. When he emerged from the fog, his hands and knees were bloodied from trying to catch hold of the rough stones over which he'd tumbled. With his feet, he finally caught the trunk of a gnarled pine that hung over a drop.

Legai's chest heaved with fear and exertion as he perched against the tree and tried to ignore the pain in his hands and knees. When his breathing finally returned to normal, he searched for the traces of the trail he and his men had climbed. It was nowhere to be seen.

He traversed across the scree, trying to descend slowly. He fell a dozen times before he reached a narrow plateau where he was able to rest again. His hands were so lacerated that the pain was unbearable when he tried to grasp anything to keep from plummeting down the mountainside. Blood from his knees oozed through his tunic.

He crossed the plateau and saw the waterfall where he'd sent his men to their deaths, and got his bearings. Now he was on the other side of the water, and he knew it was impossible to cross. He climbed down the hillside to the pool where three of his men had met their deaths.

Cha Legai found a large flat stone at the side of the pond, sat and bathed his legs and hands in the frigid water. He ripped strips of cloth from the hem of his tunic and wrapped them around his hands. While he sat there, he looked up the mountainside to the churning clouds and shuddered. The water numbed the pain, and before long he was able to stand and continue his journey.

An overwhelming dread enveloped him as he neared the place where he and his companions had camped. The thought of facing Captain Doit-soh filled him with both fear and determination. Legai listened for the sound of the corralled wolacs, but heard nothing. He crept to the site of the camp and found it deserted. The only sign it had been occupied were the stinking piles of wolac droppings around the camp's border. Cha sat on a log and contemplated what to do next.

His deliberation was interrupted by a sound in the trees. He sprang to his feet as quickly as his injured legs would allow, and hid in the willows at the side of the encampment. He had no weapon to defend himself with, and even if he'd found a sword, he probably couldn't grip it with his injured hands.

He held his breath and tried to become invisible. The sound repeated. Legai slipped through the willows, flattened into the shadows, and crept up the hillside. A small deer vaulted out of the scrub and dashed through the trees. Legai muffled a scream and waited for his heart to stop trying to break through his chest. He leaned against a tree trunk and breathed deeply to calm himself. He looked at the ground and realized he was on a trail that wound through the woodland, so he slipped further into the shadows and waited.

When Legai was certain he was alone, he weaved along the trail for some time without reaching anything that looked familiar. He was just about to reverse when he rounded a corner and saw the opening of the cave that had started him on his pursuit up the mountain. A gust of wind rattled the pines above him and swirled around his face. Legai found the mouth of the cave still protected by the thicket of wild raspberry bushes covered with wicked thorns. After testing them with his wounded hands, he realized there was no way to pass through them. But he remembered a fallen fir tree he had passed a few hundred yards down the trail.

Cha retreated to the fir and found two substantial branches that had broken off when the tree crashed to the ground. Each had smaller branches covered with flat, flexible needles. He gritted his teeth and dragged the two branches up the trail to the thicket, and placed them across the raspberry bushes. He crept across them to the mouth of the cave. A few of the thorns stuck him as he crawled over the fir branches, but he was successful in his quest. Lest anyone else should follow him, he dragged the branches into the cave.

When he had first entered the cave, his troops had determined that the men they were pursuing had abandoned it, and they had left almost as quickly as they'd come. Now he had time to explore.

A root from a tree above him had forced through the unforgiving stone and hung like a rope from the roof of the cavern. Legai hit the root with his cheek, and collapsed to his knees in pain. He ran his fingers across the cave floor and found that it was covered with black sand and small stones. His knees screamed as he forced himself to stand. He stuck his hands in front of him and shuffled forward. He had not gone far into the inky blackness before he began to hear faint sounds of hammers striking steel. He reached the back of the cavern and saw a gleam of light down a tunnel to his right. Crouched, he moved up the tunnel until he saw the charred remnants of a door. He stepped through the portal and looked down on Abadon's forge room far below. Unsure as to how he would be received, he tiptoed down the steps cut into the chamber wall. He had nearly reached the floor of the room when one of the overseers spotted him and called out an alarm.

Across the chamber a wolac was harnessed to a cart, and it began to squeal when the alarm was sounded. Two guards stationed near a door behind the wolac rushed to Legai with tsenils at the ready.

"Who are you?" said one of the guards.

"I am Lieutenant Cha Legai."

The guards laughed.

"Unlikely," said one of them. "Captain Doitsoh reported his death when he returned from the summit." He pressed the pointed tip of the battle ax into Legai's ribs. "Now who are you, really?"

Legai felt a shiver of dread race down his spine like a rivulet of icy water.

"Do I look dead to you? I was left for dead, but as you can see, I have recovered."

"So you say," the guard growled. "How do we know this is not some trick?"

"If you will take me to Captain Doitsoh ,he can vouch for me."

"That would be an easy solution if he were here. Unfortunately he and his men have left to deal with a problem in the mines of Hagade. He is not expected back for at least a fortnight." He jabbed Legai with the tip of his tsenil. "But I think you knew that and are being a trickster."

"There are others who can confirm my identity."

The two guards conferred briefly.

"You may be who you say you are," one of them said, "but we must be certain. Put your hands behind your back."

Legai did as he was told, and his wrists were bound with a leather thong. He was marched to the back of the cart, a loop placed around his neck, and the other end tied to a stave that rose from the bed of the cart. He stood there until the gong sounded twice and the blacksmiths put down their tools and lined up to leave the room. The massive door was swung open, and the men shuffled up the tunnel on the other side of the portal. When the men had passed, the wolac pulled the laden weapons cart after them dragging Legai behind. His knees had stiffened, and he struggled to remain on his feet as the wolac increased its speed.

He had nearly reached the limits of his endurance when the march ended. He was untied from the wagon and led into a room which provided some comfort for the jailors guarding the prison cells arranged in adjoining hallways. One of his captors led him across the room, where he was forced to stand against the wall while the guards conversed.

One of the doors leading to the cells opened, and a stocky man backed into the room, dragging a metal cart behind him. He pushed the cart into an alcove before facing the rest of the men in the room.

"Lieutenant! What are you doing here? I thought you were dead."

"Gah, you know this man?" one of the guards said. "Are you sure?"

"Aye, this is Lieutenant Legai. We served together in the assault on Atsanh, many years ago." He crossed the room to where Legai stood. "I heard you had died."

Legai took a deep breath. "I was wounded, but I survived. It is good to see you again, Gah." He looked past the man, to where the guards stood. "You see, I told you the truth."

"So you say." The guard crossed the room and untied Legai's hands. "But there are still many questions to be answered."

Legai tried to rub his wrists where the leather had cut into them, but his fingers were too sore.

Gah saw the cloth strips wrapped around his hands. "What happened?"

"I had some difficulty coming down from the summit."

"Let me get you some salve." Gah retrieved an urn of ointment from a cupboard attached to the wall, then began unwrapping the bandages from Legai's tortured hands.

Blood had seeped into the cloth and glued the strips to his lacerated palms. When Gah pulled the strips loose, Legai's hands began to bleed again. He bit down on his lip to keep from screaming in pain. Gah applied salve and wrapped his hands with clean strips.

He faced the guards. "Leave him with me until his hands have healed."

The two guards nodded, grabbed biscuits from the side table, and left the room to return to their post. Gah filled a basin with water and began washing Legai's knees. Then he applied more ointment.

"Come. Let me show you a place where you can rest."

Legai limped after his old companion. He was led past a curtain made of animal hide, to a small room which contained a narrow cot.

"Sleep, my friend. And when you awaken, you can tell me how you survived."

CHAPTER 39

G AH PUSHED THE METAL CART WITH ITS RUMBLING WHEELS, to a shaft that ran up to the scullery, and pulled on a thin rope that hung on one side. Above him, he could hear the tinkle of the tiny bell attached to the other end of the strand. Soon a wooden cabinet was lowered from the kitchen to the floor in front of him. Gah opened the doors of the container and removed the usual bowls of lukewarm soup and a basket of hard rolls. He placed them on his metal cart before pulling on the cord again. The cupboard was pulled back up the shaft as Gah pushed the meal cart toward one of the doors leading to the cell blocks. He paused long enough to pull the leather curtain back and check on Lieutenant Legai, who had slept for twelve straight hours. He was beginning to stir, so Gah cleared his throat.

"Lieutenant, are you awake?"

Legai's eyes flew open, and he struggled to focus on Gah's face. "What?"

"I need to deliver the food. I'll bring you something to eat when I return."

Legai threw his legs over the side of the cot. "Let me go with you. I need to move, or my knees will stiffen even more."

"As you wish." Gah pulled open a door and pushed the cart down the narrow corridor.

Legai followed on wobbly legs. Soon they reached a guard seated at a low table. He had a mug of mulled cider and a slab of rare beef on a plate.

"Who is this?" The guard jabbed the tip of his knife toward Legai.

"Lieutenant Legai," replied Gah. "He is recovering from some severe wounds."

"Legai? I thought he was dead."

"Not quite," Legai replied.

Gah pushed the noisy cart down the polished stone floor. When they reached the first cell, he removed one of the bowls of soup and pushed it through a slot in the bars. Legai looked through the bars and saw an elderly man crouched in the corner on a straw mat.

"What has he done?" he said to Gah.

"He is a rebel from the town of Aravah."

"Rebel?"

"He refuses to pay homage to Prince Abadon."

Legai wrinkled his forehead. "For that he is imprisoned?"

Gah shrugged. "All I know is that I bring them food twice a day." He shoved the cart ahead to the next cell.

As they passed each cell, Legai studied the occupants. Many were old men, some middle-aged, and the last three appeared to be in their late teens.

When they had completed their course, Gah pushed the empty cart back to their starting point.

"We'll have to go collect the bowls in a few minutes." He sank down onto a three-legged stool.

Legai retrieved another stool and sat next to him. "Gah, have you ever questioned Abadon's rule?"

Gah scrunched his nose. "No. Why?"

"Sometimes it seems a little harsh."

"Life can be harsh. But without Abadon we'd have no security." Gah paused and contemplated the backs of his hands. "Can you imagine anything worse than falling under the rule of that lying, thieving Johona? Just look at how many men have perished fighting his forces." He spat on the ground.

Legai rested his head in his bandaged hands. "I suspect you're right, Gah. But as I think back on the battles we've fought, I cannot remember one where Johona's troops were the aggressors."

"That may be true. But had we waited for them to attack us, we'd have been in jeopardy of losing our lands."

"Gah, what if we're wrong? What if what we've been taught isn't true?"

Gah shook his head. "What has made you think this way, Lieutenant?"

There was a signal from the scullery shaft. Gah scurried across the room and pulled on the signal cord. Another cabinet full of food appeared. He loaded it onto his metal cart and pushed it toward another door.

"You worry me, Lieutenant." He opened the door and proceeded down another corridor.

Legai followed him, and once they had passed the guard station, they approached the first cell. Legai looked in and saw a woman kneeling on the pallet in the far corner.

"Women?"

"Aye, one block for the men, and another for the women." Gah shoved a bowl of soup through the slot in the bars.

"And what have they done?"

"Same as the men. They won't swear allegiance to the prince."

They continued down the corridor, the only sound that of the rumbling cart and the metal plates being thrust through the cell doors. Once they had finished, they returned the cart to the chamber they'd left minutes before.

"Must a prince rule by force?" Legai said.

Gah rubbed his chin with stubby fingers. "How else would he rule?"

"You may be right."

Gah pursed his lips. "I've often wondered why the prince allowed these peasants to live on the foothills of his mountain. No doubt they were spies who reported to that fiend Johona. It did not surprise me at all when we were ordered to burn their town."

Legai leaned his elbows on the table. "And now they are all locked in cages."

"Aye, but all they need to do is pledge fidelity to the prince, and they'd be released."

"To do what? Their town is burned. Their cattle destroyed. What do they have to look forward to?"

"That is their problem, not mine. If they had given up the man we sought, their punishment would not have been so severe."

Legai could see he was not making any headway with his friend. But

the argument had convinced Legai even further that he and his compatri-
ots had been misled.

"Perhaps it is the pain I feel that is making me so contrary" he said. "If
you do not mind, I think I will sleep some more."

"Of course."

Legai stood from his perch and trudged toward the alcove, where the
cot was.

He pushed back the curtain. "Gah, were there no children in Aravah?"

"Aye. They are being taught the true doctrine each day by the overseers.
They are being kept from the evil influence of their parents."

"I see." Legai laid on the cot, but sleep would not come. *How could I
have been so blind?*

Legai tossed and turned for an hour. He heard Gah leave to retrieve
the bowls and then return. After what seemed an eternity, he forced himself to his feet and pushed aside the curtain. Gah was sitting on the stool,
writing with a quill pen on a strip of parchment. When he heard the curtain open, he turned toward Legai.

"I thought you were sleeping, Lieutenant."

"Sleep eludes me, Gah."

"Perhaps it is the pain from your injuries."

"Perhaps."

Gah stood and shuffled to a cabinet mounted on the wall, then
removed a key from his pocket and unlocked it. He inspected several bags
before removing one.

"This is a sleeping draft. It may help." Gah poured a mug of cider from
a flagon on the table, and added a pinch of powder from the bag. "Here,
try this."

Legai drank the potion and handed the cup back to Gah. His legs felt
like lead, and he had to fight to keep his eyes open. Like a drunken man,
he staggered back to the cot and drifted off to sleep.

CHAPTER 40

Tsalix struggled to decode the message Asur was sending him. Once Asur knew Tsalix understood the code his pace increased. After their brief liberation from their cells, there was much to discuss, and even though it was laborious, there was nothing else for them to do.

Asur had assessed Kwercus's condition and let Tsalix know that he had tried to ward off the guards with his ax, but had been knocked off his feet by a blow from a cudgel that had bruised his legs. Day by day the bruises were healing and his strength was returning.

The sound of the food cart caused them to stop tapping. This time, two men accompanied the cart—the usual beefy man, and another who seemed injured himself. Once they retreated Tsalix sent a message.

"Who?"

"Don't know," Asur replied.

While he drank his soup and gnawed on his roll, Tsalix tried to think of a way to escape. He removed the talisman from his purse and studied it. It remained cold and lifeless. His initials remained a flat gray color.

As he replaced it in his purse, his fingers brushed against the vial. He removed it and turned it over in his hands. *Earth,* he read on its black surface, but he couldn't think of any way it could help them, so he put it back.

Tsalix retraced the routes he had taken within Mount Jinee. He knew that if they were to escape their cells, the tunnels in the mountain were guarded.

His mind wandered to the brief episode in the sunlight. The way to the courtyard was guarded by a steel door that could only be opened from the outside once the proper sign—a medallion worn around the guard's neck—was shown.

Tsalix could see no solution. Even if they were able to reach the courtyard, the spiked fence would corral them.

He sighed deeply, knelt and placed his ear against the wall. After removing the talisman again, he tapped a message to Asur.

If we reached the courtyard, how could we escape?

A pause that stretched into minutes before Asur replied, *I don't know. Fence a problem.*

Ponder, Tsalix sent.

As he lay on the straw tick, he continued to deliberate the problem. If they could get over the fence, they would face a long fall to the steps that were cut into the mountain. And if they survived that fall, the sentinels from the palace would certainly pursue them down the stairs. On the other hand, if they tried to head toward the forge room and take the other fork in the tunnel, they'd end up having to avoid the men in the armory to escape to the outside. Then they'd be faced with the same problem of getting down the stairs without being caught and returned to prison—no doubt, with fresh wounds.

Tsalix tossed and turned on his bed as he fell into a troubled sleep. In a dream he heard a voice—*No task given to you will be too great. There will always be a way to succeed.*

His eyes flew open. "I believe you, my king. But what is the solution to this problem?"

CHAPTER 41

Cha Legai awoke refreshed. He had no idea how long he'd slept, but his hands and knees felt much better than they had before he'd fallen asleep.

He removed the bandages around his lacerated flesh. The scabs were beginning to itch. Some had attached to the dressing and pulled away from his hands, leaving raised red scars. Still, he could flex his fingers for the first time since his precipitous travel through the clouds. He bent his knees and found that the pain was much less than it had been.

Legai drew back the leather curtain and entered the room. Gah was sitting on his customary stool, writing in a ledger with a quill pen. He heard the sound of the curtain being drawn and turned.

"Lieutenant, how do you feel?"

"Much better. How long have I slept?"

"Most of the day, I fear. It is almost time for the evening meal."

The bell sounded down the shaft from the kitchen. Gah shuffled to the opening and tugged on the slim strand of rope. Within a few minutes, he had lowered the food and moved it onto the metal cart.

"Would you like to rest some more? Or would you like to accompany me again?"

Legai nodded. "I think it would do me good to stretch my legs. I'll join you, if you don't mind."

"Of course." Gah pushed the cart toward the door to the women's cells.

Legai stepped in front of him and opened the door.

"Thank you," Lieutenant."

Gah pushed the cart down the corridor until they reached the guard station, where two men sat at a table, playing a game of Troefcall, and barely paid any attention as Gah and Legai passed by.

"We'll bring you your dinner soon." Gah nodded.

The two men grunted in response.

The laden cart reached the first bank of cells, and Gah removed the metal bowl and slid it through the opening in the cage. An old woman, white haired and toothless, retrieved it, along with the hard roll. She immersed the roll in the liquid and turned it with skeletal fingers, trying to soften it. Legai studied her as Gah pushed the cart to the next cell. Certainly she posed no danger to Abadon.

Legai shook his head as he caught up with Gah. By the time they reached the end of the cell block and reversed their course, Legai was nearly in tears. The women he had seen were gaunt and haggard, obviously suffering.

"Gah, my friend, how long will they have to stay?"

"Until they come to their senses and bow to the prince."

"Why? They pose no peril to Abadon. They can barely stand they are so weak."

Gah pushed the cart into place to load it with food for the men's cells before he turned to Legai.

"Lieutenant, if we are to live in peace and security, we must eliminate any hint of disobedience. These stupid people from Aravah cling to their foolish traditions, like rust to steel. And if we are going to scour that rust and polish the steel, we must have their total allegiance. Certainly you understand that."

Legai plopped onto one of the three-legged stools. "Can we force people's fidelity?"

"We'll see when the first one dies. Then the others will see their stubbornness is futile."

"Must it come to that?"

Gah seated himself on one of the other stools and gazed into Legai's eyes. "Lieutenant, why do you doubt? Haven't you always followed orders without flinching?"

Legai thought of the terror he had felt when he hadn't been able to hold onto the chain and had fallen, screaming down the vent in the mountain.

"Yes, I have," he replied.

Once the cart was loaded again, they proceeded down the men's cell block. When they reached the last three cells, Legai noticed the men in them were considerably younger than the rest.

"Who are these three?" he said.

Gah shrugged. "I know not. They were captured within the mountain. Two were armed, and they were relieved of their weapons." He started pushing the cart back down the hallway. "But whoever they are, they're just as stubborn as the rest."

Gah moved on, but Legai dragged his feet and stopped at Asur's cell.

"Who are you?" he whispered.

Asur moved to the bars. "Asur Longtooth," he whispered.

"Why are you here?"

Apparently Legai's whisper was too loud, and one of the guards barked down the corridor, "Silence!"

Asur drew back from the bars, and Legai caught up with Gah.

They passed by the two guards who were sitting at a table, sharing a flagon of wine.

"Lieutenant," one of them greeted, as Gah and Legai lumbered past.

Once they were seated, they sat in silence for several minutes.

"Do you want to go with me to pick up the empty dishes?" Gah said.

"I think I'll wait for you here. I may be overdoing things." Legai held his hands up in the flickering light of the torch.

The scabs and scars were vivid.

"As you wish." Gah pushed the cart through the doorway to the women's cells and closed it behind him.

Legai went to the cabinet from which Gah had removed the bag containing the sleeping draft, but found it locked. He examined the lock and determined it was too sturdy for him to open it with anything but a key. He returned to the stool, sat and leaned against the wall. A plan began to form in his mind.

By the time Gah returned with the empty bowls from the women's cells, he knew what he had to do.

"Gah, I'm finding it difficult to sleep. Do you have more of that sleeping powder?"

"Aye." Gah removed the key from his pocket and unlocked the cabinet, then mixed a pinch of powder with a mug of cider and handed to Legai. "That should do it, Lieutenant."

"I think I'll take it to the cot. Last night I barely made it before I fell asleep. But I think I'm getting better. It might be time for me to leave and rejoin my regiment."

Gah nodded. "I still have the men's dishes to pick up. I suspect you'll be asleep before I return. Good night, Lieutenant."

"Good night, my friend. I feel much better, so I'll be gone by morning." Legai pulled the curtain aside and stepped into the nook.

He heard the door to the men's cells open and close. He counted to ten before he drew the leather back. The room was empty. He hurried across the floor to the table where Gah recorded his duties. His cup of cider was half-full. Legai rushed back to his bedroom and poured the cider into the chamber pot beneath his bed. He replaced it with the sleeping potion from his mug, then repositioned it on the table. He scurried back to his cot and pretended to be asleep.

When Gah returned, he pushed the cart into place and then returned to his record keeping. Legai waited with butterflies fluttering around in his stomach.

Thump!

Legai pushed the curtain aside and saw Gah lying on his side, snoring. He bent and removed the key from Gah's pocket. Once he'd opened the cabinet, he took down the bag of sleeping powder and prepared four mugs of cider. He returned the bag to its place, locked the cabinet, and put the key back in Gah's pocket.

He had barely finished his preparations when the signal from the kitchen rang. He tugged on the rope, and soon the guard's meals appeared down the shaft. Legai arranged the plates of food on a tray, but replaced the flagons from the kitchen with the mugs of cider he'd prepared. After lifting the tray to his shoulder, he to the door that led to the women's cells. A couple minutes later, he finished his task and headed to the guard station in the men's cell block.

Legai returned to the room where Gah lay sleeping on the floor, and waited ten minutes before returning to the women's cell block. The guards had fallen asleep and were slumped over their table. The cards from their game of Troefcall were scattered on the floor. Legai removed the ornate key from its hook on the wall and hurried down the passage to the cells.

He applied the key to the first lock and swung the door open. It screamed a grating sound that echoed through the block. The emaciated woman within the cell struggled to her feet. She pushed the snow white hair back from her face.

"Who are you?" she wheezed.

"A friend," Legai replied.

"Where are the children?"

Legai paused. "I know not."

"We cannot leave without the children." The old woman sank back down on her pallet.

"Don't be foolish. This may be your only opportunity to escape."

"Not without the children. Without them there is no future."

Legai turned to the next cell, inserted the key, and pulled the door open. The woman inside squinted as she tried to focus on his face.

"Have you brought the children?"

Legai called down the corridor, "I can free you from your cells, but these two refuse to leave. What shall I do?"

A chorus replied, "Where are the children?"

He shook his head. "If you won't leave, I can't help you."

"Then you must leave us." The old woman in the first cell gasped as she dragged her cell door shut.

Legai retreated past the guard station, shaking his head. "What is wrong with these women?"

He paused at the guard station leading to the men's cell block long enough to confirm that the guards were still sleeping, before continuing to the first cell. He inserted the key and dragged the door open. An old man was curled on his straw pallet. He barely had strength to stand.

"Come, old man. I've opened your door." Legai extended a hand to help the man to his feet.

"You've brought the children?" the old man said.

"No. I know not where they are. Why this obsession with the children?"

The man inspected Legai's black tunic. "You wouldn't understand. But without them we cannot leave." The man slumped back to the floor.

"Do any of you want to be free?" Legai called out.

"We are free," the old man replied.

Legai looked at the gaunt creature at his feet. "Free? You're locked in a cell deep within a mountain. How can you say you are free?"

The old man smiled. "We are free because we have not surrendered our will to the tyrant." He coughed. "That, too, may be hard for you to understand. But we are free."

Legai shook his head. "No, I don't understand." He pushed the cell door shut before continuing down the hallway.

A vision of the young men in the last three cells appeared in his mind. He hustled down the corridor until he stood in front of Asur's cell.

"And you. Must you wait for your children? You are barely older than a child yourself."

Asur grasped the bars of his cage. "I have no children. But escaping from this cell does not mean escaping from this unholy place."

"At least it is a start," Tsalix said, from the adjoining cell.

"Aye," said Kwercus, from across the passage. "We can accomplish nothing from within our cells."

"At last, someone who will listen to reason." Legai opened their doors and was joined by the three prisoners.

"Now what?" said Asur.

CHAPTER 42

"Are things progressing as we desired?" Elosha said to his wife.

"Perhaps not as quickly as we'd hoped. But yes, all is now in place." She stood from her throne and stepped off the dais.

A gentle breeze blew through the open window, brushing her silver hair behind her. Nadlee placed her hands on the window sill and gazed over the fruitful meadows of Hayeli.

"This is such a beautiful, peaceful place. Why can't our son Abadon accept his role? Why does he cause such heartache and bloodshed? What did we do wrong in raising him?"

The king moved to her side and encircled her waist with his hands. "There is no easy answer. He has used his agency to create chaos instead of peace and order. What he may not know is that with every decision comes a consequence—whether it be for good or ill. His pride has caused this schism between us, and all we can do is love him and hope for a change in his demeanor. But I fear it will not come."

"How can two brothers be so different?"

The king drew her close to him. "I know not. But I know that you gave each of them an equal measure of your love. We have not chosen their paths. They have."

Queen Nadlee wiped a tear from her cheek. "Oh, how my heart cries out for both of them."

Elosha lowered his head until his chin rested on his chest, and heaved a sigh. "At least our three young friends are progressing."

"Yes." She gave a hint of a smile. "Do you think they need help?"

"Tsalix will find a solution. He has a quick mind, and strength of will. There is great trust among the three of them."

The silver gong was struck to announce a visitor, and the two of them turned to see their eldest son, Johona, walk into the throne room. He bowed his head to his father and embraced his mother.

Elosha beamed. "What brings you here, my son?"

"A report on the uprising at Hagade."

Elosha and Nadlee returned to their thrones.

"Please be seated," the king said. "Then proceed."

Johona sat next to his father and began his report. "We arrived with our troops after hearing of the unrest in the mines of Hagade, and found my brother had sent troops to quell the turmoil. Captain Nash Doitsoh was leading the fray. He had removed the men from the mine and chained them to posts that lined the street, through the town. When we appeared, Captain Doitsoh withdrew his men and placed them on the hillside above us, trying to get the advantage. What he did not know is that we had anticipated this move, and had placed the majority of our men on the plateau above the mines. Thus Doitsoh's troops were below them, while I brought a smaller force into the town. We waited until the sun set before springing our attack from the top of the hill. This meant Doitsoh's men were looking into the setting sun as my men descended. When they turned to defend themselves, our smaller force at the base of the hill was able to create confusion among his men. The battle was fierce, but it was not long before Captain Doitsoh withdrew what remained of his men and retreated to Mount Jinee. We pursued them until we feared he would be able to muster a much larger force and return to do battle."

The king stroked his chin. "How many men were lost, my son?"

"None of ours were killed, but many suffered wounds."

"And Abadon's troops?"

"Nearly two dozen fell to the sword. Only a few escaped without injury."

"What about the people of Hagade?" said Queen Nadlee.

"All are free. Of course they are worried my brother will send a bigger force to punish them. And they may be right."

Elosha pursed his lips. "The sound of war is on the wind. Abadon will not take lightly his defeat at your hands. Not only will he likely scourge the town of Hagade, but he will try to wreak revenge upon you. He has never been able to take defeat. Even when he was a small boy, he had to best you in every contest, and I know deep in my bones that he will not let this debacle go unchallenged."

Nadlee placed her hand on her husband's arm. "If things are accelerating, perhaps we do need to help our young friends. They bear the solution to the problem at hand."

Elosha pondered what his wife had said. "Have faith in Tsalix, my dear. I cannot help but believe he will find a way to return with the talisman. He is, after all, a Silverthorn."

Nadlee smiled. "At some point you will have to explain his lineage to him."

"At the appropriate time."

CHAPTER 43

"A RE THERE ROPES ANYWHERE NEAR?" TSALIX SAID TO CHA Legai.

"Perhaps. I am not as familiar with this level of the fortress as I am with other areas."

Once Tsalix, Asur, and Kwercus were standing in the corridor, Legai pushed the cell doors closed and locked them.

"Wait here, and I'll see what I can find," he said.

While Legai hurried down the row of cells, Tsalix followed him until he was outside his father's cell.

"Father."

His father smiled and reached through the bars and hugged his son. "You found the message I left in the chimney stones?"

"Aye." He hugged his father in return. "Now we have to leave you and try to complete the task Elosha has given us."

"I understand, my son."

"Tell mother I love her and will try to return to free all of you."

Tears ran down his father's face. "Go, my son."

Tsalix returned to where Kwercus waited. Asur had taken time to say goodbye to his father as well.

Asur put his hand on Tsalix's shoulder. "You have a plan?"

"Perhaps. If our mysterious benefactor succeeds in finding ropes, we may be able to scale the fence and then lower ourselves to the landing below."

"Then what?" Kwercus shook his head. "Certainly we will be pursued down the stairway."

Tsalix nodded. "I see no other way. If there is a better option..."

"None that I see," Asur whispered. "I wonder who opened our cells."

They heard footsteps echoing off the walls, and Legai reappeared, dragging two heavy coils of rope behind him.

"I hope this will do," he said.

Tsalix nodded. "They look substantial enough." When he took the hank of rope from Legai's hands, he saw the scars and scabs. "You are injured."

"I am healing. All will be well soon."

Asur grabbed the other coil of rope. "We have one other problem. How do we get the guard to open the door? And what do we do with him?"

Tsalix looked in to Legai's eyes. "Do you know where the medallion that opens the door is kept?"

Legai shook his head. "I do not. Can you describe it to me?"

Kwercus said, "The jailor had it around his neck, remember."

"Start carrying the ropes to the doorway," Legai said. "I'll see if I can find the medallion, and join you there."

The three young men began dragging the heavy ropes down the passageway that led to the courtyard beyond the steel door. The journey was a long one. Once they reached the door, they waited until Legai strode up to them. Dangling from his fingers was a medallion on a chain.

"Is this it?" he said.

"Aye. At least, I think so," Asur replied.

Tsalix took the medallion from Legai. "We'll know soon enough." He walked to the door and raised his fist to pound on it.

"Wait!" Kwercus said. "What do we do with the guard once the door is opened?"

Legai knelt and looked at the hinges on the door. "It swings inward. Once the door begins to open, let me handle the guard."

Tsalix pounded on the door and held the medallion up to the peephole, which opened and closed before the heavy door began to open. Legai stood next to the door, and as soon as it opened far enough for him to reach through the opening, he grabbed the door and pushed it open. The guard was leaning against the door, pushing it with both hands, and the sudden movement threw him off balance. As he pitched forward, Legai hit him on the back of his head with a wooden cudgel he'd removed from his waistband. The guard fell to the floor with a thud. Legai dragged him into the tunnel, and as soon as the three freed prisoners were in the courtyard, he pulled the door shut.

Tsalix uncoiled one of the ropes, formed a double loop in one hand, and with the other tried to throw the strand over the spiked fence. It was too heavy and fell short. He coiled more of the rope in his hand and tried again, but it dropped at his feet.

"Let me try," Kwercus said. "I'm more used to working with ropes when I cut timber and haul logs."

He stood back further from the fence and threw the rope. The end of the rope flew over the fence, but the weight of the strand behind it pulled it back onto the courtyard floor. He tried a second time, with no success.

Tsalix looked around the courtyard for something to aid them. Beside the guard's station was a metal bucket. He picked up the pail and looked inside. The guard's partially eaten lunch lay in the bottom. Tsalix dumped the food out and tied the end of the rope around the bucket's handle.

"Find me some stones to fill the bucket," he said.

Five minutes later the bucket was half-full of small rocks.

"Stand back." Tsalix swung the bucket around his head.

He stepped back from the edge of the courtyard and let out more and more rope until he was sure he had enough to reach beyond the top of the fence. The whirling bucket made a swishing sound as it spun around Tsalix's head. He let the bucket fly, and it cleared the top of the fence by a foot or two. The bucket slammed into the metal pickets like a gong. Tsalix fed more rope, and the pail rested on the landing below. He fed the free end of the rope through the bottom of the fence until it reached the bucket. There was still ten feet of rope lying on the floor of the courtyard.

"Can you hold the rope while I climb the fence?" he said.

"Aye." Kwercus reached through the fence, grabbed the hanging rope, wrapped a loop around his body, and leaned back. "Go, my brother."

Tsalix grabbed the rope, wrapped a loop around his foot, and began to climb. Kwercus planted his feet and held the rope taut while Tsalix climbed to the top of the fence. Once he swung himself over, he hung from the top of the fence until Kwercus could shift his weight to the strand Tsalix had climbed. Tsalix grabbed the rough rope and slid down to the landing below.

"Let me pull the rest of the rope through," he called.

Once he had accomplished that, he tied off both ends of the rope to the iron handrail that guarded the edge of the staircase. Asur appeared a few moments later as he vaulted over the top of the fence. Soon he was standing next to Tsalix on the landing.

In the courtyard Kwercus turned to Legai. "Your turn, my friend."

Legai shook his head, "I cannot go with you." He held out his hands. "I would like to join you, but I fear I cannot climb up the rope, and certainly not lower myself."

"If you stand on my shoulders, you can almost reach the top of the barrier," Kwercus said. "Then if you can balance yourself, you can tie a loop in the rope, put your foot in it, and I can lower you to safety."

"But why would you do that?"

"You have freed us from prison. Will you not let me return the favor?"

Legai looked at his wounded hands. "I hope I do not fail you."

Kwercus called down to Tsalix and explained what he intended to do. A moment later he boosted Cha Legai onto his shoulders. Legai reached up and grasped the iron rail that ran around the top of the fence. The cold metal burned his wounds, but he gritted his teeth and slid one leg over the bar between two of the pickets. Tsalix had already untied the bucket and retied a loop in the end of the rope. Kwercus drew the rope up until the loop was just below Legai's foot. He slid the rest of the way over the fence, slipped one foot into the loop, and grabbed hold of the rope. The rough rope scoured scabs from the palms of his hands as Kwercus let him down to safety.

Tsalix tied off the end of the rope, and a few seconds later, Kwercus stood with the other three men on the landing.

"Now what?" he said.

"Now we get rid of the rope." Tsalix freed one end and pulled the other side of the rope until the heavy coil lay at their feet.

They lifted it and dropped it over the side of the mountain.

As soon as it disappeared, Tsalix said, "Haste. We must climb down these stairs before our escape is discovered."

An alarm bell rang above them, and the sounds of men rushing down the stairway above met their ears. The four of them dashed down the stairway. Tsalix's purse bounced against his leg. He thrust his hand into it to keep the talisman from bruising his thigh, and felt a warm pulsation from the black vial labeled *Earth*.

As they rounded a corner and came to another landing, he withdrew the vial from within his tunic and opened the seal. The small black flask throbbed for a moment, and then a cascade of dirt began pouring from its neck. In a few seconds, a mound of earth filled the landing and the staircase above for a dozen or more feet, blocking those who pursued them.

"Move, move!" Tsalix said.

Legai stood frozen, his mouth agape.

"There is no time to gawk," said Tsalix. "It will buy us a few precious minutes."

"But how did you do that?"

"Later," Tsalix pulled Legai after him, down the staircase.

A half-hour later they reached the bottom of the steps and continued their flight.

"Where shall we go?" Asur said. "We know there are soldiers on the Plain of Wonadsi." He wiped his brow with the back of his hand. "I think we should retrace our steps on the footpath beneath the high plateau."

"Nay, my young friends," Legai said. "Captain Doitsoh has been sent to Hagade. There has been rebellion in the mines. If we go that way, we will certainly run into his men."

Kwercus stroked his chin. "I have often cut timber from the forests on the top of the high plateau. Although there is no road, I know the forest well. I would suggest we make our way around Hagade and avoid a confrontation with Captain Doitsoh."

The others nodded, and soon they were moving through the charred remnants of Aravah, on their way to the path that led them to the top of the range. The climb was hard, and they had no provisions with them, but no one complained.

The moon sank behind the ridge of the plateau as they approached the end of their climb.

"I know where there is water." Kwercus gasped for breath.

The others followed him into a copse of trees. The air was cool and sweet, scented with pine. They reached the spring and guzzled the water before sitting on a fallen log.

"Rest a few minutes," Kwercus said. "Then I will take you to a cavern where we can spend the night. The opening faces away from the villages below, and if we make sure the wood is dry and does not send up smoke to give away our position, I believe we can build a fire to warm us." He squinted into the darkness.

Less than an hour later, they were gathered in a small cave. Kwercus had proven his woodsman skills by gathering dry needles and wood and starting a fire in the mouth of the cave. Its light cast shadows on the cave walls behind them. The four men huddled together, absorbing its warmth.

"I am sure you are as hungry as I am," Kwercus said, "but I can offer little for dinner. In the morning we should be able to find some berries to eat. It is still early in the season, but I'm sure we won't starve." He added more wood to the fire.

The floor of the cave was covered with several inches of sand, and once a few pebbles had been removed, they were able to lie down comfortably. Occasionally some small animal made noise, scurrying through the underbrush, but the night was peaceful.

They had been lying there for several minutes when Legai said, "May I ask you a question?"

"Of course," Tsalix replied.

"I tried to release all the prisoners."

"Yes?"

"They would not go."

"It is probably a good thing, for we could never have gotten all of them over the fence."

Silence for a moment, before Legai rolled over on his side. "But that wasn't the reason." He stared into Tsalix's eyes. "They would not go without the children. Why?"

Tsalix wrinkled his forehead. "Because who would take care of them? They are our families."

Legai lay silent for several minutes, and Tsalix thought he had fallen asleep.

"I don't understand," Legai said. "Would not the overseers take care of the children?"

"Overseers?"

"Those who raise and teach the children until they are old enough to take care of themselves."

Tsalix reflected on Legai's answer. "Did not your parents raise you?"

"Of course not. I know not who gave birth to me. As soon as I was born, I was placed with an overseer who taught and trained me." Legai paused. "Is it different with you?"

Tsalix thought back to the love and warmth he had been surrounded with in his home.

"Oh, yes, my friend. Very different." He yawned. "Perhaps we can explain as we travel tomorrow." He closed his eyes, and soon drifted off to sleep.

Legai could not sleep. Too many questions racing through his mind. *Parents? What a novel idea.*

CHAPTER 44

ABADON STORMED AROUND HIS THRONE ROOM WHILE HIS servants cringed against the walls.

"Escaped! No one has ever escaped before," he bellowed. "How many? Who were they? How did it happen?" He spun around, his cape swirling around him, as he pointed at the guard kneeling before him.

"Three, my liege."

"And?"

"I know not their names. They were three young men who crept into the armory and were captured."

"Really? When did this happen? Why wasn't I informed?"

The guard tried to calm his quavering voice. "They seemed harmless."

Abadon circled until he was standing behind the trembling warrior. He drew his sword from its scabbard and placed the point against the back of the man's neck. Sparks of red flashed from the jewels encrusting the hilt.

"And how did they escape?"

"Somehow they deceived the doorman at the courtyard. He was found unconscious behind the door. Once they were in the courtyard, they scaled the fence."

"I thought the fence was impossible to climb," Abadon boomed.

The guard cringed at the point of the sword on his neck. "We all believed that to be true. How they accomplished it we do not know." Sweat coursed down his back.

"And why were they not recaptured on the staircase?" Abadon pushed the point of the sword harder against the yielding flesh.

Drops of blood trickled down the man's neck, and tears ran down his cheeks.

"My liege, a huge pile of dirt filled the stairway. Where it came from, I do not know." The guard was shaking. "It took nearly an hour to dig through. With every shovelful we removed, more seemed to appear. By the time we were able to pursue the men, they were gone."

"Fools!" Abadon screamed.

He lifted his sword to the left, and with a swift backhand, decapitated the kneeling guard. The severed head skidded across the floor, while the body slumped amidst a pool of blood. Muffled screams filled the room from the others, who quailed against the walls.

"Remove him and clean up this mess." Abadon gestured to his servants. "Perhaps I am surrounded by fools, and I must deal with this myself." He swirled his cape around him and stomped out of the room.

Behind him, his shuddering servants removed the body and began to clean up the wide puddle of blood on the throne room floor.

Abadon slammed the door behind him, rattling the stained glass windows in the ante chamber. He wiped the blood from the blade of his sword on one of the curtains, and replaced it in its sheath. As he paced across the polished floor of the small room, he tugged on his pointed beard while considering what to do next.

No one had ever escaped from the dungeons. Everyone had eventually sworn fealty to him and been released so they could be educated and retrained to serve him, the one true master.

Many minutes passed before he had calmed enough to pull open the door and re-enter the throne room. The servants were swabbing the last vestiges of blood from the floor. Abadon's entry caused the men to redouble their efforts.

"Where are the priests?" he hissed. "Summon them with the Book of Laws."

"At once, Master." The vizier raced out of the room and returned with the three priests in tow.

One of them carried a heavy leather-bound book.

"Your majesty." The three men bowed, their long beards nearly touching the floor.

Abadon sat on his throne. "I seek your advice."

The three men nodded. One of them adjusted the black sash around his red robe while they waited for the question. Abadon stroked his beard wondering how much to reveal to the priests.

"What is the penalty for escaping from the dungeon?" he said.

"It depends, Master, on why the person was being held," replied the senior priest.

The other priests nodded.

"What was his crime?"

"Treason."

"Ahh."

The three men opened the book and searched through several pages.

"According to the Book of Laws," said the senior priest, "a person guilty of treason is punished by death. No one has ever escaped before, so there is nothing listed concerning that."

They closed the book and stood silently.

"There is another matter you can help we with," Abadon said. "In all your wisdom, how might you suggest we find those who have escaped?"

The three priests conferred among themselves.

"We are not trained in such matters," the senior priest said. "However, the keeper of the columbary, Chee Danzie, has disciplined many of his feathered friends to do amazing things. There may be birds trained to seek prey. Beyond that, I fear we cannot help you."

"Away then." Abadon dismissed them with a sweep of his hand.

The three men backed out of the throne room.

"Vizier, bring me this Chee Danzie."

"Yes, my liege." He bowed and left the chamber.

A few minutes later he reappeared with a tall, thin man dressed in a forest green tunic, a heavy leather apron, leather leggings, and thick gloves. The man appeared startled when he was led before Abadon. He sank to his knees and bowed his head.

"Arise," Abadon said. "It is said that you have trained your birds to do many tasks. Is that so?"

Chee Danzie nodded. "Yes, my master."

Abadon stroked his beard. "Three young men escaped from the dungeon."

Danzie was in utter disbelief.

"Can any of your charges help me find them?"

Danzie thought for a moment. "Perhaps. There is one of my pets, Sidii, who is skilled in locating prey. She has great strength in her wings and can fly high. From that vantage point, her keen eyesight allows her see even the smallest mouse on the ground. Sidii may be able to find your escaped prisoners if I can explain to her what they look like." He looked into Abadon's face. "Can someone describe them to me?"

"Summon the other jailor," Abadon said. "He can describe these men to your Sidii."

Chee Danzie shook his head. "Only if they speak her tongue. It has taken me most of my life to learn how to communicate with my charges."

Abadon waved his hand. "Then have him describe them to you, and you translate."

The jailor was thrust into the room. He sank to his knees.

"Stand up!"

The jailor pushed up to his feet and stood on quivering legs.

"You saw the men who escaped?"

"Aye."

"Go with this man," Abadon pointed at Chee Danzie, "and describe them to him so he can talk to Sidii."

The jailor creased his brow. "Aye, my Master."

Chee and the jailor backed out of the throne room and climbed the east tower of the castle. When they reached the top of the spire, Chee opened the door of the room. Inside, several dozen birds were roosting on wooden perches. When the door opened, all of them began to twitter.

"I don't understand." The jailor shook his head. "Who is Sidii?"

Chee crossed the room and untied the leather jesses wrapped around the legs of an enormous hawk.

"This is Sidii." He placed her needle-sharp talons on the leather glove encasing his left arm, and stroked her plumage with his free hand.

The bird cocked her head and looked at him with one ebony eye. Chee's neck muscles tightened while he pursed his lips and issued a "*kree-ee-ar*."

The hawk responded in kind.

Chee turned to the jailor. "Tell me what these three prisoners looked like."

The jailor took one look at the bird's talons and sank back away from the bird.

"All three were young men. One had shaggy blond hair, one had red hair, and one had black hair. The blond-haired youth had a heavier build than the other two."

Chee began a series of chirps and rasping notes to the bird.

He turned to the jailor. "How were they dressed?"

"In simple tunics. One of them had a sword, and another an ax. But both were taken from them."

Chee nodded and spoke to the hawk again.

Then he turned to the jailor. "That is not much information. Is there anything else?"

The jailor shook his head. "No. You must realize we have so many prisoners that it is hard to keep track of them all. And so many of them look alike."

Chee stroked the hawk's head and spoke, giving it a few last-minute instructions, before he carried onto the balcony. The great bird sank against his glove, then sprang into the air with a rush of its wings. While the two men watched, the bird cleared the battlements and began ascending with powerful strokes. Soon it was but a small dot in the sky. She circled for a few seconds before streaking off to the southeast.

"When will it return?" said the jailor.

"By nightfall. We shall hope it brings us news, for our master does not like failure, as you know."

Chee led the man back down the staircase, toward the main floor of the castle.

CHAPTER 45

KWERCUS AWOKE, STIFF AND SORE, AND TRIED TO STRETCH the kinks out of his body. During the night, the small fire had burned out and a hint of frost covered the ground outside the cave.

Kwercus left the others sleeping and scouted the area for food. He'd traveled a short distance when he found a winterberry bush covered with purple fruit the size of the tip of his pinky. He picked the berries until he had two handfuls of the succulent fruit. He returned to the cavern just as Tsalix emerged.

"Here, Tsalix, have some breakfast."

Tsalix accepted the fruit. "I'll share," he whispered.

"Nay. There is plenty for all."

While Tsalix ate the mouthwatering berries, Kwercus returned to the spot where he'd found the winterberry bush. Soon he returned with two more handfuls. Asur and Legai were standing outside the opening to the cave as he approached. Kwercus split the berries between the two of them before retreating into the forest. A few minutes passed before he returned with more fruit. When they had eaten their fill, the sun was just appearing over the eastern skyline.

"Kwercus, you are a lifesaver." Tsalix smiled. "Now we must rely on you again to lead us through this forest."

"Aye. We'll travel as quickly as we can, but know this. The forest is dense, and there is no road. I think, too, that we must stay away from the cliffs to our left, lest we be seen by the villagers below."

They began moving single-file through the nearly impenetrable foliage, with Kwercus in the lead. Asur was directly behind him, and Tsalix and Legai brought up the rear. Little sunlight reached the forest floor, and the towering trees cast heavy shadows on the band.

"Tell me your names," Legai said to Tsalix. "I am Cha Legai."

"I am Tsalix Silverthorn. Asur Longtooth is next, and Kwercus Strongheart leads. We are from the village of Aravah, which is no more."

Legai's eyebrows shot up. "But you are dead!"

"Hardly," Tsalix replied. "Why would you say such a thing?"

"It is said you were killed when Aravah was burned."

"Who told you that?"

"I don't remember. It was spoken by many people."

They continued to travel in silence for nearly an hour.

"Last night you spoke of being raised by your family," Legai said. "This is totally foreign to me. Could you explain?"

Tsalix looked back over his shoulder. "Perhaps it would help me if you could tell me your story. You spoke of overseers. What was that like?"

Legai pondered his response for several steps. "It is said that when I was birthed, one of the priests took me to the edge of the parapet and examined me for any flaws—"

"Flaws?"

"Aye, a crooked leg, a birthmark. Anything that was less than perfect."

"And then what happened?"

"If a flaw was discovered, the baby was dropped from the battlement to the valley below."

The other three remained silent.

"Since I had no flaw, I was returned to the care of an overseer who took care of me until I could fend for myself." Legai rubbed a raised scar on his left bicep, where once a lash had struck him. "I was then put into school, where I was taught discipline and how to fight so I could defend my master." He cleared his throat and spat into the undergrowth. "When I was sixteen, I was assigned to my legion, where I served...until recently."

Tsalix cast a glance over his shoulder. "But have you completed your service?"

Legai dropped back further behind Tsalix. "There is no end but death. I have begun to question whether I am committed to the right side of the battle."

They continued their hike for several minutes.

"Is there more to your story?" said Tsalix.

"Nothing important." Legai wondered if he should explain what had happened to him on Mount Jinee, but decided that it was too hard to believe. "Tell me what is different in the way you were reared."

"I was born to the Silverthorn clan for the Sweetwater clan in the small village of Aravah," Tsalix said. "My father was a herder, and my mother a weaver. When I was growing up, my father often took me with him to spend time with the animals. It was assumed I would take after him, as he had taken after his father and grandfather. My mother taught me to read and write in the evenings, within our home. I suppose I would have become a herder had not the call come for able-bodied men to join Johona's army. When I was sixteen, I accepted the call and became part of his defensive forces. After two years in his service, I completed my tour of duty and returned home." He glanced back at Legai. "There is nothing special in my life." He gestured toward Kwercus and Asur. "My friends have similar stories, although Kwercus is a woodcutter, and Asur a dairy farmer."

"You were not compelled to enter the army?"

"Nay, neither Asur nor Kwercus chose to join."

Legai mulled over what he had heard. "You herded your own animals?"

"Of course. We needed them for food and raiment." Tsalix knitted his brow. "Did you not farm and herd?"

Legai shook his head. "Nay. The slaves did that."

Kwercus raised his hand and brought them to a stop. "We are approaching Nanish, the mine above the town of Hagade. It would behoove us to be silent so we are not discovered."

He turned toward the west and crept through the trees. They reached a clearing in the woods a short time later, and Kwercus signaled for a break. They sank down onto fallen logs that encircled the open spot.

"There is a spring a few minutes ahead of us," Kwercus whispered. "It supplies the water to Hagade and is safe to drink. Once we have rested and slaked our thirst, we will be in an even more heavily wooded part of the forest. We will have to travel slowly and carefully so we do not injure ourselves. The canopy is so substantial that little light reaches the ground, and there are many fallen branches and burrows that might trap our feet." He shifted his gaze to Legai. "If you are going to continue on with us, now is the time to decide. For in a few more minutes of travel, you will not be able to find your way back without my help."

Legai drew a circle in the dirt with the toe of his boot. "I have no one to return to. And once they find that I helped you escape, my life will be worthless." He looked over his shoulder, back toward Mount Jinee. "If you'll have me, I'll join your troop."

"So be it," said Tsalix. "Carry on, Kwercus."

CHAPTER 46

S IDII CLIMBED THROUGH THE AIR AND CIRCLED MOUNT JINEE. She emerged on the southeast side of the mountain, where the Swamp of Miasma met the edge of the Plain of Wonadsi. She rode the thermal currents that rose from the plain.

As the sun moved higher, Sidii's picked out encampments of troops below, with her keen eyesight. She noted the black and scarlet tents of Abadon, and the four colored ones of Johona. Higher and higher she soared, until the men below looked like ants crawling across a tan, wrinkled fabric. Turning her head from side to side, she searched for three men who were separated from the rest of the troops. With the escape less than two days before, she was sure they had not traveled as far as Shayeksten, the Desert of Desolation. A rising draft sent her even higher, and to compensate she folded her wings against her sides and plummeted toward the earth. The sun rose higher as she reached the edge of the desert. She wheeled and began a flight back toward Mount Jinee.

Midday passed, and Sidii felt pangs of hunger. Below her, on the plain, she could see a rabbit hiding in the shade of a clump of grass. She moved behind her prey, folded her wings against her body, and dropped from the sky. At the last second, she extended her talons and flared her wings. The impact broke the rabbit's spine, and Sidii grasped the quivering victim with her talons as she stroked with her wings and carried it to a branch of a salt cedar near the edge of an arroyo. She held the prey with one foot, and her perch with the other, while she sliced strips of flesh from the rabbit's warm body with her beak. It took but a few minutes until she had finished her feast and lifted her body into the air again.

Her third and fourth passes over the Plain of Wonadsi were just as fruitless as the first two. The sun was sinking low in the western sky when she wheeled past Abadon's palace and began a final foray down the western margin of the plain. Beneath her the waters of the Tohkal River glistened like a silver braid. She passed high above Hagade and saw a small line of soldiers heading toward Mount Jinee. High on the hillside, two groups of men were passing each other near the mouth of the goldmine as the day shift returned home and the night shift reported to work. She circled above them, searching for three men who did not belong.

Sidii hovered over the village of Bitahkiz and watched while the villagers wandered back and forth among the shops and their homes. She spotted a red-headed person and swooped down until she saw it was a woman. Sidii stroked her wings and flew higher. The sun set as she flew past the village of Atsanh, to where the Tohkal River emptied into the Sea of Tabass. The air was cooler and less turbulent. She turned one last time and began her return flight over the high plateau. Baffled and discouraged, she glided through the darkening skies.

A glint of light caught her eye and she swooped downward. Four men were gathered around a small fire. The flickering firelight barely illuminated them, but Sidii thought three of them matched the meager description she had been given by Chee Danzie. Who the fourth one was remained a mystery.

She floated above the men, assessing them, before she lifted higher and sped for home.

A gibbous moon had risen in the eastern sky, and cast its faint glow over the side of Mount Jinee as Sidii glided through the window that led into the aerie. She settled on her perch and preened her feathers with her beak. Several of the other birds called out a greeting to her. When she lighted on the roost, a small silver bell that hung beneath it sent out a sibilant chime.

Chee Danzie entered the room a moment later.

"My sweet," he said, before changing to her language.

He asked about her success, and she reported to him the sighting of not three, but four men.

"Where?"

"On the high plateau between Bitahkiz and Atsanh," she screeched.

"You have done well." He stroked her head. "Here is your reward." He placed strips of raw meat in her dish, along with a cup of water.

Once he had taken care of the hawk, he retreated down the staircase, to the guards outside the throne room.

"Halt!"

"I have news for Prince Abadon," Chee said. "News about the men who escaped the dungeon."

"Wait here." The guard knocked on the door to the ante chamber, and soon the vizier answered. "This man claims he has news for our master."

"What kind of news?"

"Of the men who escaped," Chee said, from behind the guard.

"One moment." The vizier closed the door behind him.

Chee tapped his foot while he waited, wondering if the success of this mission would gain him favor with Abadon.

The door opened.

"Come with me." The vizier gestured for Chee to follow him.

Once they entered the throne room, the door was shut behind them. Abadon stood gazing out the window, into the gathering gloom of night. A dozen blazing torches lit the throne room with their flickering flames.

"Speak," he said, without turning.

"Master, the men are on the high plateau between Bitahkiz and Atsanh. However, there are four of them. Not three, as was reported."

"Four?" Abadon spun around. "Who is this fourth man?" He pointed at the vizier. "Was I not assured that only three had escaped from the dungeon?"

"Aye, my master." The vizier prostrated upon the floor. "I will inquire of the jailors."

"Do it!"

The man scrambled to his feet and backed out of the room. Once the door shut, Abadon turned his attention to Chee.

"You have done good work this day. You are due a suitable reward." He gestured for Chee to approach him as he reached into his purse and extracted a handful of gold coins. "Take these."

"Thank you, my prince."

"But I require one last thing of you."

"Anything."

"Never speak of this to anyone again. For if I find you have done so, I will exact punishment. Am I clear?"

Chee wrinkled his forehead, wondering why this must be kept secret.

But he was wise enough say, "As you wish, my liege."

"Now go. There is work to be done."

As Chee Danzie backed out of the room, Abadon sat on his throne and contemplated his next move.

"Where is Maii?" he said to the vizier.

"Always awaiting your command."

"Send word that he and his companions have work to do. Tell him where our defectors are located, and give them reign to solve the problem."

"As you wish, my liege." The vizier scurried down the hallway, to the stairway that led Maii's apartment.

He knocked on the door, and a moment later a tall, dark-skinned man opened it.

"Maii. Your special talents are needed."

A feral smile crossed the man's lips. "Really? What is wanted?"

"There are four men crossing the high plateau. Our master would like you and your kin to...intercept them."

"And?"

"Do what you do best."

"As you wish." Maii strode down the hallway, pounded on three other doors, and beckoned to his brothers. "We have a task to fulfill."

The four of them traversed the castle halls until they were at the top of the ten thousand stairs. They stood in a circle, each one's arms around his brother's, and tilted their heads back in the light of the moon. They started to quiver. Then their bodies began to change.

A moment later Maii raised his head and howled. Where there had been four men, there were now four huge coyotes. With a last call to the moon, they descended the stairs, on the way to their quest.

CHAPTER 47

K WERCUS SAT ON THE FALLEN LOG, HIS BACK TO THE FIRE. While three of them warmed themselves, the fourth took turns facing away from the flames to be the lookout.

Kwercus sighed. The next day's journey would be the most difficult they had faced. Once they passed above Atsanh, they would have to descend from the plateau to the plain below. Only once had he made this journey, and that time he had brought the necessary equipment to rappel down the cliff face. This time they had nothing to help them but their wits.

Kwercus placed his hands behind his head and looked at the pewter sky. The moon was rising in the east, and the last vestiges of sunset lingered. A flicker of motion caught his eye. He focused his attention on the tiny spot moving above them. It circled, then fled to the north.

He turned to his brethren. "I fear we are discovered."

The other three leapt to their feet. "Who?"

Kwercus pointed up. "A hawk circled above us before streaking toward the north. I think it was no accident."

Tsalix pursed his lips. "How long will it take for pursuit to arrive?"

"It has taken us the better part of two days to travel this far," Legai said. "Even if a force is sent out tonight, we have that much lead."

Tsalix turned to him. "You know much better than I how Abadon will respond."

"He will likely send a troop of ten or twelve men." Legai shrugged.

"But we rarely traveled on the high plateau. With no trails to follow, who knows how long it will take for them to catch up with us."

"We have made good time," said Asur, "because Kwercus knew where to lead us. Do we dare sleep here tonight and then press on in the morning?"

"It has been a hard march, and we are weary," Tsalix said. "I would suggest we sleep a few hours and then be on our way."

The others agreed, and soon they were trying to make themselves comfortable around the fire.

Neahsja the owl sat on a branch of a tree overlooking the four men. She listened to their conversation before raising one foot and scratching behind her ear. Unseen by either Sidii or the men, she gathered as much information as she could before furling her wings and flying into the night sky. The moon was climbing high as she slipped through the window of the aerie, and hooted a call to her keeper. Although it was nearly midnight, a few minutes later her message was being delivered to Elosha by his chamberlain.

"This is troubling," said the king. "Although I hate to wake him, please have Johona join me in my chambers."

"As you wish."

Ten minutes passed before Johona joined his father and mother in the throne room. He sensed the urgency and seated himself.

"My son, word has reached me that Tsalix, Asur, and Kwercus are traveling with a fourth companion toward our home. They are on the high plateau and have been discovered by your brother. No doubt he will send soldiers to capture them. Or worse."

"I do not wish to interrupt, my Father, but if I know Abadon, he will send Maii, the coyote, and his brothers to intercept them. They move faster through the forests than men."

Elosha considered this for a moment. "You are right, my son. Why I did not think of that reveals my age." He turned to his wife. "What would you suggest, my dear?"

Nadlee frowned. "Perhaps we need to fight fire with fire. Has not Shush, the great bear, and his brothers just awakened from their winter sleep?"

"Aye. And a powerful force they are." Elosha turned to his son. "Send word to Shush that our friends are in danger and could use their protection."

"As you wish." Johona stood, bowed his head to his parents, and strode out of the room.

CHAPTER 48

THE MOON HAD SET, AND DAWN WAS A COUPLE HOURS AWAY when Tsalix roused his companions. The small fire had burned out and left only ash. In the chill darkness, they picked through the forest. Kwercus led the way, although the blackness kept him from moving more than a crawl.

An hour passed, and they entered a small clearing. Above them faint starlight cast pitiful shadows. Kwercus raised his hand and signaled for a rest. The dew covered brush had soaked their clothing, and they shivered in the cold. A dozen rocks the size of sheep rested in the grass-covered space. The four of them sat, each on his own stone.

"I have taken us away from the edge of the plateau," Kwercus said. "I think it will be safer here, for we stand no chance of being seen by the people of Atsanh, nor would this be the way our pursuers would expect."

The others nodded.

"There is a problem that lies ahead, however."

"What is that?" Tsalix said.

"We are nearing the end of our journey on the plateau. A few miles ahead, we leave the forest and the plateau swings west. We will be well-above the valley floor, and the cliffs are steep. Without ropes I know not how we will descend to the plain."

"There must be some way," Legai said.

"I'm sure there is," Kwercus replied. "But I'm not sure what it is."

Legai stretched his arms above his head, and his back popped. "There are few, if any, soldiers sent to the high plateau, for that reason. There are few ways to climb up or down from the rim, but I know there are some ways. We may have to search awhile, but I am sure we will find a place to escape."

"Have faith," Tsalix said. "We will find a way."

"I think we have another problem," Legai said. "If, as we suspect, there is someone pursuing us, we have no weapons with which to fight."

"Then we'll just have to stay ahead of our foes." Asur gave a grim smile.

"Then we'd better move on." Kwercus pushed to his feet.

The four of them moved across the clearing, and had just reached its edge when they heard something. Kwercus spun around just in time to see a huge furry beast explode into the opposite side of the clearing. Close behind it three more creatures sprang into view. Kwercus dropped to one knee and felt for a stone to throw. He found one the size of a peach and stood back up, ready for the onslaught. The four animals pawed the ground, saliva dripped from their open maws, while an unearthly growl filled the air. They prowled towards the men.

"Maii and his brothers," Legai whispered.

The furry fiends advanced across the clearing, their yellow eyes glowing demonically. When they were about ten feet from Kwercus, they stopped. The leader motioned with his head, and the other three fanned out to be able to attack from four directions.

Kwercus drew his arm back, ready to cast the stone. Tsalix moved next to him and held a rock as well. Maii snarled, drew his legs under him, ready to spring, and looked at the other coyotes, waiting for his signal. He fixed his gaze on Kwercus, opened his mouth, and launched into the air. Kwercus hurled the rock. It caught the huge coyote on his chest and diverted his path. He landed on the ground next to Kwercus, rolled over, and prepared to sink his teeth into Kwercus's leg.

The undergrowth next to Tsalix erupted in a burst of leaves and twigs as an enormous bear surged into the opening. He rose on his hind legs and let out a roar before dropping to the ground and turning toward Maii. The coyote ignored Kwercus and focused on his new adversary. With his tail drawn under him, the coyote tried to circle the bear, looking for an opening. The other three coyotes abandoned their positions and joined their leader in circling their new foe.

Kwercus signaled to his companions to follow him as he led them further into the forest. They had traveled only a few steps when they heard something else approaching, and halted. Three more bears rushed past them, into the clearing, growling. The four men paused long enough to see one of the coyotes being tossed into the air while it yipped. The others had disappeared into the woods from which they'd come, with the bears in hot pursuit.

The sun was near the eastern horizon, and the light within the forest was improving as Kwercus dashed through the trees. In the distance behind them, they could hear the sounds of a battle being waged.

"It is good we had help," Kwercus said. "Though where it came from, I know not."

"Aye, our fortune is in the hands of our protectors." Tsalix followed Kwercus through the dense forest.

They traveled without a break, often looking over their shoulders, until the sun was straight overhead. Kwercus led them to a small spring, where they refreshed. The head of the spring was surrounded by berry bushes, which provided aid to their rumbling stomachs.

"It will be good to find something else to eat," Tsalix said.

"Atsanh is almost directly below us," Kwercus whispered. "This spring feeds the last branch of the Tohkal River. A few miles ahead, it forms a waterfall that drops into a basin that empties into the river."

They traveled a short distance when the ridge they were following veered to the west. The forest thinned, revealing the edge of the plateau and a drop of nearly a thousand feet to the plain below. In the distance to the southeast, they could see the Sea of Tabass and Mount Litso, and to the east their destination, Mount Deschee. The small stream they had followed merged with a larger one and plunged over the edge of the cliff. The sun shining on the fan of spray that obscured their vision of the pool below created a striking rainbow. To their left they could see the edges of the village of Atsanh, far below. Straight ahead and to their right, the cliffs plunged in a drop to the floor of the plain.

Kwercus brought them to a halt.

CHAPTER 49

Captain Nash Doitsoh knelt before Abadon's throne. His head was bowed and his mane flowed around it.

Abadon sat with his chin in his hand. "How many did we lose?" he said, icicles forming every word.

"Twenty three, my master." Doitsoh bowed even lower.

"Twenty three? How did this happen?"

Doitsoh knew Abadon wanted no explanation. He merely wanted to draw out Doitsoh's pain before he was punished.

"Their forces were split in two, and we were caught in the middle."

"You were caught in the middle?" Abadon stroked his pointed beard. "How could that happen?"

"We were out-maneuvered."

"Really? The great Captain Nash Doitsoh was out-maneuvered. By whom?"

"Johona," he spat. "Your vile brother."

Silence hung in the room like a velvet cloak. Servants pushed into alcoves in the walls as the storm brewed. Abadon sank lower on his throne while Doitsoh continued to kneel before him.

"I am not a cruel master, Captain." Abadon sneered. "But I am surprised you were defeated by a much inferior force."

Doitsoh said nothing.

"What about the miners who were revolting? What has happened to them?"

Doitsoh kept his head down. "They seemed to have worked it out among themselves."

Abadon creased his forehead until his dark eyebrows formed a single line. "So sending our forces was a mistake?"

Doitsoh sensed the trap. It was Abadon who had sent the forces. If Doitsoh said that was a mistake, he was vilifying his master. Yet if the miners had worked out their problems without his intervention, the invasion was certainly not needed. Either way, he was doomed.

Doitsoh remained silent.

"I am going to give you one more chance, Captain Doitsoh."

Nash rose his head slightly.

"Three days ago, three men escaped from the dungeon," Abadon said.

"What? How?"

"How they did it is not important. Somewhere along the way, they've picked up a fourth miscreant. I have learned that they are on the high plateau, and I've sent Maii and his pack to take care of the problem."

Doitsoh nodded.

"Go retrieve the bodies. Take whatever men you feel you need to accomplish the task. Bring them back so that I may see who these foolish souls are."

Doitsoh nodded again.

"But do not fail me again, Captain." Abadon drew out the last word. "If you do, I cannot be responsible for what happens."

"I will not fail."

"Then go." Abadon waved him away with the back of his outstretched hand.

Doitsoh rose from his knees and backed out of the throne room.

Light was fading as Doitsoh and five others mounted their wolacs and began climbing the switchback trail to the top of the high plateau. Each carried enough provisions for a week in saddlebags that hung over the narrow thorax of his steed.

None of the men, but one, had ever been on top of the high plateau. Corporal Bisodih had traversed the plateau when he was an adolescent, more than fifteen years before. Doitsoh had chosen him to lead them in their retrieval mission.

By the time they reached the top of the trail, the sun had set and the moon had risen over the eastern horizon. The wolacs eyes were adapted to seeing in darkness, and they moved ahead at a steady pace. The men fought to stay awake and alert as they traveled through the night. Below them lay the mines of Nanish, above the village of Hagade. Doitsoh felt bitter bile rise in his throat as he thought of the defeat he had met there a week earlier.

Onward they plodded, until at daybreak they were passing above Bitahkiz. Doitsoh called a halt. They dismounted and ate breakfast from their provisions.

"We have made good time," Doitsoh nodded at Corporal Bisodih.

"It gets more difficult from here on. The forest is much denser, and we will have more trouble getting through." Bisodih took a bite of the biscuit in his hand. "We may have to tether the wolacs and continue on foot."

Nash considered this for a moment. "Let us continue as far as we can on our steeds. Then, if necessary, we will leave them."

After a brief stop, they continued onward. As Bisodih had predicted, they had gone less than a mile before the trees and undergrowth were so dense that the wolacs couldn't force through. The men dismounted, filled rucksacks with food, and continued on their way. Corporal Bisodih led the men, looking for any signs that someone else had passed this way, but saw none.

They were becoming more and more weary with each passing hour. It had been more than a day since any of them had slept. Finally, as they entered a small clearing, Captain Doitsoh ordered a rest stop. They sank to the ground, leaned back on their packs, and fell asleep.

When the sun reached its zenith and streamed down into the opening, it awakened Doitsoh. His golden eyes fluttered open, and he pushed up to his feet.

"Let's go," he barked.

The other five awakened, stretched and yawned. They stopped twice more during the day to eat meager meals. At twilight they had passed above Bitahkiz and were partway to Atsanh.

"Does it seem peculiar to you that we have seen no sign of our prey?" Doitsoh said.

"Aye," replied Corporal Bisodih. "We do not have much further to go until we reach the end of the plateau."

Doitsoh stopped. "If Maii has taken care of the problem, we should see some evidence. Keep a sharp eye."

They entered a small clearing. In the center of the opening were the remnants of a camp fire. Nash signaled for a stop. He knelt and thrust his hand into the ashes.

"Cold." He rose. "Still it is evidence that someone has been this way." He looked at the drooping figures of his men. "Let us stop for the night. Without our wolacs to guide us through the trees, we are at a standstill. We will continue in the morning." He knelt and removed the rucksack from his back.

The others followed suit, and soon the six men were struggling to find strength to prepare a meal before falling asleep.

The next morning they arose before sunlight, ate breakfast, and continued their quest. They were on their way for less than an hour when Corporal Bisodih raised his hand.

"There was a struggle here." He pointed to broken branches, twigs, and leaves on the ground.

The men fanned out and began searching through the dense undergrowth. The scent of death was everywhere.

Nash Doitsoh pushed back a giant fern and halted. Lying beneath the fern was the broken body of a coyote. Its throat had been ripped open, and two of its legs were broken, the bones protruded through the skin. The forest floor was black with congealed blood.

"Over here," Doitsoh called.

The others came to his side.

Doitsoh ground his teeth. "It appears our adversaries may be stronger and better armed than we thought."

A half-hour later, they discovered two more bodies, each mangled.

"Be on alert," Doitsoh said, as they moved forward.

CHAPTER 50

T SALIX LAY FLAT ON THE GROUND NEXT TO THE HEAD OF THE waterfall and looked straight down at the valley floor far below. He searched for any way that the four of them could descend from the top of the plateau. Except for a few scraggly bushes whose roots had forced into shallow cracks, the cliff face was smooth and undisturbed.

He slid backwards and pushed to his feet. "I see nothing that can help us."

"Perhaps we should continue along the plateau to the west," Asur said. "There may be a better way."

"Perhaps," replied Kwercus. "I have not explored the ridge that way. The one time I came this way was before we brought the rope necessary to rappel down the cliff, and even then I sported many bruises from my adventure." He looked at the edge of the plateau as it disappeared to the west. "Who knows what lies that way?"

"There seems to be little other choice," Tsalix said.

The four of them stepped back from the edge of the rock and maneuvered along the edge of the plateau as it turned to the west. The sun warmed their backs as they scouted for some way to reach the plain below. They traveled for over an hour before they reached a spot where it appeared that another waterfall had coursed down the cliff. But now the channel was dry. Where the water had eroded the rock, it left a cleft about a yard wide.

They looked over the edge of the plateau, into the shadow below.

Cha Legai examined the vertical walls. "I believe we can go down where the waterfall cut the rock."

"How?" said Asur.

"By putting our backs against one side of the cleft, and our feet on the other. It will be slow, but it can be done." Legai looked again at the rock chimney. "There are two problems...maybe three." He lay down and inspected the rock channel again. "First is the problem of getting into position to begin the climb down. While the first three will have someone to help us, the last climber will be on his own. Second, we will have to go one at a time so that if rocks are dislodged, they won't fall on anyone below."

"And the third problem?" Tsalix said.

Legai took a deep breath. "Well, we really can't see all the way to the bottom in the shadow. We might get partway down the cliff and find that the cleft does not continue all the way to the bottom...or gets too narrow."

Kwercus shaded his eyes. "I see no other way." He shrugged. "I'll go first."

Tsalix put his hand on his friend's shoulder. "Kwercus, if you get partway down and can go no further, will you have the strength to climb back up?"

"I don't know. But I do know that there are likely pursuers at our back, and if we can't get down off the plateau, our lives are not worth much anyway." He walked to the edge of the cliff, lay on his back, and slipped his feet into the channel. "Give me a hand."

Tsalix and Asur each grabbed a hand and helped Kwercus wedge himself in the chimney. Inch by inch, he began to lower himself. He slid his back and shoulders down the rock and moved his feet down the opposite side. The others lay on the solid rock and watched as Kwercus worked down the chute. He paused frequently to regain his strength, and eventually disappeared into the shadows that enveloped the bottom half of the cliff.

Well over an hour passed before his triumphant call echoed from the floor below.

"I've made it." The faint call echoed up the cliff.

"Who's next?" Tsalix said.

"I'll go," replied Asur.

Tsalix and Legai helped him into the channel, and watched as he descended slowly. He was not as husky as Kwercus, and his slight frame allowed him to slide more easily down the chimney.

"Be careful," Tsalix called. "There is no need for haste." Asur grunted a reply as he disappeared into the shadow.

The sun was climbing high into the sky when a second call echoed up the cliff.

"You go next," Legai said. "Join your friends, and I'll follow." He helped Tsalix into position.

"Are you sure you can do this alone?" Tsalix said.

"I must. Now go."

Tsalix began inching down the channel. The muscles in his legs ached from being in such a cramped position, but he ignored the pain and continued downward. Kwercus and Asur called their encouragement to him as he reached the shadowed portion of the descent. When he got to the talus slope at the bottom of the cliff, his friends embraced him. The three of them called up to Legai.

On top of the plateau, Cha lay down on his back and slid his legs into the chimney. His toes reached the far side, and he continued to slip forward until his hips slid over the lip. Panic seized him as he tried to find something to grasp but found nothing. He slid his body into the chimney, and with a burst of terror, pushed backward with his feet, lodging himself in the cleft. His body trembled.

From below, the other three cheered him on. Legai caught his breath and then began the slow descent. He was well into the shadowed part of the journey, only a dozen feet or so from the floor, when a shower of pebbles fell from the top of the plateau. He heard the rattle of the stones and wedged himself in the narrow opening while he covered his face and head. The small rocks pummeled his body.

He looked to the top of the cliff and saw the silhouette of Nash Doitsoh framed in the opening. In his hands was a boulder the size of a watermelon. Legai's legs were burning from the effort to crawl down the chimney, but he hurried to reach the ground. With a roar that carried down from the plateau above, Doitsoh released the stone.

Legai pulled his legs to his chest and dropped to the chimney floor. His breath was knocked out of him by the cobbles beneath him. Tsalix grabbed him under his arms and dragged him to safety as the falling boulder pulverized the smaller rocks before bouncing down the talus slope.

"Are you all right?" Tsalix said to Legai.

"Bruised, but no bones broken, I think."

"Who was that on the plateau?"

"Captain Nash Doitsoh, my former commander."

Tsalix felt a pulse of terror race down his spine. "Then we must make haste. He will surely pursue us."

The others nodded and started down the talus slope. The going was treacherous. The rubble beneath their feet was unstable, and they often found themselves falling to their knees. But they eventually reached the bottom of the slope and continued around the cliffs, to the place where the waterfall carved a basin. They guzzled down some water before crossing through the tall grass to the split main road. To the south it led to the Sea of Tabass. To the east was the path that led to the village of Chushka, at the base of Mount Deschee, forty miles ahead.

CHAPTER 51

NASH DOITSOH ROARED IN FRUSTRATION, WHILE HIS MEN cowered behind him. Below he could see the four fugitives as they scrambled down the talus slope at the base of the cliff. The packs containing the ropes and other climbing equipment were with the wolacs, more than a day's journey behind them. If he sent his men to retrieve them, by the time they returned, their prey would have a two-day head start.

Anger boiled in his blood as he watched the figures reach the plain, then disappear from sight, around the corner of the rockface. His nimble mind raced to find a solution. He knew that if he returned to Abadon empty-handed, there would be a heavy price to pay.

Consumed by fury, Doitsoh spun around. "Any ideas?" he spat.

Corporal Bisodih's voice trembled. "If we continue to the west, there is a gentler slope." His hand shook as he pointed. "It is not the same direction we might wish to follow, but it is said that we might be able to climb down to the valley."

"How far?" barked Doitsoh.

"Half a day, at most."

With a final look over the edge of the precipice, Captain Doitsoh gritted his teeth.

"Lead on."

Bisodih started a march westward along the top of the plateau. The ground was strewn with pebbles and cobbles that slipped and skidded under their feet, keeping them from moving as fast as they'd have liked.

They paused only once for a few minutes to eat a meal before continuing on their way.

The sun was low in the sky, casting giant shadows, when they finally reached the spot Corporal Bisodih had remembered. The slope was steep and the footing unsure over rocks deposited by a landslide decades before. Bisodih gingerly placed his weight on a boulder, only to feel it move under his foot, then plunge down the incline, bounding and clattering over the rocks below.

"We must be careful," he said. "But it is a way down."

Captain Doitsoh grunted a reply and then ordered the men to begin their descent. It was slow going as the scree moved beneath their feet, but after more than an hour of slipping and sliding, they reached the bottom of the slope with only a few scrapes and bruises. The sun had set, and dusk was giving way to total darkness.

Doitsoh considered the situation. He knew the men he was pursuing had a half-day's lead on him, and he was anxious to catch them, but he and his men had had little sleep in the past two days and had been pushed to the end of their endurance.

Reluctantly he called for a halt and announced that they would rest for a few hours before continuing their pursuit. The men sank down, opened their packs, and ate their rations. A chill wind whispered through the camp. They drew their cloaks around them and soon were asleep.

Above them on the high plateau, a lone coyote howled a funeral dirge.

CHAPTER 52

THE TRAIL TO CHUSHKA WAS WELL-MARKED, AND EVEN
though the night was upon them, the four men continued at a brisk
pace. Their stomachs complained. The last time they had eaten was the
handfuls of winter berries on the top of the high plateau. Here on the
edge of the Plain of Wonadsi, there was nothing that was edible. The
promise of aid once they reached the village kept them moving forward,
along with the fear of pursuit.

"How much longer?" Legai said.

"We have traveled nearly ten miles," Kwercus replied. "The village lies
another thirty miles ahead. We should reach Chushka by mid-morning.
And I promise you, the people there will feed us."

"That is one promise I'll hold you to," Legai said.

Two hours passed before they stopped for a rest. Legai squinted into
the darkness and looked back up the trail they had covered.

"He will be on our tail," he said.

Tsalix rubbed his chin. "Do you think they had ropes?"

Legai shook his head. "I know not, but I do know how determined
Captain Doitsoh is when it comes to fulfilling his quest. It is said that he
will stop at nothing." He thought of the command he had been given on
top of Mount Jinee that had sent him plummeting down the vent to what
he was sure was his death. "He will pursue us to the very end." He nodded.

"Then let us be on our way." Tsalix rose to his feet. "Without arms we
must find help, or perish."

They hurried down the path. Fatigue slowed their feet after another couple hours, and they sank to the ground for a brief rest. To the side of the trail, low thorn bushes and cheat grass grew, making it uncomfortable, if not impossible, to sit anywhere but on the path itself. The four of them rested silently, each consumed with his own thoughts. The moon was setting over the rim of the high plateau, and the first evidence of sunrise—a gray glow to the east—told them that daylight would soon be upon them.

"We have a ways to go," Tsalix said. "Are you rested, my friends?"

"Aye." Asur forced himself to his feet and dusted off the seat of his tunic. "Let us be off."

With a glance over their shoulders, the four men continued down the trail toward Chushka. Although their stomachs grumbled, thirst became their enemy.

"Is there water anywhere?" Legai said. "My mouth is as dry as a wizard's wit."

"Nay. Not until we reach the village," replied Kwercus.

"How much longer, then?"

"Less than two hours."

The sun broke over the eastern horizon, and they had to squint as they moved toward Chushka. After another hour, the landscape began to change as spots of green were interspersed with the dried dun of the plain.

"We are nearing the town," Kwercus said, through sun dried lips.

"That is good news," Legai croaked.

"See." Tsalix pointed. "The village is in sight."

The four of them picked up their pace with the hope of refreshment soon. Before long they spied a man working in his field. He also spotted them, and waved. He left his plow and crossed the newly turned earth to the fence line that ran alongside the road.

"Welcome." He smiled. "What brings you to Chushka?"

Tsalix tried to wet his lips, but failed. "We are returning to Hayeli after completing a quest for the king," he wheezed.

The farmer raised his eyebrows. "What kind of quest?"

"One we were sent on by King Elosha," said Tsalix. "We have succeeded with the first part of our journey." He glanced back over his shoulder. "However, we are being pursued by some of Abadon's men."

"How many?"

"We know not. The force seemed small, but..."

"Then we must sound the alarm." The farmer pushed the bottom strand of fence with the heel of his boot, while he raised the other foot, crouched, and stepped through to the path. "Come." He strode down the path.

The four of them followed.

Within a few minutes, they reached the edge of the village, which was just coming to life in the early morning.

The farmer led them to an inn. "You'll find refreshment here while I alert the mayor."

A tub of fresh water stood beside the door to the inn, and the four of them scooped handfuls to their parched lips. The innkeeper heard the commotion and appeared a moment later.

"Good men, what brings you to our village?"

Tsalix was guzzling from the tub, and he stopped, wiped his lips with the back of his hand, and explained their quest. He had barely finished telling of Abadon's men when an alarm bell sounded through the town. The innkeeper spun on his heel and rushed back inside the building. A few seconds later, he reappeared, buckling a sword around his ample waist. Other men were congregating on the main street of the village, each with a sword, spear, or bow.

"I suspect you are hungry," the innkeeper said. "There is bread and sausage inside. There are waterskins as well. Eat your fill quickly, and then continue on your way."

"We cannot thank you enough," Tsalix said.

"It is nothing."

The four of them entered the inn and grabbed a slab of bread and piece of sausage.

"I suggest we eat on the way," Asur said.

"Aye," replied Tsalix.

As they left the inn, they saw a tall, imposing man striding toward them.

"Hail!" he said. "I am mayor of Chuska. Tell me of the threat that approaches our peaceful village."

For a third time, Tsalix explained their mission and the pursuit by Abadon's men.

"You know not how many?"

"Nay. A small force, we believe."

"We will be ready," the mayor said. "You best continue your journey. You have a steep climb ahead of you."

Legai turned toward the mayor, with a puzzled expression. "Why do offer such aid to us?"

The mayor straightened to his full height. "It is not only to protect you and the king. We fight for our homes, our wives, and our children. Now go."

The four of them returned to the pathway and continued on toward Hayeli, on the top of Mount Deschee. Tsalix watched over his shoulder as the mayor placed the armed men in spots that would provide an advantage over their pursuers.

"I would not like to be Captain Doitsoh," Legai said. "If he is wise, he will abandon this cause. He is sure to lose."

"Yet he is determined," Kwercus said. "Did you not say he would pursue us to the bitter end."

"Aye."

The path continued up the slopes of Mount Deschee, and before long they had lost sight of Chushka. Tsalix's heart felt lighter as he realized the end of the first part of his quest was near, although he was still worried about what was happening in the village below.

CHAPTER 53

C APTAIN NASH DOITSOH EXAMINED THE TRAIL AND SAW THE
faint imprint of sandals in the hard-packed dirt.

"They are not far ahead," he said to his men. "We have made good time
in our journey. It is time to inspect your weapons and assure a victory."

Every man checked their sword to make sure it slid easily from its scabbard, and adjusted every knife for quick retrieval.

"We are less than a mile from Chushka. One never knows what might
befall us there, although there has never been any resistance in the past."

The outlying farmlands were green and verdant. Cattle grazed the
fields. There was no hint of alarm. The pathway wound around a thumb
of rock on the south, and as the men marched single file around it, they
could see the village of Chushka ahead. The sloping hill on their right was
shrouded in shrubs and trees, while to the left the pastures ran to the edge
of the Plain of Wonadsi.

"I see nothing standing in our way," Doitsoh said. "We will make short
work of our task this day."

They continued a half-mile before they saw someone standing in the
middle of the trail. On both sides of him were heavy thickets of thorn-
bush. Captain Doitsoh raised his hand, and his soldiers stopped behind
him.

The man stood still with his arms crossed, blocking their advance. He
appeared to be unarmed.

"Spread out," Doitsoh said. "We do not know what this man means."

The five men behind him fanned out as they approached the single figure. When they were within a hundred feet, Doitsoh stopped again. The man stood motionless.

"Stay here," Doitsoh whispered to his men. "Provide cover, if needed." He marched forward until he was within a sword's length from the solitary man. "Let us pass," he growled.

The man shook his head. "You are not welcome here. Leave now if you value your lives." He uncrossed his arms and pointed back down the trail.

Doitsoh looked around him and saw no one. "And if we choose not to leave?"

"It would be wise if you did. This is your second warning."

Doitsoh placed his hand on the hilt of his sword and began to slip it from its sheath.

"I would not advise doing that." The man stared at Doitsoh. "We seek nothing but peace, but if you force a fight, you will suffer the consequences. This is your last warning."

"Really." Doitsoh sneered, then began to laugh. "And what will happen? Will you fight me without a weapon?" He drew his sword free of its scabbard and waved it in the air.

His men moved forward in support.

"So be it." The man raised his arm, and before Nash could wield his sword, an arrow struck him in the arm.

From the hillside a great roar went up, mingled with the whistling of a hundred arrows seeking targets. In the blink of an eye, Captain Doitsoh's five soldiers fell dead to the ground. He turned, raised his shield for protection, and raced back down the trail, blood dripping from his arm wound.

A second flight of arrows followed him. Enraged and terrified, he continued his flight. Only when he had covered a half-mile did he sink to his knees. He grasped the shaft of the arrow, gritted his teeth, and with a howl that echoed from the hillside, pulled the barbed point from his arm. Blood gushed out of the wound. Doitsoh fumbled in his rucksack and found a strip of cloth, which he wound around his wounded arm. He pulled a knot tight using his good hand and his teeth, and eventually the bleeding slowed.

Doitsoh evaluated his position. He had seen his men fall at the hands of these foul followers of Johona. There seemed to be no pursuit from the village, but he was exposed, weak from loss of blood, and without any support. To the south, on the other side of the foothills, was Shayeksten, the Desert of Desolation. While to the north was the Plain of Wonadsi, where many of Abadon's troops were stationed. If he could find one of the emplacements, he would find aid.

Doitsoh felt susceptible as he knelt at the side of the trail. He forced himself to his feet and stumbled into the trees that covered the low rise to the south. When he felt hidden, he forced himself to drink from his waterskin and eat part of his rations. Fatigued gripped him as he sat in the shelter of the spruces, and before long he stretched out on the ground and slept, unaware that he was being watched by a dozen pairs of eyes.

The bodies of Captain Doitsoh's men had been retrieved by the men of Chushka and carried back into the town, where they were prepared for burial.

The mayor looked at the fallen soldiers and shook his head. "Why wouldn't they listen?"

CHAPTER 54

NASH DOITSOH'S EYES FLICKERED OPEN. THE MOON HUNG IN the sky above him. His arm ached, and his lips were dry and cracked.

How long have I been asleep? He reached for his waterskin and struggled to raise to a sitting position, but he seemed pinned to the ground. He tried to roll on his side when he saw the two arrows that had been driven through either side of his cloak. He pulled them from the ground and sat up. Attached to the shaft of one arrow was a scroll of parchment tied with a leather thong. He untied it and strained to read the script by moonlight.

Your life has been spared that you might know we seek only peace.

Doitsoh's heart beat wildly. He rose to his feet and scanned the surrounding trees, but his head swam and he sank back to the ground. He took a deep breath before rising slower. There was no movement in the forest around him. The message was clear—he had been at their mercy, and they had let him live. He shook his head, and his mane riffled in the nighttime breeze. It was beyond his understanding why he had been spared.

Trembling, Doitsoh headed out of the woods and to the trail that led to Chushka. He felt for his sword. It had been removed, as had his tsenil and knife. He was unarmed and clearly at the mercy of these people. Although he could see none of them, Doitsoh had the feeling he was being watched.

He looked across the tended field to the Plain of Wonadsi. In the distance he could barely see flickering firelight. He lifted his waterskin to

his lips and was surprised to find it full. Likewise, the rations in his pack
had been replenished. Fighting dizziness, he staggered onto the trail and
began his trek toward the distant camp.

Nearly an hour passed before he reached the edge of the pasture and
entered the plain. As he descended from the hillside, he could no longer
see the glimmering light far away. Onward he trudged, hoping he was
traveling in the right direction. He tried to find a solution to the problems
he faced. Even if he located an encampment, he would eventually have to
return to Jinee and report to Abadon. He had failed once, and had been
warned not to fail again.

Rage rose within. How could he have let those mere boys slip through
his fingers? Who was the fourth man with them? Who were they, anyway?

The moon sank low in the western sky, sending silvery shadows across
the landscape as Doitsoh stumbled across the Plain of Wonadsi. As the
glow of sunrise painted the mountains to the east, he sank to the ground
and ate some of the food that had been placed in his pack. His mind
began to churn as he wondered why the people of Chushka would give
him food.

Is it poisoned? He spit the mouthful of food out on the ground and
waited, but nothing happened. After waiting a half-hour with no evidence
that the food had been doctored, he gave into hunger and scarfed the food
down.

The sun was climbing into the sky when Doitsoh struggled to his feet
and continued moving toward where he thought he had seen a fire the
night before. He was weakened from the loss of blood, his arm ached, and
sharp pains racked his shoulder, but he plodded on, hoping to find aid.

The sun was setting when he heard the squeal of a wolac. Doitsoh
raised his drooping head and scanned the plain. He tried to call out, but
his lips were cracked and his tongue was swollen. He made a mere squeak.

As Doitsoh raised the waterskin to his mouth and gulped the water,
the sun's rays painted a brilliant pattern in the sky. Then a shadow crossed
his face. He shaded his eyes and squinted into the sunset to see a wolac
climb out of the arroyo to his left. Astride the beast was a soldier with a
spear in his hand.

"Who goes there," the man growled, as he examined the creature
standing before him.

The lion-headed man seemed familiar.

"Captain Nash Doitsoh. My men were ambushed, and I alone escaped."

The man dismounted and approached Doitsoh, his spear at the ready.

"What brings you to this part of the kingdom?"

"A mission from Abadon."

The soldier was close enough to see that Doitsoh wore the black and scarlet tunic of Abadon.

"Where are you going?"

"To seek aid. I am alone and unarmed."

"Aye, I see no sword in your scabbard."

For the first time, he noticed the blood-soaked rag around Nash's arm. "You've been wounded."

The man put aside his fears and helped Doitsoh to the wolac, which knelt and allowed the two men to mount.

"Camp is this way," the soldier said, as the huge beast turned and began a steady lope across the plain.

Once in camp Doitsoh's wound was cleaned and dressed, and he was fed and given an empty tent in which to sleep. He lay awake on the cot, considering his next move. If he returned to Jinee, he was sure Abadon's punishment would be severe—perhaps even death. Besides, he was angered that these men had escaped him, and he wanted revenge.

It was clear that they were traveling to Hayeli, on Mount Deschee, but was that their final destination? If it was, Doitsoh had no hope of finding them, for he was a single warrior against an entire city. But if they were only visiting, he might track them again and recover his honor.

Doitsoh fell asleep trying to find a solution.

By morning he decided he needed to stay with the camp until his strength returned. Then he would see if he could find any trail of his foes and complete his task. The camp blacksmith could supply weapons, and he would be back on the hunt again. Perhaps he would try to enlist the aid of his people. They were a mighty race who lived just outside the kingdom, on the far side of the Sea of Tabass.

Of course, there was the problem of returning home if a price was still on his head. Perhaps he could enlist the help of some of the men in this camp.

Whatever he needed, he would find it.

And his pursuit would be swift and deadly.

CHAPTER 55

TSALIX LED HIS SMALL TROOP UP THE TRAIL THAT ENCIRCLED Mount Deschee. His heart was light, knowing they had escaped Abadon's men and completed the first of the challenges before them.

Tsalix slipped his hand into his purse and felt the smooth, warm black talisman. He removed it and looked at the *TS* engraved in its surface. Instead of the gray, lifeless letters he had last seen, they now glowed again.

He returned it to his pouch. All day they traveled upward, until the four of them reached the arch that spanned the main road, with its welcoming sign.

"I have never seen such beauty," Legai whispered. "Everything is perfect."

"It is indeed a wonderful place." Tsalix smiled. "Come. Let us report the success of the first leg of our quest."

They strode toward Elosha's castle, whose alabaster towers gleamed in the sun. Along the way they were greeted by many of the townspeople, who welcomed them to their city. Legai was dumbfounded by the peace and order he saw.

Eventually they reached the white fence that surrounded the castle and the white-robed gatekeeper.

"Ah, Masters Silverthorn, Longtooth, and Strongheart, it is good to see you again. And who might this be?" He pointed his staff toward Legai.

"His name is Cha Legai. He is a friend we met along the way. He was a great help to us."

"Then welcome, Master Legai." The gatekeeper gave a gentle bow in Legai's direction. "I suppose you'd like audience with the king?"

"Aye," Tsalix replied. "Although, after our long trip, we are hardly dressed to enter his presence."

The gatekeeper nodded. "I believe we can offer aid." He stepped into gatehouse, and a mere moment passed before two young women appeared. "Please follow them, and they will help you prepare to meet the king." He bowed again. "It is wonderful to have you here. I hope your quest was successful."

Tsalix nodded. "At least, the first part of our journey."

An hour later—bathed, shaved, and dressed in clean clothing—the four of them were led to the throne room. King Elosha and Queen Nadlee sat on their thrones. Tsalix and his companions knelt before them.

"Rise, my great, young warriors." Elosha lifted his hands. "And introduce me to your friend."

"This is Cha Legai, my liege. We were imprisoned in Abadon's dungeons within Mount Jinee, and Cha secured a key and opened our cell doors. He has traveled with us on our sojourn from Jinee to Deschee."

Nadlee smiled as she looked into Cha's eyes. He returned her gaze, and deep within the recesses of his mind, he tried to figure out why she looked so familiar.

Tsalix reached into his purse and removed the talisman. It pulsed in his hand as the engravings glowed.

"We have succeeded in retrieving the first stone." He offered it to the king.

"Well done. You have been faithful in crusade." Elosha took the talisman and placed it on a pedestal behind the throne. "It will rest here, awaiting its two brothers." He returned to his throne. "Now please be seated and tell me of your adventures." He knit his brow. "I wish I could tell you that the other talismans will be easier to retrieve, but they may prove equally as difficult to obtain."

Kwercus raised a hand. "But no matter how difficult, we will succeed, your majesty."

A broad smile creased Elosha's face. "I know you will. I have great confidence in you. And the rewards will be greater than you can imagine."

Over the next half-hour, the three of them described their expedition while Cha Legai sat silent. When they finished recounting their tale, Nadlee beamed and turned to Legai.

"And what about your journey here?" she said. "I sense you have traveled a more difficult route. Tell us your story."

Legai shrank down into his seat. "I fear there is much in my life that is unpleasant."

Nadlee and Elosha smiled at him.

"The past is behind us," she said. "It is the future that is important."

Legai told his story, omitting only the parts that were too painful for him to recall. Awash in shame, he looked at the floor, unwilling to meet Elosha's gaze.

"My son," the king said. "You have been a good friend to my young charges. Without you, they could not have succeeded. It is good for you to have seen the error of your ways, but do not dwell on the past."

"What will become of me?" Legai said.

Elosha beamed. "We welcome you to Hayeli. I think you will find peace and comfort here."

"Am I not to continue on the quest?"

Elosha shook his head. "Nay, my son. It is for these three alone." He spread his hands toward the three young warriors. "But you will be embraced by the people of our city, and the day will come when you will have a quest of your own."

Nadlee rose from her throne. "Now you must be weary. Please go rest, for tonight we will have a banquette celebrating your success." She looked at Tsalix. "There is something that bothers you?"

"Aye, my lady." He took a deep breathed. "With Cha's help, the three of us escaped. But the rest of my village—men, women, and children—are still imprisoned in Abadon's dungeons."

Nadlee clenched her jaw. "I cannot understand my son's will. All I can tell you is if you succeed, all will be well." She sat. "Please trust me."

Elosha rose to his feet. "Yes, my sons, trust. As difficult as that may be. Now rest. For three days from now, you will leave on the second part of your adventure as you travel to Mount Tsood. The way is arduous, and it will require all of your wits and strength to complete the task—but you will."

Sensing they were being dismissed, the four of them left the throne room and strolled toward their apartments. Legai was silent as they moved down the alabaster hallway.

"What is wrong?" Tsalix said.

"I have never felt emotions such as these. Why am I so sorrowful at parting company with you? And why have I been accepted into this community without hesitation? I have been raised to fear these people, and yet they have welcomed me without question. I just find it hard to understand."

Tsalix put his hand on Legai's shoulder. "You'll learn, my friend. As for us leaving, it must be so. We'll look forward to a reunion when we return from Mount Tsood, with the second talisman."

"Between here and Mount Tsood is Shayeksten, the Desert of Desolation." Legai shuddered.

"Aye, but we will cross it one way or another."

Legai shook his head. "I have been there. Terrible heat, lack of water, and poisonous fumes await you."

Tsalix straightened to his full height. "I, too, have been on its edge. But we will succeed. We must."

FORTHCOMING TITLES IN THIS SERIES

TSALIX SILVERTHORN AND THE DESERT OF DESOLATION
TSALIX SILVERTHORN AND THE MAELSTROM OF TEARS
TSALIX SILVERTHORN AND THE GLITTERING PEAK

AVAILABLE BOOKS

CayellePublishing.com

 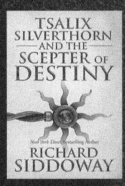 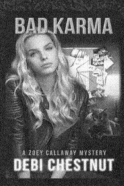 

amazon.com

COMING
SOON

CayellePublishing.com

CPSIA information can be obtained
at www.ICGtesting.com
Printed in the USA
FSHW011319010820
72446FS